Copyright © 2018 Charles Hugh Smith
All global rights reserved in all media
ISBN-13: 978-1724939661
ISBN-10: 1724939661

First edition published August 2018

Oftwominds.com
P.O. Box 4727
Berkeley, California 94704

The Adventures of the Consulting Philosopher
The Disappearance of Drake

A novel

Charles Hugh Smith

To Cindy, for giving me the freedom to write what I longed to read for my own amusement.

Chapter One

"I can't believe it—you actually have a client."

The Consulting Philosopher shifted his substantial weight on the office's velvet draped divan and looked up from the tattered paperback in his hand at the astonished expression on his assistant's endlessly charming face.

"Your wonderment is exceeded only by my own, JP," he replied, his deep voice easily audible in every room of the sparely furnished flat. "But let's reserve our absolute astonishment for a client's payment of cash."

Sitting up, he smoothed the front of his golden-dragon-emblazoned red robe and asked, "And who is this mystery client who has broken the curse of cruel mockery we've suffered since putting out our consulting shingle?"

"I don't know, but she must be really desperate," JP exclaimed, and the Consulting Philosopher chortled ruefully. "Your steadfast faith in the value of my services is the shield that protects me from the slings and arrows of outrageously unfair fortune."

"Of course I have faith in you," the young woman replied earnestly. "But nobody pays for philosophy."

"You may well be correct in that," he muttered. "It's nothing short of miraculous that I'm not swathed in orange robes, rattling my begging bowl outside the fruit vendor's stall."

Arising to pace his usual figure-eight route in the office's faded blue Persian rug, he said, "After all, look how Goethe toiled as manager of a great estate for years, or the destitution, relieved only by gifts of sake, endured by Ryokan in his hovel atop Mount Kugami."

"You just made a small fortune in the stock market," his assistant blurted, destroying his attempt at self-pity. "Goethe and Ryokan should be so lucky."

"Trading options requires the utmost application of disciplined philosophy," he countered, and then sighed theatrically. "Nobody pays for what they don't value. And so I'm forced to extract value from a mindless market."

"Nobody feels sorry for you," JP said sharply, and her pout was too delicious to overlook.

"I absolutely adore the way you immediately annihilate my every attempt at feeling sorry for myself. Wild things don't feel sorry for themselves, and I'm grateful to you, JP."

"Why don't you teach me how to make a small fortune in the stock market?" she retorted.

"I did distribute a handsome slice of my winnings to you," he noted in a wounded voice.

"You are very generous," JP said in her delightful Mandarin-tinged accent, "but the fisherwoman wants to learn to catch her own fish."

"Now we're finally making progress," he thundered. "You want to master trading, and the pathway to that mastery is through philosophy. I am teaching you, dear clever and bighearted JP, but you don't yet recognize the lessons."

Pausing at the window to gaze out at the windswept waters of San Francisco Bay, he continued, "Why just yesterday I spoke at length about a particular insight of your countryman Zhuang Zhou, a Taoist insight that is a direct pathway to mastery of volatility and risk. But you were bored by the discourse, I saw it in every fiber of your being."

Cutting off her protest, he continued. "I understand, truly I do; yours was the boredom of someone whose primary interest is practicalities. You are a practical young woman, anxious to make her own way in the world under her own power. I recognized this in you in the first moments of our first meeting, and that is why I outbid every other conceivable employer you might have contacted. I admired your drive, your bright intellectual light, and your sincerity, by which I mean the particular Chinese character known as *makoto* in Japanese, which combines sincerity, truth and authenticity in one splendid unity. I admire you enormously, JP, and I want the fisherwoman to catch whatever fish she desires in her net."

Blushing most fetchingly under this weight of praise, JP looked down and said quietly, "I really don't see how some dusty old Taoism helps you make money."

"That is the trick, isn't it?" he said softly, and then shifted gears. "Did the mystery client make a general inquiry, or did she ask for an appointment?"

"An appointment."

"And how did you respond?"

"I told her your schedule was booked but we'd try to squeeze her in."

"Excellent. And that's no exaggeration, given my current analysis of Alexander the Great's philosophy of warfare. It's devilishly interesting work, comparing his principles with those of Grant and Nelson. Quite different characters, of course, facing considerably different military challenges, but it's fascinating to ponder the unifying themes. If you want to master risk and volatility, there's almost no better place to start than Alexander, Nelson and Grant, though I suppose Genghis Khan and Napoleon must be included as well."

The bent figure of an elderly man emerged from the entry doorway, surprising both occupants of the office. "Poppycock, everything you told that greedy girl is poppycock," he berated the Consulting Philosopher. "You don't use Taoism to make your money. I've watched you. You don't have a system."

"I have the system of no systems," The Consulting Philosopher countered. "And please stop sneaking in so soundlessly. You get all too much satisfaction from startling me."

"Don't con the girl. You trade on instinct," the old man snarled. "That can't be taught. I'm waiting for you to crash and burn, but you're a lucky devil."

"Instinct is the Tao, that's the whole point," the Consulting Philosopher said sternly. "And though it can't be taught, it can be learned. *Praxis* becomes intuition which becomes instinct."

"Poppycock," the old man replied. "And that greedy girl will get what she deserves—nothing."

JP pouted most fetchingly and the Consulting Philosopher sighed. "For someone of Chinese heritage, you have an astounding lack of appreciation for the graces and wisdom of your culture."

The elderly gent grunted and waved the comment off as if it were an annoyingly persistent wasp. "You exaggerate everything. I'm only part Chinese." Gazing at JP, he added, "They're all greedy, the younger generations. All they want is money."

"I take it you lost at online poker again?"

JP politely muffled a laugh and the foul mood of the elderly gent deepened. "Have your fun at my expense, Caverlock. When you're wiped out and can't afford to have your pretty little Chinese assistant around, don't come to me looking for sympathy."

"Dicky, you're ruining a very rare and precious good mood. JP informed me the consulting business has its first client. Two years of patience has finally been rewarded."

"Must have been a wrong number," Dicky scowled.

JP corrected him. "It was an email."

"OK, a wrong email," Dicky replied sourly.

The doorbell chimed, and all three exchanged anxious glances. "Dicky, I can't let your foul mood destroy my enterprise. Lock your polyglot Pacific self away in the spare room or you shall lose the only mahjong partner you'll ever have who loses so often and so gracefully."

As Dicky shuffled reluctantly away, Caverlock hissed, "And JP is not greedy. She merely wants to make her own way."

Turning to his slim assistant, he eyed her from head to toe, taking in her long black hair, blue jeans and teal-hued blouse. "We must give a positive impression of competence, and if not competence, then confidence will do. JP, have you ever worn a dress to work here?"

"No."

"I thought not. A pity. Some variation of the California denim office attire would be most welcome."

Sniffing the air, he asked with restrained anxiety, "Is the scent of our morning incense still in the air?"

The doorbell rang again, and he stage-whispered, "JP, pull your glorious tresses into a businesslike ponytail in the event this is the mystery client. If it is the client, usher her in, offer her green tea or Sumatran coffee and then sit beside me. Take copious notes about her and what she says on a yellow legal pad. If you reckon I missed something important, speak up or I shall be very cross."

Straightening the sleeves of his dragon-emblazoned red robe, Caverlock readied himself with a deep breath. Straightening her glossy black ponytail as instructed, JP whispered, "Why do you let that horrible old man around?"

"To remind us of what we must never become," he whispered back. "Now take a deep breath and answer the door."

Chapter Two

Female voices filtered in from the entry, and a moment later JP led a striking young woman into the office. Beyond youth but far from middle age, she was not as tall as JP or Caverlock; her expression betrayed her nervousness, but her lack of makeup and erect posture gave a strong impression of self-control. Her dark hair was cropped to her shoulders, and she wore a bright yellow dress with black trim, a summery impression quite at odds with the autumn caution of her manner.

Taking in the multitude of paintings and prints adorning the walls and the bookshelf crammed with travel mementos and artful tchotchkes, she turned to Caverlock. Her hazel-green eyes widened as he approached to greet her warmly with a formal handshake.

"Delighted to make your acquaintance, Miss…"

"Victorine Greenwell."

"Ah, an excellent name," he replied. "I must disclose that my middle name is Victor, so we have at least one small commonality."

Unsure how to respond, Victorine turned to the expansive windows and gazed out at the windswept Bay. In profile, the source of her attractiveness became clearer; her features were agreeable, her mouth fetchingly kissable if one was invited to do so: but it was her green-brown eyes, alive with an uncommon intelligence, which rendered her magnetic.

"A blustery May day," Caverlock commented, but their client remained silently pensive. JP cleared her voice and asked, "May I get you some green tea or coffee?"

Before their guest could respond, Caverlock said, "I hand-grind the Sumatran coffee myself, adding some Ka'u beans to brighten it up a bit. The green tea is aromatic and a revelation."

"Green tea, thank you."

As JP headed for the kitchen, Caverlock instructed, "JP, let's use those *wabi-sabi* Japanese tea cups, thank you."

Turning to Victorine, Caverlock remarked, "Let me assure you that everything said here is in the strictest confidence, and nothing is audio-recorded. We have only our written notes."

By way of small talk, Victorine said, "You have quite an eclectic collection of art."

"Flotsam and jetsam, really," Caverlock said modestly. "I'm drawn to things with a philosophic connection of course, though I confess the connection is often obscure. For example, I love that print of a British folly, a faux Greek temple ruin built for the amusement of 19th century gadabouts. To me, it evokes Hume and Athens, quite a combination."

JP set the rough-glazed earthen-colored cups on the room's round inlaid teak table, and the three sat down in utilitarian Shaker style wooden chairs.

"Now let's hear your situation, Miss Greenwell, in whatever context you reckon most insightful."

Victorine sipped the green tea and gazed appreciatively at the earthen glazed cup.

"I'm not really sure why I'm here," she said hesitantly.

"Ah, well, then we're all on the same page," Caverlock exclaimed, and the first hint of humor softened his guest's tense expression.

"I suppose it was 'leave no stone unturned.'"

"An excellent strategy," Caverlock assured her. "Now just imagine us as trustworthy friends and go from there."

Victorine paused hesitantly and then steeled herself to begin. "My fiancé Drake Darcy went missing ten days ago. I contacted the police first, of course, but the missing persons bureau found nothing—no police reports of an unknown victim, no abandoned vehicles, nothing."

"But of course you didn't stop there," Caverlock prompted her.

"I hired two private investigative agencies and they both reached the same conclusion. Worst-case scenario, Drake died accidentally in some remote location or was murdered." Pausing to regain her composure, she said, "Their second theory is that Drake chose to leave his identity behind and assume another one elsewhere, possibly overseas."

Resolutely continuing her account, she said, "The police told me it's not that uncommon."

JP looked up from her notetaking and Caverlock said, "And so failing to locate Drake, you find it difficult to resume your life without knowing what happened to him."

"Yes," Victorine said. "I can accept he made a new life somewhere, but I'd like to know why."

Caverlock sipped his tea appreciatively. "I take it you find the worst-case scenario unlikely."

"Drake is not a secretive person," Victorine explained. "He didn't trek off alone in the wilderness, he did things with friends or with me. As for being murdered, of course some horrible chance meeting could have occurred, but there's no evidence of that."

"And how is his family taking this?"

"They're devastated," Victorine replied. "He's everything his family values: generous, thoughtful, diligent, bright, ambitious, loyal. His sister is distraught; they're very close."

"They've undoubtedly hired their own investigators," Caverlock said, and Victorine nodded confirmation.

"No evidence of other intimate relationships, no digital crumbs from bank accounts or social media?"

"Nothing."

"Nothing erased before he vanished?" Caverlock asked.

"Nothing. It's as if he walked into a time warp. There was a half cup of coffee on his desk at home, his dirty laundry is in the hamper, his deleted email wasn't even emptied, and his mobile phone was on his desk."

"Most curious," Caverlock commented. "I take it Drake is employed?"

"Yes, at a marketing firm here in the city."

"Has he been there long?"

"Since he graduated from university," Victorine replied. "He's a senior vice-president now."

"A remarkable achievement," Caverlock observed. "Does he travel much in his position as senior VP? Domestic? Overseas?"

After a thoughtful pause, Victorine answered, "He travels regularly to Washington D.C. because the firm has contracts there, and occasionally to Europe and Asia."

"Have you ever accompanied him on these trips?"

"No. They're usually just a few days and there's no time to play. He's promised me we'll go for a real vacation later this year."

Her measured demeanor broke, and she looked down until she recovered control.

JP looked up from her notes and said, "Sorry to ask, but have you set a date for your wedding?"

"Yes, in September," Victorine replied.

Caverlock nodded thoughtfully before breaking the grim silence. "Naturally, people have suggested you to get psychological counseling as the solution to this terrible puzzle, and naturally, you've refused to accept that as the end-game."

"Yes."

Unable to sit any longer, Caverlock eased from his chair and began his figure-eight pacing on the faded blue Persian carpet. "Unconventional problems require unconventional means, which is why you're here."

Victorine considered this and replied, "Yes, I suppose that's right."

"I preface my comments in this manner because my approach may strike you as beyond the boundaries of what we might call conventional unconventionality."

Victorine pondered this disclaimer and said, "You have my permission to pursue any line of inquiry that you feel has any chance of success."

"Thank you," Caverlock replied. "I discern two paths which we should pursue simultaneously. One is Wittgenstein. Now you as remember from

Philosophy 101, Wittgenstein reckoned that all the great philosophic problems could be solved by the study of language. He changed his mind later in life, but that is not our focus here. I propose that you turn over all of Drake's correspondence going back at least a year, not just including intimate correspondence but especially intimate correspondence. Are you able to do that?"

Victorine blanched but steadied herself. "Yes, if it's absolutely necessary."

"It is absolutely necessary, for just as Wittgenstein intuited, if something other than a tragic bolt from the blue occurred, then the language of his correspondence must hold subtle clues that will be visible to those who grasp Wittgenstein's core insights."

Victorine accepted this and JP's eyes widened in mild surprise.

"Wittgenstein was not limited to abstractions," Caverlock observed. "He built a house with his own hands. This inquiry is intensely and entirely practical."

Swinging round to the window, he said, "Next, we must dig deeper into the digital trail left by Drake, for the world is now digital and even an aging dinosaur such as myself understands it is well-nigh impossible to erase all digital fingerprints."

"The private investigators already looked into that," Victorine said, and Caverlock waved her statement aside. "They only looked for the obvious bread crumbs. They've found none, which is of monumental importance. I am confident no one looked at the meta-level and meta-meta-levels because few have the skills to do so."

"And you do?" Victorine asked with visible skepticism.

"No. but I have a fellow who does. Unfortunately he doesn't come cheap. What is your budget for this inquiry?"

The question flustered Victorine and she bit her lip again. "I paid the private investigators by the hour. I have some resources, and Drake's family might help once I've spent all my money." Glancing uncertainly at Caverlock, she asked, "Will it be terribly expensive? I don't know that I can sell my flat quickly enough."

"We would never let you sell your flat to pay us," JP announced, and her sympathies were clearly fully engaged.

Caverlock gave her a reprimanding glance and said, "We will certainly endeavor to keep expenses to an absolute minimum, but some travel may be necessary."

Victorine withdrew her checkbook and asked, "Will a month of my salary be enough to start?"

"Thank you for your trust in us," Caverlock remarked. Turning to hide his wink at JP, he accepted the check and folded it in his robe pocket.

Victorine's tense expression softened into a faint smile. "I trust you will return any money that isn't spent directly on the investigation."

"Of course," Caverlock replied. Glancing at JP, he added, "In fact, your funds will be held in escrow, untouched, until the investigation yields some satisfactory results. However I feel obliged to mention the possibility, however remote, that expenses may far exceed this initial retainer."

JP frowned in disapproval, and Caverlock strode to the bookcase. "JP, you need only summarize my comments here, which will serve as disclosures I deem necessary for Ms. Greenwell to understand."

Pausing by the shelving, Caverlock gazed contemplatively at the chaotic mix of hardbound and paperback books and the profusion of mementos before speaking. "When I was a boy, I contracted a chronic illness and was delivered—dumped might be more accurate, but considerably less charitable—to my aunt's rural abode for the many months of slow recovery."

Touching a hardbound volume of Aristotle's works, he said, "My aunt was kindly, her husband less so, and they were away most of the day working. Their house held only four books: a weathered Bible, an untouched single-volume encyclopedia, and two well-spattered cookbooks. With nothing else to occupy myself, I read the Bible cover to cover, then the encyclopedia and then the two cookbooks. This left me with a curious curiosity and a knack for rather decent scratch scones."

Victorine shifted uncomfortably on the wooden chair, and Caverlock said, "I apologize for the roundabout discourse, which JP tolerates out of the goodness of her heart, but there is a purpose here."

Taking a small cast bronze skull from the shelf in his hand, he said, "Alas, poor Yorick, a fellow of infinite jest and most excellent fancy."

Setting the bronze piece down, he resumed his pacing. "Two biblical stories apply to your case, Miss Greenwell. The first is the account of an adulteress confronted by an accusatory mob. The conniving officials seek to convict Jesus by his own words by asking him to pass judgment on the poor woman, who by the rules of the day would be stoned to death by the assembled mob of men."

Caverlock stopped and turned to face his client. "Jesus knelt down and traced some figures in the dirt, which to our great loss went unrecorded. He then said, 'let him who is without sin cast the first stone.' And in this way, he provoked each man's conscience to serve as judge. Convicted by their own consciences, the mob dissipated, and Jesus forgave the woman but asked her to sin no more."

Victorine absorbed this performance with subdued interest, and Caverlock continued. "My point here is that we must be prepared to forgive what many might view as unforgivable. We do not know the circumstances of Drake's disappearance or decisions, but until we know the full circumstances, we must assume he acted in good faith to make the best possible choices given the situation."

Victorine accepted this without comment and Caverlock stopped by the picture window to gaze at the flags along the Embarcadero billowing in the breeze.

"The second story relates to Jesus arising from the dead. While we may reckon his disciples and friends were overjoyed by this miracle, they were in fact terrified to find the rock closing His tomb pushed aside and His resting place empty."

Caverlock turned to gaze at Victorine. "My point is two-fold. We must be prepared not only for the worst possible news, but to be dismayed to our core by what we find."

His sober tone caused JP to lose her reserve. "We don't know anything yet, so why scare us with these stories?"

"Actually, JP, we know quite a lot already. We know that nothing we know adds up. People do vanish, but with sufficient effort and time, some bits of evidence—physical, digital, accounts of witnesses, security camera footage, and so on—generally turn up. Yet conventional investigations have found nothing. That in itself is peculiar. No, I think we already have enough in hand to conclude that the waters are deeper and darker than the other investigators have suggested."

Victorine's expression telegraphed alarm, and Caverlock said, "It would be irresponsible in the extreme to dismiss what we do know. Don't you see the structure of contrivance? The cold cup of coffee, the undeleted emails, the lack of any trail of crumbs—it's too perfect to be spontaneous."

Warming to the topic, he said, "As Merleau-Ponty observed, we are experiential beings. If Drake, by Miss Greenwell's account a non-secretive person, set out to remove every trace of his disappearance, how could he carry it off so flawlessly on his first attempt?"

Caverlock approached the two seated women and paused theatrically. "As Husserl noted, there are limits to science as an epistemological discipline. The relevant text, for your edification, JP, is titled *The Crisis of European Sciences and Transcendental Phenomenology*."

His deep voice filling the room, he said, "My point here is that we are dealing not just with observable evidence but with a web of unseen forces." Looking directly at Victorine, he said, "Drake struck you as not a secretive person. That makes him the ideal person to hold secrets."

JP's looked up from her yellow legal pad at Victorine, whose expression betrayed her surprise. "Doesn't it strike you as peculiar," Caverlock continued, "that someone clever enough to orchestrate such a thoroughly puzzling disappearance would fail to leave a trail of evidence that suggested a conveniently believable explanation?"

Picking up his rough-glazed tea cup, Caverlock drained the contents and set the cup down with enough force to rattle the tabletop. "Just as Plato's famous cave holds only shadows, we have only shadows. And my point here is that what's missing is more important than what we see. Put yourself in Drake's shoes. For some reason, he feels compelled to disappear for a time. Others may assume he has disappeared forever but there is no reason to assume it is anything other than a temporary fix to a very pressing problem."

Refilling his tea cup, he said, "The first thing you would conjure up is a plausible cover that explains your sudden disappearance: an urgent business trip, an old friend is terribly ill in some distant jungle, that sort of thing. The very last thing you would do is arrange such a perfectly mysterious disappearance that everyone would immediately start investigating your whereabouts. There is nothing more alarming than an inexplicable vanishing, and so the person doing the vanishing would avoid that at all costs. Yet this is what we have: a carefully contrived disappearance."

Victorine shook her head in a show of skepticism. "But wouldn't there be some evidence of Drake's secret life, if that's what you're proposing?"

Caverlock resumed his pacing. "I realize the suggestion that your knowledge of your fiancé is imperfect is disturbing, but you must confess that Drake, or whomever arranged his disappearance, has all but issued a cry for help. How else can we explain the extraordinary lack of a cover story or a trail of crumbs that lead to a plausible explanation?"

Victorine's tone was again one of alarm. "Are you suggesting someone spirited Drake away?"

"I am simply observing that this disappearance has been carefully contrived to send a meta-message, and that this contrivance might be the work of Drake or of an organization—perhaps his employer or some organization as yet unknown."

Caverlock resumed his restless pacing and said, "JP, make careful note of this. The very core of philosophic inquiry is to ferret out the unstated assumptions hidden within a narrative and expose them to the bright light of logic—not just formal logic, but the logic of one thing following another in a sequence which makes sense. Even the most ineffable mysticism of the Taoists follows a narrative from specific assumptions about the way the world works."

Gazing at the two women, he added, "I relish your skepticism, for you are questioning my questioning. And this is how we progress."

Returning to the cluttered bookshelf, Caverlock scanned the rainbow of paperback spines. "I would dearly love to find a particular quote by Tacitus at this juncture, but alas." Picking up a small fabric camel from the shelf, Caverlock toyed with the memento while he spoke. "What are we to make of the absence of action from Drake's employer?"

"But I didn't say anything about his employer's actions," Victorine protested.

"Precisely," Caverlock replied. "A key employee vanishes without a trace, and the employer performs an empty round of suitably anxious handwringing but does nothing you reckoned worthy of reporting."

"They said they were letting the authorities handle the investigation."

"Of course they would say that," Caverlock replied. Setting the miniature camel back on the shelf, Caverlock asked, "Would you say that Drake was a well-organized person, tidy about record-keeping and money, that sort of thing?"

Victorine pondered the question and replied, "Yes, he's well-organized, but not to the point of being obsessive."

"Splendid," Caverlock said. "I presume he has his own flat, and that you have the key?"

Victorine nodded, and he issued her instructions. "I need you to bring every scrap of paper in his home desk, a complete copy of every file on his laptop and every text in his mobile phone and his private correspondence with you—letters, emails, texts. This afternoon would not be too early. Time may be of the essence."

Arising from her chair, Victoria said, "I'll do my best to get it all here before five."

JP set her legal pad and pen on the table and escorted Victoria to the entry. Caverlock turned the pad around and read JP's first neatly printed note: "Client looks like a movie star."

JP returned to the office and gave her employer an appraising look tinted with admiration. "You're better at this than I thought."

The Consulting Philosopher smiled broadly and commented, "I have endeavored, largely with little success, to reveal that philosophy is the most suitable foundation for tackling complex problems. Now you finally get to see philosophy in action."

Caverlock's cheerful demeanor faded and he added somberly, "JP, I strongly suspect this case is a monstrous iceberg adrift in a stormy sea. As yet we only faintly discern the visible 10%, and we see that only through a thick fog. We shall need every moment of your waking time and every spark of your prodigious intelligence to sort through the mass of evidence that will be delivered to us this afternoon."

A creaking of the hardwood flooring announced the return of Dicky from his involuntary banishment. "I saw your client," he announced with satisfaction, as if it were a moral victory over the forces of repression. "Quite a looker."

Caverlock responded forcefully to the intrusion. "I can always count on you to reliably give voice to the coarsest animal spirits," Caverlock commented as he brusquely shooed Dicky out to the entry. Dicky's parting shot was cut off by the slamming of the heavy carved-wood entry door, and Caverlock returned to the office muttering epitaphs in a foreign tongue.

"JP, be sure to lock the deadbolt when you come and go. We must keep Dicky out of the flat for the duration of this case."

His young assistant registered her satisfaction with this banishment and asked, "Where do we start?"

Pacing to the low side table adjoining the divan, he opened an age-darkened metal box whose surface had the texture of coarse sandpaper. Sorting through rolls of euros, renminbi, yen and dollars, he withdrew a thick roll of bills bound by a rubber band. Peeling off a sheaf of bills, he handed the cash to JP and instructed, "We start with restocking provisions.

We shall need to keep our strength up, and so please get whatever brain food you desire in Chinatown, with an extra portion to share with me, and buy a box of my favorite *char sui bao* from that hole-in-the-wall bakery, you know the place. We also need fresh ginger, *yao choy* and scallops for the wok, kimchi, *sato imo* for my *nishime*, which I recall you viewed quite favorably, and please snag whatever you need for your superb braised green beans and *Ants Climbing a Tree*. Oh, and have the delivery service conjure up four *lau-laus* and a container of poi. We shall undoubtedly be eating in for the next few days."

Chapter Three

JP sat cross-legged in the middle of a semi-circle of neatly separated piles of papers occupying the center of the office floor. Exhaling in frustration, she said, "I don't even know what I'm looking for."

The Consulting Philosopher wordlessly completed his tai chi routine on the faded blue Persian carpet and stood in silence for a moment before replying. In contrast to JP's blue jeans and floral poppy-patterned blouse, Caverlock wore gray slacks, a black belt around his ample waist and a button-down pinstriped Oxford shirt.

"Let's be grateful that the tax code has trained everyone in business to automatically save every receipt, no matter how trivial. At least we have material to work with."

Kneeling down beside his assistant, Caverlock said, "We're not looking for something, we're looking for holes in the narrative that don't make sense." Taking up a loose pile of receipts, he methodically glanced at each one. "Consider this trip to Paris. Business class airfare, a night in a hotel in the 16th arrondissement, a TGV ticket stub and then another night at an airport hotel three days later."

"You see the holes, JP? Why a small hotel in the 16th, which is not convenient to the airport, train stations or their client's offices in the 7th? And where did Drake go for the three missing days? We have a TGV stub to Nimes in the south and nothing else."

JP arched her back in a feline stretch, and her long glossy black hair shimmered as she resumed examining the documents. "Maybe he's having an affair."

"That's one possibility," Caverlock agreed, "but his lover would have to jet around the world meeting him in various places on limited occasions. Hardly the ideal romance."

"Maybe he's with a different woman each time, or with a man," JP said.

"I admire the breadth of your suspicions, we must leave no possibility unexamined. Any of these would leave a trail of bread crumbs—a receipt from a meal, a text message, an email. Secret lives add a layer of complexity that's difficult to manage, and leakage is inevitable. The less the leakage, the likelier that some organizational protocols are in place to limit the leakage."

"I don't follow you," JP said.

"Think about leading a secret life, JP. Managing occasional secrets comes naturally enough, but managing a complicated secret life takes practice," Caverlock explained. "This is why organizations have protocols for employees to follow. If we can't find any leakage between his secret life and his ordinary life, then the odds favor his secret life is an organizational one."

JP's eyes widened. "You mean like a spy."

"Not necessarily a spy, but performing some duty or service that must remain confidential. It could be a corporate role, for example, above and beyond his visible position."

"But he could be a spy," JP insisted. "He went to Washington D.C. more often than anywhere else."

"D.C. is a hub of all sorts of government business and technology," Caverlock replied. "The odds of him being caught up in an official intelligence web are low."

"But the odds go up if we don't find bread crumbs."

"Yes. But one trail such protocols can't cover is our everyday use of language. This is why I'm poring over his texts, emails and letters to Victorine. You have the easier task, JP, despite its many difficulties. You are seeking unexplained holes in travel itineraries and trails of bread crumbs that don't match the official narratives of a business trip. I am seeking the equivalent of neutrinos, subtle changes in his vocabulary and tone that would indicate some internal conflict or crisis coming to a head."

Tapping her tablet computer approvingly, he said, "We can't organize all these threads without a database. So enter each question we have—why the small hotel in the 16th arrondissement, where did he go from Nimes, where did he stay in the south, and so on—and whatever we know about the cover story: the client in Paris, any reports he filed on the trip, and so on. Then we can start cross-referencing correspondence and receipts, and start filling these gaping holes."

Caverlock clambered to his feet and pensively scanned the gray skies above the bay.

"We have an epistemological inquiry here," he said, and his deep voice once again filled the room to bursting. "Epistemology is the study of how we come to know the world around us, and ourselves, and in this case, a man we have yet to meet and his life leading up to a most mysterious disappearance."

Warming to the topic, he said, "When we say we know someone, what are we claiming to know? Not just various bits of data, but the story of their life, a narrative that ties together their motivations, goals, values and primal urges, and exposes their weaknesses. How do they handle errors of judgment and the misfortunes that come with living? And most importantly, how do we come to learn all this?"

Turning to JP, he exclaimed, "I have the most astounding thirst for a strong coffee. May I get you a tea or coffee?"

"OK," JP replied noncommittally as she flipped through another pile of receipts. "I see what you mean. His trip to Tokyo is also full of holes."

"Splendid," he remarked. "Patterns may emerge. But our larger puzzle is why Drake was drawn to a secret life in the first place, and what he extracted from leading that life."

Entering the kitchen, Caverlock put on the electric kettle and then placed his bulk in the doorway. "JP, I make very few non-work-related demands of you, but could you crack open the window when you're having those pungent pickles with your congee in the morning? I would tuck into them myself later in the day, but I'm not prepared for that particular assault at dawn."

"Sorry, boss," JP replied, but her tone undermined the sincerity of her apology.

Emerging some minutes later with two white coffee mugs on a lacquer red tray, Caverlock set the tray on the round inlaid teak table and said, "JP, please join me for a short break from your arduous task."

JP arose, bent down to stretch, effortlessly touching her toes and then took a chair opposite her employer. "And I struggle to touch my knees," Caverlock noted wistfully as he handed her the mug. "I made it with sweetened soy milk, as you like it, and here are some of those Hong Kong biscuits you favor."

While JP crunched on a thin cookie, Caverlock flopped onto the divan and returned to the topic of the moment. "Now this is critically important to our work, JP, so pay strict attention. If you devote yourself to this case for the next few days, I promise to give you an immensely insightful lesson on how to make boatloads of cash in the markets."

JP nodded and sipped her coffee appreciatively. "We have two points here," Caverlock began. "The process of knowing ourselves and other people is not like the process of learning grammar or how to construct a boat. The human mind and experience is opaque, unknown not just to observers but to ourselves. The human mind does not have a nice little transparent library of traits, conflicts, motivations, and so on. There is no book that gives us perfect knowledge of an individual. We must parse all this out the hard way, by objective observation and an intuitive search for truths, truths which may change as the individual changes."

Caverlock cracked one of the cookies in half and dipped a piece in his coffee. "My second point is the average person assumes this is a job for psychology, which seeks to categorize individuals with test results, as data is reckoned to be more reliable than other means. But data collection is blind to the deeper dilemma of how do we come to know how and why a person ends up in a place where disappearing is the only viable solution?"

Sipping his coffee, Caverlock continued. "You are young, but you have lived long enough to observe that people claim to hold certain goals and values dear, but their actions reflect entirely different goals and motivations. Our own conscious motivations may not align with what we actually choose to do."

Gesturing at JP, Caverlock said, "You mentioned spying. Some spies thrive on the illicit thrill of getting away with betraying the trust of others. That their secret life is morally reprehensible seems to add to its appeal. Others go down what appears to be a modestly intriguing path that leads, step by step, into a thicket they cannot escape. I fear we can't make any real progress unless we can assemble a collage of Drake's motivations, goals and the forces that have apparently swallowed him whole."

Caverlock paused reflectively, and added, "We can know all sorts of data about him and know absolutely nothing about him or his situation."

Arising from the velvet-draped divan, mug in hand, Caverlock gazed at his youthful assistant. "JP, we haven't discussed your family much, have we?"

JP shrugged and bit into another cookie. "My family is normal," she said. "Not interesting."

"Yet I know your father is still alive."

JP nodded noncommittally, and Caverlock's deep voice softened. "You never speak of him as you do your Mom, your Aunty and your maternal grandmother, and so I know he isn't part of your life."

JP took a sip of coffee and tried to mask her growing discomfort.

"I would be bursting with pride if I had a daughter as fine as you," Caverlock said, and the sincerity in his voice electrified the air. "I don't know that I can ever fully forgive him for not appreciating you."

JP looked down, and Caverlock added, "That's probably why I enjoy serving you so much. As I was unappreciated as a child, I recognize it in you. People love you, but they don't appreciate you. And I cannot help but appreciate you."

Returning to the divan, Caverlock said, "You see, this is how it works. Each person can only know others through the lens of their own experience and self-knowledge. We can only come to know Drake and Victorine though the imperfect lens of our own experience."

JP wiped the tears from her eyes and chided him. "You're a bad boss. You made me cry."

"Yes, I deserve to be punished, and so I'll force myself to open a bottle of champagne at day's end."

The mobile phone laying on the inlaid table chirped, and Caverlock hastened to answer it. "Ah, Carlito, at last we speak. I have a critically important project for you that pays handsomely."

Caverlock listened and then said, "Yes, come over immediately. Fifteen minutes will be enough."

Ending the call, Caverlock remarked, "I don't believe you've met Carlito. Or does my memory fail me?"

"No," JP replied.

"He's young, about your age I would reckon."

JP was silent, and Caverlock considered the absence of a reply. "JP, if you have a boyfriend, or acquire one, I'd be grateful if you'd bring him round—or her, if that's the case. I promise not to pry, and to be on my best behavior. I would be honored by your trust."

"Boss, I'm trying to concentrate."

"Sorry," The Consulting Philosopher apologized. "Of course you have an absolute right to privacy. Forgive the intrusion, I suppose reading Drake's love letters to Victorine put me in a romantic frame of mind."

JP set down the receipts and submitted to the temptation of curiosity. "Don't you feel bad, reading their private letters?"

"Not really," he replied. "I put myself in an objective frame of mind and remind myself this is a serious business. Besides, I have my own romantic experiences, and so I'm a sympathetic reader."

JP stole a glance at Caverlock. "Have you been married?"

"Twice," Caverlock answered. "Once for practice and later as a necessity."

"For practice? Did she think it was practice?"

Caverlock smiled at JP's righteous indignation and said, "No, of course not. We were drunk with infatuation, supremely confident it would last forever, and that our lives would be drenched in creative endeavors and splendid adventures. We would be intellectual free spirits like Simone and Sartre, minus all their sordid affairs."

"And what happened?"

"Youth ends," Caverlock said with unaccustomed simplicity.

"Do you have any photos of her?" JP asked, her curiosity now fully piqued.

"I suppose I do," Caverlock replied a subdued voice. Taking up a folder, he shuffled through folded papers. "This is modern intimacy," he remarked. "Hand-drawn hearts on Post-It notes, snippets of conventionality in phone texts and an occasional love letter typed out on a computer."

Extracting one longhand letter, he remarked, "The French put great store in handwriting, as do I. One must never give a typed note the same veracity as the hand-written one."

Unable to resist, JP arose and came to look at the letter in Caverlock's oversized weathered hands.

"JP, what is the Chinese word for 'inscrutable'?"

JP shrugged and read the longhand letter with intense concentration. "Do you think he really loves her?"

"Actions speak louder than words, and he abandoned her without explanation for what we hope was a very pressing reason—pressing enough to overcome his attachment to her." Stabbing a line with his index finger, he said, "But words are still important. Here is the most interesting line: *'I'm drawn to the mysterious and inscrutable, and long to know all of you.'*"

JP puzzled over the line. "Why is that more important? Because it's poetic?"

"True, there is something of the German Romantic here, a line self-consciously composed while listening to the *Moonlight Sonata,* far from the object of one's affection, or even a bit of Russian passion, something a character in Pushkin might say, or even Pushkin himself."

Caverlock's brow furrowed, and he murmured, "But remove the 'long to know all of you' and it has the pre-ordained qualify of Augustine, a force that cannot be denied. He could be describing the urge that drew him into a thicket he cannot escape."

"Boss, you're talking in circles."

"Just thinking out loud, JP. Why didn't he just write 'mysterious' and leave it at that? Why use 'inscrutable'? Why not 'enigmatic' or 'inaccessible'? Is he describing Victorine, our reserved and intensely private client, or is he describing himself?"

"Boss, you're going overboard. It's just one line. What about the rest of the letter?"

"The rest is also interesting, of course, but I've read all his letters, emails and texts, and he never used 'inscrutable' elsewhere, and certainly not in a line designed to be profoundly romantic to a woman who would, beneath her controlled exterior, be moved by his desire to know all of her, not just the attractive surface bits that have drawn a host of shallow suitors."

"How can you read all that in one line? You're just making stuff up," said JP accusingly.

"Not at all, JP. He's telling her that he recognizes she has uncommon depth, that is to say, an internal life rich in complex feelings, observations, dreams and self-awareness, and that unlike her other suitors, who seek a conquest or trophy, he must know all of her, even the parts she has kept private from everyone else, lest they trample her most secret and fragile gardens."

"No wonder your first wife fell in love with you," JP remarked. "You can really talk."

Caverlock made a slight bow in recognition of her praise and continued his analysis. "My second wife also loved me, and I was besotted with her, but let's focus on Victorine and Drake. Recall that what we're seeking are the truths that delivered Drake to his as yet unknown fate."

Handing JP the entire page to read, Caverlock said, "He's also telling her that he is drawn to the mysterious and inscrutable as a general rule, not just to her. In other words, whatever has ensnared him was also a challenge, just as she is."

Taking up his figure-eight pacing once again, Caverlock concluded, "And so we discern a declaration of his ontological core, who he truly is, and perhaps a subconscious plea for understanding and forgiveness. In a way, he could be telling her, *I am drawn to the mysterious and inscrutable, including this secret project; please forgive me, for it is as unstoppable as my desire to know all of you."*

Caverlock continued pacing in silence, and JP carefully returned the letter to the folder.

"Victorine is profoundly disturbed not just by his disappearance," Caverlock said with conviction, "or by the terrible awareness that he has successfully hidden his secret life from her, but by the possibility that his attraction to mysterious challenges is far stronger than his love for her. That is, even if he surfaces, he'll soon be off chasing another mystery, or even worse, another inscrutable beauty."

"I'm starting to hate this guy," JP murmured darkly.

"Now JP, let's be charitable. I am sure the unhappiest moment of Drake's life was leaving Victorine with nothing but an unnerving vacuum. The conflict within him must be crushing."

JP swept her long hair over her shoulder and began twisting it in a ruminative braiding.

Pausing in front of his slim assistant, Caverlock said, "Who is to say that each isn't testing the other's devotion? After all, his disappearance throws down a challenge to Victorine. Will she seek him out, or abandon him?"

"We still don't know what his secret life is about, or why he disappeared," JP observed. "Shouldn't that be our focus?"

The doorbell rang, and Caverlock brightened. "Yes, and perhaps we can now make progress on that front."

Chapter Four

Carlito entered the office clasping a laptop computer, a slim figure charged with nervous energy, and Caverlock gazed at him with unconcealed amusement. A pork-pie hat clung precariously to his curly pile of dark hair, wire-rimmed glasses framed his expressive brown eyes, and he wore a pin-striped suit jacket over what appeared to be a Hello Kitty pajama top. His tan shorts ended at the knee, exposing his tanned calves to the chilling vagaries of San Francisco weather, while his lizard-green running shoes sported several tears from long use.

JP arose to meet the new member of the team and Carlito gaped as if she'd alighted by magic on his lonely desert island.

"Carlito, my assistant JP, JP, Carlito," Caverlock said, stressing the "lee" syllable in Carlito's name as if he were saying *Lolita*.

"Nice to meet you, JP," Carlito said politely, removing his hat, and JP looked down modestly as she accepted his proffered hand.

"The Caveman didn't mention having an assistant."

JP was unable to restrain a laugh at this nickname and Caverlock sighed. "Carlito is full of witticisms, which we forgive due to his fine character and mind."

JP glanced with amusement at The Consulting Philosopher and said, "You do look like a caveman."

"I see you'll get along most grandly," Caverlock muttered, "at my expense." Turning to the young man, he said, "Carlito, satisfy my curiosity and explain how you came to your most interesting outfit."

Carlito shrugged twice, his high level of energy dictating two shrugs where one would do for most mortals. "In a hurry, grabbed a coat to stay warm and a hat because I like hats."

"You possess a most charming disregard for the opinions of others regarding your attire," Caverlock said with visible admiration. "Perhaps you will inspire JP to vary her sartorial routine."

JP made a pouty face at her employer, who flourished a mock bow.

Gazing at the orderly piles of papers on the floor, Carlito said, "What's the job? I have 15 minutes."

Caverlock sketched the mysterious disappearance and the lack of evidence, and handed Carlito a thumb drive with the files retrieved from Drake's computer. Carlito sat down at the table, inserted the drive in his laptop, waited like a coiling spring for the transfer to complete and then began clicking through documents.

"Here's a couple of things," he said, and Caverlock replied, "Already? You astonish me."

As JP and Caverlock looked over his shoulder, he highlighted lines in the source code of a web page.

"This is his online resume. Look at this URL in the source code. This link to The Trans-Pacific Council is only visible in the source code; it doesn't show up in the web page."

"Fascinating," Caverlock muttered, and Carlito continued. "Here's a site map for his website. There's no link to the map on his page, but here's a link in the site map to the Commodities Board of Governors."

"Maybe it was a coding error that they didn't show up on the web page," JP suggested, and Carlito drew an X in the air with his hand. "No coding error. They were intentionally buried."

As JP and Caverlock absorbed this, Carlito clicked to the database of Drake's wearable fitness monitor. "This guy is pretty fit, but what's interesting is the GPS data, which he probably didn't know he could turn off. He's been out walking or jogging in Bangkok, western Japan, Paris and southern France, Shanghai and Pingyao, China."

"Where in southern France?" Caverlock asked.

Carlito referred to a map on the screen and answered, "Saint Martin du Fort" in English pronunciation. Caverlock repeated the name in French, *Sah Martahn du for*, glanced at the map and added, "Buried deep in the Cevennes. And where in Japan?"

The young man pointed to the digital map. "Kujiranami," Caverlock said. "Niigata prefecture. Ridiculously cold in winter."

Leaning back, Caverlock said, "Curious places for a marketing man to visit on business trips."

"Perfect for rendezvous with secret lovers," JP noted. "That would explain why there's no receipts."

"Possibly," Caverlock agreed. "But the expense and difficulty in arranging these rendezvous are high. Would a young man on the verge of marrying a fine young lady arrange assignations in such remote places? If he wanted to betray her trust, couldn't he do so in the cities he visited?"

"He could be paying or accepting bribes," JP said.

"Perhaps," Caverlock said. "But even bribes would be more easily transacted in cities. We may have to visit these remotes places to learn the truth. Drake has erased the direct digital trails, but left indirect clues, such as these organizations. The overriding question is why. Were these inserted without his knowledge, or did he leave us these bread crumbs?"

"Depends on who has admin rights to his website," Carlito said, "or who's root on the server that hosts his site."

"Carlito, your fifteen minutes have passed," Caverlock noted. "Perhaps you can perform some meta-magic on these organizations' digital fingerprints, and narrow the GPS data to addresses in these corners of the world."

Carlito snapped his laptop closed, gave JP a longing smile and sprinted for the entry.

"He's smitten," Caverlock observed, and JP blushed slightly.

The Consulting Philosopher arose and began pacing. "Our work now comes into sharper focus. Look for any cash receipts from Bangkok, Japan, China and France, and I'll pore over his texts and emails for any references to people, places or activities in these locales. Next, make a list of all the key employees of these organizations, research their resumes and affiliations, and let's see if we can't find some connections between these organizations and Drake's employers—or his family."

As JP returned to the circle of papers, Caverlock said in an uncharacteristically muted voice, "A deep game is being playing here, and we must be careful not to follow the bread crumbs into blind alleys—or a well-camouflaged steel trap."

Chapter Five

Deftly picking up a single inch-long piece of savory green bean with his chopsticks, The Consulting Philosopher pondered it briefly. "We are of course eating crude oil that's been converted into food," he noted conversationally, and then served himself another helping of JP's braised green beans. "Less than 5% of the work growing, harvesting and distributing these delights is performed by humans. The rest is work performed by our energy slaves, otherwise known as fossil fuels."

"Does he always talk like this during dinner?" Carlito asked JP.

JP was working her way through a healthy portion of Caverlock's wok-fried scallops and *yao choy* with single-minded intensity, and she nodded an affirmative response to the young man's question.

"By which you mean a discourse on a real-world topic of great importance," Caverlock countered. "Yes, I always talk like this. A working philosopher is interested in how the real world functions. Philosophy is first and foremost a profound curiosity about the real world, and the only way to truly explore the world is to master its workings with one's own hands and mind. This is of course the foundation of the Tao."

Taking in JP's brisk clean-up of the remaining stir-fried scallops, Caverlock said, "I have succeeded when JP devours my cooking. There is no greater compliment than JP's appetite."

As JP studiously ignored her employer's self-satisfaction, Carlito's attention strayed to the hardwood box on the Shaker-style dining table that held chopsticks, forks, spoons and rolled napkins in separate compartments. Examining the intricate notched corners and use of two different woods, Carlito commented, "Where did you get this? I like it."

"I made it, of course," Caverlock replied. "I have a small shop in the basement which relieves the tiresomeness of pondering abstractions. Which brings us to the day's discoveries. What concrete facts have we pried loose?"

Politely wiping her lips with her neatly folded napkin, JP said, "I found some interesting things in an envelope of loose receipts. A cash receipt for two nights in a youth hostel in Bangkok, but no sign of any airline tickets to Thailand. Then, a restaurant receipt from Adeline, Australia, but no credit card or checkbook entries for a ticket to Australia. A hotel bill in Ukraine, and a café receipt from Canada. I couldn't find any other travel expenses, or any entries in his phone calendar or work notes about going to these places."

"Remarkable," Caverlock said. "Excellent work."

"It looks like he paid cash for airline tickets," JP continued. "There's only a few travel agencies left in Chinatown that take cash. I don't think *laowai* even know about them."

"Yes, there's a cubbyhole travel agency on the second floor above the bakery you like. I doubt any *laowai* has ever stepped foot in it. But our Mr. Drake is no ordinary *laowai*. It might be worth visiting them and asking if your sister's *laowai* boyfriend, Mr. Drake, bought a ticket with cash earlier this year."

JP's puzzlement dissolved as she grasped his suggested path of inquiry. "OK, I get it. Pose as being interested if my poor sister's *laowai* boyfriend is cheating on her."

"Yes," Caverlock continued. "We want to know if he bought tickets with cash, and if he traveled with a companion or companions, that is, if he bought multiple tickets." Arising to clear the dishes, Caverlock explained, "An inquiry without context will arouse immediate suspicions, and the clerks will tell you nothing. But in the context of familial concern about a cheating *laowai* boyfriend—who can resist helping a distraught sister?"

"If he used cash," JP said, "where did he get it? There should be big withdrawals from his accounts. But the bank statements Victorine gave us show very few ATM withdrawals, and those were for small amounts. Maybe he has a secret account Victorine doesn't know about."

"That's somewhere between possible and likely," Caverlock agreed. "The other possibility is that he traveled on private aircraft."

Carlito could no longer restrain himself and he blurted, "That's more likely than you know. These groups he's connected with are full of heavy hitters. I did a quick scan of the groups' leadership, and there's a connection to Drake's father, who's linked to charities and alumni groups that are networks of Old Money, government agencies, tech and financial bigshots—the classic interlocking networks."

"A family connection," Caverlock said as he stacked the dishes in the sink. "Now that's a new and intriguing wrinkle."

Moving to the refrigerator, Caverlock removed a pink bakery box and placed it on the table. "JP, would you be so kind as to serve our guest his choice of the scrumptious pastries you bought on your shopping spree?"

As JP retrieved dessert plates from the kitchen's glass-doored cabinets, Caverlock returned to the table and said, "Carlito, would you please distribute the dessert forks from the box you admired while I attend to the beverages?"

Ruminating while he rummaged through the liquor locker and assorted packages of tea, Caverlock said, "If I were a gambling man, I'd lay odds that our Mr. Drake has also traveled to London, the Caribbean and Switzerland, either alone or with others."

"I almost forgot," JP said excitedly. "He did buy some fancy headphones in Switzerland with cash. How did you guess he'd been to Switzerland?"

Networks have nodes," Caverlock replied. "In the networks Carlito described, London and Switzerland are financial nodes, and the Caribbean is an offshore banking node."

Caverlock filled the electric kettle and loaded a round red-lacquered tray with bottles of port and cognac and the accoutrements to brew single cups of coffee. Setting the tray on the dining table, he mused, "No credit or debit card records. That speaks volumes. Here the world is going to digital money with a vengeance and Mr. Drake skulks around with cash. Why is he hiding in such a clumsy fashion? It's so much more effective to hide in plain sight. How difficult would it have been to arrange a cover for these trips?"

Carlito was vibrating with the urgency to share his trove of information but Caverlock restrained him with a calming gesture. "Let me finish this thought, Carlito, and then you shall have our undivided attention."

While JP set out the glazed fruit tarts on small white plates decorated with cranes, Caverlock busied himself with preparing a well-used Japanese teapot adorned with a pattern of maple leaves that seemed to be floating on the breeze.

Arranging the matching tea cups, he said, "The problem of knowledge is knotty. There is how we come to know things, what we call epistemology, and the limits on what we can know, at least with certainty."

Turning to his youthful compatriots, he murmured, "By all means, pour yourselves a spot of port or cognac to accompany your dessert. But pay attention, this is critically important to the ultimate success of this investigation."

Neither of the young people partook of the spirits, and Caverlock half-filled a tea cup with the amber-colored port, inhaled the aroma and continued. "We're bedeviled by overlapping problems of knowledge. Drake knows all sorts of things we are seeking to know, but it seems entirely likely that his knowledge is imperfect by design, meaning those at the heart of this intrigue may have given him imperfect knowledge to encourage or perhaps coerce his participation."

The electric kettle clicked off, and Caverlock turned to his audience. "Coffee, anyone?"

Carlito said, "Decaf for me," an unsurprising choice given his vibrating energy, and JP said, "Tea, thank you."

Caverlock measured out the coffee with rough precision and filled the filter with steaming water before resuming his discourse. "Our epistemological problem is obvious: how can we gain knowledge of a purposefully obscured situation? How can we sort knowledge from falsities intended to mislead us? There are no clear pathways."

Handing Carlito the cup of coffee, he motioned to the milk and sugar on the tray and arose to pace the compact kitchen. "What troubles me is the clumsiness of Drake's disappearance. Was it purposefully designed to be clumsy, and if so, with what intention? To appear like the work of an amateur? Or is it the clumsiness of an anxious amateur, who reckons the best way to sort a crushing problem is to simply vanish? How can we explain the choice to disappear, while leaving an assortment of clues lying about for us to find, rather than cover his travels with a coherent narrative? Had he conjured up a plausible cover story, it wouldn't seem odd at all to find receipts for headphones or cafes. If these travels were designed to remain secret, it would have been wiser to hide in plain sight."

Returning to the table, he poured the remaining hot water in the teapot and retrieved his teacup of port. "It's also possible that leaving the receipts lying about is a subconscious sign of turmoil regarding his participation in this project, whatever it may be, or the unconscious detritus of a guilty conscience."

JP had cut her raspberry tart into four neat quarters, and was reserving the final portion to enjoy with her tea. "You mean he's done something he feels guilty about?" she asked.

"Possibly," Caverlock replied. "To paraphrase Carl Jung, whatever we leave hidden in our unconscious guides our life, but we call it fate. In other words, though we attribute our path to fate, we're actually guided by unexamined forces and conflicts within us."

Sipping his teacup of port, Caverlock said, "Jung was much more a philosopher than a psychologist. He understood the complexity of the human soul, and that human experience is a maelstrom of reactions to real-world dilemmas and shadowy inner dynamics."

Draining the teacup in one gulp, he paused in blissful appreciation before continuing. "This is why I'm persuaded that Drake's disappearance—if it isn't the result of a cruel accidental death that remains undiscovered—has roots not just in whatever project he pursued on these trips abroad but in his inner life. Perhaps he has doubts about tying the knot with Victorine. There may be family conflicts that are playing out beneath the surface, or obligations that he is rebelling against. We cannot know—the problem of knowledge again—but we must remain alert to the volatile mixing of his unconscious drives and his real-world crises. And the one bedrock we have is that if he is not lying in a shallow grave in some remote and awful place, he is in crisis."

Setting the teacup down with a definitive thud, Caverlock concluded, "And so we have three basic possibilities: One, his clumsy disappearance was designed by professional handlers to appear to be the work of an amateur, for reasons that are unclear. Two, Drake is so far over his head that disappearing struck him as the only solution available, and the clumsiness is the result of his hurried leaving. Three, Drake disobeyed instructions and either purposefully or subconsciously botched his disappearance, leaving clues that would only be found by those looking at metadata and doing the irksome work of sorting every scrap of paper in his home and every file in his digital archives."

JP gazed up from her cup of tea and said, "It could be as a simple as him leaving everything behind to be with another woman."

"We remain alert to that possibility," Caverlock replied, "but it seems to me that Drake is in the midst of an existential crisis, one that melds his betrothal to Victorine, his professional life, his family dynamics and this secret project. He may feel like a character in Camus' *The Plague*, beset by a spiritual illness he could not cure."

Turning to JP, he said, "You are focused on the possibility of another woman, and certainly romantic tangles are a remarkably reliable source of secrecy, betrayal and intrigue. But again paraphrasing Jung, people will do any number of absurd things to avoid facing their own souls. One reliable manifestation of this is people doggedly pursue self-ruination. In this case, if Drake is attracted to another woman, this may have romantic roots, but it could also be a means to cancel his marriage and create all sorts of unnecessary and absurd crises so he doesn't have to face his own soul."

"You're saying he's cheating on Victorine and wants to be caught?" JP asked, and Caverlock replied, "I understand your skepticism, but you are young and have yet to witness humanity's seemingly irresistible urge to self-destruct. It's entirely possible that this mystery is based on Drake subconsciously choosing to disrupt his life in the most extraordinarily destructive fashion to escape some internal dilemma, even as he is blaming Fate for his travails."

Carlito was uncharacteristically subdued, pushing the remaining crumbs of his strawberry tart around his plate, and Caverlock filled the void. "It doesn't add up, does it? A young man with a beautiful fiancée, a loving family and a brilliant career vanishes, apparently of his own free will, but leaves a handful of scattered clues for those with a mind to look for them."

Carlito broke his silence. "He might have been forced, and the clues were just happenstance. Why else would he leave his phone and laptop behind?"

"Excellent point," Caverlock said. "Did either of you find any evidence suggesting the clues were planted?"

"The receipts were stuffed in an envelope in a box of old papers," JP said. "Would you count on someone sorting through such a mess?"

Carlito shook his head like a wet terrier. "Nobody cleaned his laptop or phone. His browsing history, texts, voicemail, all untouched."

"Or so we're led to believe," Caverlock noted. "As you say, why leave his most essential digital tools behind, unless their being left behind served a purpose? Is there any evidence that he has a duplicate phone, laptop and credit card? Maybe these are simulacra intended to persuade us his disappearance was sudden and unplanned."

The two young investigators had no ready reply, and Caverlock said, "Correct me if I'm wrong, but the only secure digital file is one that's unconnected to the Internet."

Carlito quickly interjected, "Correct."

"Old-fashioned paper may well play a critical role here," Caverlock said. "it cannot be accessed remotely, which leads me to believe the evidence we seek is overseas, and the only way we're going to find it is to go to these obscure corners of the world in person."

JP's eyes widened in surprise. "You mean we're going to spend Victorine's money visiting all these places?"

Caverlock assessed her mix of hope and disapproval, and said, "Don't worry, dear frugal JP, we shall travel as stoics on Victorine's money, only steerage, cattle cars and crusts of bread, and we'll use my personal funds for epicurean splurges. But if Victorine truly wants to get to the bottom of the disappearance of her Drake, she will have to pay our expenses. Is your passport current?"

JP searched her memory and nodded affirmatively and Caverlock turned to Carlito, who blurted. "I don't even have a passport. And I don't have time for jetting around. I'm overbooked."

"Nonetheless, we may need you for brief periods, and so you must submit an expedited passport application tomorrow. Consider the possibility that the mystery boils down to a distant computer in which all connectivity has been disabled. That is the digital equivalent of a locked file cabinet. JP and I might be able to force open the locked file cabinet, but not the locked computer." Caverlock poured a splash of port in his teacup and turned his attention the blueberry tart on his plate. "Carlito, the stage is yours."

The sudden prospect of overseas travel dissipated Carlito's natural energy, and he paused circumspectly before speaking. "The tools I used search for all the network connections to people and organizations of interest," he began. "They map out the entire network, including secondary connections. We're interested in nodes, which are like nerve centers, and also dead ends—organizations and people that don't connect to anything but a single node."

Retrieving his laptop, Carlito opened the screen and brought up a complex representation of spokes and connections that looked like a snapshot of a fireworks display.

"Another tool maps email traces, media references and social media. A third one searches the dark web. Now if a person wants to be anonymous, they avoid social media. They only do incognito web searches, and pay in cash, not online. Whatever they do online is posted under pseudonyms."

Caverlock swallowed a bite of blueberry tart and commented, "And have you found such reclusive people connected to Drake?"

"Yes," Carlito replied, "and even more interesting, organizations. Look at the Trans-Pacific Council. It seems legitimate, and Drake's father is a board member. But a lot of the organizations linking to the TPC are dead-ends—they don't have any connections except to the TPC."

"Front organizations," JP said.

"Yes," Carlito confirmed. "Take this organization in France that's linked to the Commodities Board of Governors. Their site only contains one file, an academic paper on commodity pricing models. No board of directors, no email address, a bunch of web pages under construction. A dead-end."

Caverlock interjected, "So it's not just links and nodes, it's what has no links."

"Correct. The interesting part is the secondary search results," Carlito explained. "The Commodities Board of Governors appears to be quasi-official, with links to people in the Commerce and State Departments. Once we trace those connections to people outside the agencies, we get links to banks, corporations, international trade organizations, big foundations—a map of influence."

"Is Drake's father one of the digital reclusives?" Caverlock asked.

"Hard to tell," Carlito replied. "Maybe the lack of email traces and social media links are just a matter of his age. But his digital footprint is just what somebody trying to keep a low profile would have. So we don't know."

"Precisely," Caverlock said. "We know nothing of the intent behind any of this. And how about Drake himself?"

"He's got hundreds of social media and professional links, very typical of someone his age and position."

"The ideal person if the goal is hiding in plain sight," Caverlock observed. "Which makes his hasty disappearance all the more puzzling." Turning to the youthful investigators, he asked, "So how would you suggest we proceed?"

Both were quiet, and Carlito shrugged. "I've never done anything like this."

"Me, neither," Caverlock replied, "but we have philosophy and intuition as our guides."

JP stretched her arms above her head and grimaced. "It's just a bunch of unconnected stuff."

"To quote Nagarjuna, if you desire ease, forsake learning," Caverlock replied. "Our goal must be to learn as much as possible, however formidable the task. So tomorrow morning, JP, you will visit the Chinatown travel agencies and then assemble every one of these overseas receipts, so we have the precise places Drake visited. Carlito, you must somehow find time to file an expedited passport application and run a statistical analysis of your second-order data to identify the people with the highest number of connections within the network you're constructing, and overlay this with the physical locales JP has identified. Then we'll meet in the afternoon to brief Victorine."

"What about you?" JP asked, and Caverlock replied, "I shall be busy investigating Drake's family and his employer, with Victorine's potentially reluctant assistance."

Chapter Six

"What a marvelous vista," Caverlock exclaimed as he and Victorine sat down at a table fronting the Ferry Building, a table that afforded an expansive view of the silver-gray Bay Bridge and pillowy clouds wafting over the quiescent waters of the Bay.

To counter the mid-morning sun, Victorine wore a stylish wide brimmed woven hat that with her Wayfarer sunglasses lent her an air of anonymity. Her flouncy floral sundress exposed her shoulders and calves to the admiring glances of passersby, attention which she studiously ignored.

Caverlock's age-battered fedora, tailored gray jacket over an Oxford pin-striped shirt and black jeans acted as one of his uniforms in the outside world, reflecting a suitably bohemian San Francisco blend of styles and evocations of bygone eras.

Caverlock adjusted his fedora to block the sun and smiled warmly at Victorine. "As a consulting philosopher, I must start by noting that we don't control the nature of information, we only control our reaction to the information. There is nothing inherently negative or positive in the facts of the matter, it is our reaction that is positive or negative or neutral. The Taoists recommended *making all things equal*; that is, accepting every fact, emotion and reaction as equal in our own eyes."

Victorine gazed at him expressionlessly and he added, "I am concerned you may find the topics we must discuss disturbing, hence my introduction." Turning to view the blue skies and billowy clouds, he mused, "I find myself pondering the idea that a hybrid Confucianism might be in play, a Westernized version of filial piety. But I also wonder if Drake is in a narrative worthy of Kafka, a maze of mysterious punishments for the innocent."

The waiter, a towering gaunt figure with a scruffy reddish beard and spiky thatch of hair to match, arrived to take their order, and Caverlock ordered a house coffee with milk, rosemary focaccia and a cheese plate; Victorine ordered an Americano coffee.

"Forgive the intimacy of these questions," Caverlock began, "but I'm afraid they're essential. Has Drake been enthusiastically involved in planning your wedding?"

Victorine shifted slightly. "He's listened attentively, but he seems happy with what I've suggested. Why do you ask?"

The waiter loomed over them, deftly laying the table with the coffees and the warm focaccia smelling of herbs and yeast, and the plate of assorted cheeses.

"I insist you try a piece of focaccia with the Sonoma County *brobi*, and this creamy *chevre*," Caverlock said as he pushed the plates toward his guest. Victorine took a square of the proffered flat bread and carefully sliced off a triangle of the goat cheese. Caverlock gazed at her for a long moment and then broke his reverie.

Leaning forward, Caverlock said in a quiet voice, "I ask because I fear Drake is in the grip of an existential crisis that extends beyond the confines of whatever took him abroad."

Victorine's reserve sagged and she asked, "You mean this is about our marriage? Doesn't everyone have doubts?"

"There are doubts and there are doubts," Caverlock replied. "I myself had no doubts whatsoever about my youthful marriage, but that didn't mean it was destined to permanence. Doubt is a healthy thing, but then there's the other kind of doubt—the kind we keep private. Did you ever share your doubts with Drake?"

Victorine's discomfort was visible. "No."

"And did he ever discuss his doubts, if any?"

"No."

"And so we have a situation in which doubt exists but is never discussed openly," Caverlock said. "In other words, the pretense that doubt didn't exist was maintained by unspoken mutual agreement."

Victorine's discomfort increased but Caverlock pressed on. "I know this is unsettling, but do you think avoiding acknowledging doubt is a sign of healthy communication? No, of course you don't. And so you have your own doubts gnawing away at you, and you have no idea of the depth of Drake's doubts."

In a tone harsh with skepticism, Victorine asked, "Are you saying he disappeared to avoid marrying me? Is that the best you can come up with?"

"No to both questions, but hear me out," Caverlock replied soothingly. "I suspect it is not one motivation, but a confluence of motivations, all of which could be resolved in the short-term by vanishing."

Victorine remained silent, and Caverlock continued. "Which brings us to his sudden disappearance, apparently by his own hand. I have just received confirmation from my digital researcher that an anonymous account that he traced back to Drake has been active today. This suggests that either Drake is alive and well, or someone has assumed his identity, including this anonymous account that he took great pains to keep secret. If someone is using his account, it may be at his behest, or he may be a prisoner. Or as dreadful as it is to give voice to what we all fear, he may no longer be among the living. The most likely explanation in my view is that he is alive and keeping himself well hidden."

Victorine's expression evinced a mix of hope and puzzlement. "But why?"

"Three lines of inquiry present themselves," Caverlock replied, "and I will start with the most intimate one first."

Taking a slow appreciative sip of his coffee, he gazed at his comely client with uncharacteristic sobriety. "I regret having to broach this, but I cannot escape Stendhal's phrase, 'I love her beauty, but I fear her mind.' I don't doubt Drake's love for you or his honorable intentions, but you are formidable in ways you may not recognize."

Victorine looked up in surprise and he continued. "I've observed that a remarkably high percentage of attractive women don't consider themselves beautiful, as they focus on their miniscule flaws, which is ironic, given that these small flaws are the source of their beauty. Faces sculpted by plastic surgery into a doll-like perfection are sadly charmless."

Adding more milk to his own coffee, he said, "As Stendhal understood, beauty is the promise of happiness. Thus men love a woman's beauty but fear her mind. You've probably noticed how grateful men are for your physical affection, and how they wilt like lettuce in hot soup when exposed to your depths. Who are we to say what doubts Drake might harbor about living up to your measure?"

Victorine's body language expressed impatience and she asked, "What are the other avenues of inquiry?"

"The murky project that took him abroad to obscure locales, and his father's ties to that project."

The family connection visibly startled Victorine, and Caverlock cut short whatever questions she was formulating. "Forgive my role as inquisitor, but allow me to answer your questions by starting with my own questions. How would you characterize your relations with Drake's parents and sister? We must have the unvarnished truth or this investigation will surely founder."

His comely companion hesitated, and The Consulting Philosopher said, "Perhaps my guess will make it easier to start. I would guess his mother and father are cordial but controlled, polite but not intimate, treating you more as a potential high-level employee rather than as a family member."

Victorine absorbed his speculation and toyed with a torn triangle of focaccia before answering. "I wouldn't have put it so bluntly, but that's exactly how I feel. They're warm and personable with me, but it's superficial. Not because they're superficial, but because they don't seem to trust me."

"Precisely," Caverlock interjected. "Not because you're untrustworthy but because the family has assets and responsibilities that must remain confidential to maintain their utility. Revealing these connections to you would entail a very large risk while providing essentially zero upside—at least until you can be integrated into the family's shadow network."

Victorine's appetite suddenly emerged and she loaded two slices of cheese on the triangle of focaccia and consumed it in two bites.

"Is it fair to say that the family's reticence has fueled your own doubts?" Caverlock asked, and Victorine reluctantly met The Consulting Philosopher's gaze. "I suppose that's part of it."

"And they have the same reservations about you," Caverlock said. "Imagine the difficulty they face in assessing your trustworthiness and willingness to join what appears to be a consequential network of power and wealth—not just for confidentiality but for burdens much greater than mere secrecy."

Caverlock drained his remaining coffee and motioned to the towering waiter for a refill. "I strongly suspect that these burdens are at the heart of Drake's disappearance. If you'll forgive a bit of speculation, I can readily imagine Drake's doubts about your marriage resting on fears that his family's finances and ties might burden you and your marriage to the point of failure. This becomes even more likely if we imagine that Drake has only recently discovered the true weight of these obligations."

The cadaverous waiter loomed over the table and carefully refilled Caverlock's coffee. Caverlock returned the waiter's toothy grin and paused until the friendly giant was out of earshot. "I realize all this speculation must seem very tenuous, but philosophy is not limited to abstractions untethered from practicalities. The family is core to human life, and we can discern the outlines of Drake's father's ties to networks of power and influence. If asked to hazard a guess, I would say that his father gave him a family-related task that quickly moved from the shallow wading pool his father anticipated to much deeper waters. His parents are understandably distraught that he is out of his depth and has withdrawn in an attempt to sort the crisis out. Our job is to locate him and help him successfully resolve all the issues ensnaring him."

Caverlock removed his worn brown fedora and smoothed his rumpled gray-flecked hair. Glancing about the crowded dockside plaza, he returned the hat on his head and lowered his voice. "Keep your eyes on the wondrous scenery behind me for the next few moments, if you don't mind. Forgive my suspicious nature, but it wouldn't surprise me in the least to find that Drake's parents are monitoring your activities, online and in the real world, in the event that Drake contacts you before he contacts them. They could fear he might entrust you with more than they reckon he should, and perhaps they fear his judgment may buckle under pressure. I consider these parental concerns quite reasonable, so we must tread very carefully and assume we are being monitored by operatives far more experienced than ourselves."

Victorine's posture froze and Caverlock smiled broadly. "Now think of the funniest joke you've heard recently and imagine I just told it to you. A laugh out loud joke."

Victorine managed a stiff grin and Caverlock laughed. "Our attempt to feign good humor is funnier than any joke we might tell. The point here is to look as though the last thing we suspect is that we're being watched. We must understand that his parents fear our success in contacting Drake because they fear we will make matters worse through ignorance and inexperience. We must understand their fears are entirely reasonable. If Drake is adrift in deep waters, why should his parents assume either of us could navigate a treacherous Scylla and Charybdis better than they could?"

Leaning back in his chair, Caverlock took a leisurely sip of coffee and continued. "We must do the opposite of our initial instinct, which is to shy away from public places, avoid contact with his parents and stop exchanging emails about Drake—in effect, doing everything to telegraph our suspicions that we're being monitored and thus increasing their alarm. Instead, we must construct a perfectly believable narrative that confirms their expectations that we are clueless about Drake's travails."

Attracting the oversized waiter's attention again, Caverlock ordered two crème brulee and another Americano for Victorine. "Instead of withdrawing, a move guaranteed to arouse their suspicions, we must construct a persuasive cover story that obscures our investigation. Now imagine you know nothing of what I've just revealed. Wouldn't your natural reaction be to reach out to his parents to see if their private investigators have turned up anything about Drake? Of course you would. And you'd contact his workplace to see if by chance he'd contacted his colleagues."

Pressing his palms together in an isometric stretch, he said, "We must continue meeting in public, and exchanging emails and voicemails about the fruitlessness of my efforts and your rising anxiety as Drake's disappearance lengthens. You must also report these disappointing developments directly to his parents. This will provide cover for our more daring ventures."

"Such as?"

"Such as traveling overseas without telegraphing our destination," Caverlock replied. "Which brings us to the murky business overseas. I need your help in assembling the timeline of Drake's many trips to far-flung locales. He must have provided you with some cover stories while he jetted off to these far-flung locales. We can assume his trips served double-duty: a legitimate marketing meeting provided cover for some confidential business."

The Americano coffee and crème brulee arrived and Caverlock cracked the crystalized sugar crust with his spoon. "This is my favorite part," he exclaimed with childish delight. "It's like cracking open a frozen pond of warm creamy custard."

Victorine scooped up a big spoonful of the dessert and Caverlock noted approvingly, "We must keep our spirits and energy up. Let's consider his possible hideaways. Being inexperienced, Drake likely reckoned an obscure hiding place would be preferable to a teeming metropolis, and he will likely go to a place he's already visited."

Closing his eyes to savor the crème brulee, Caverlock licked the spoon clean and said, "We shall have to go abroad, JP and I, and Carlito may join us should we happen upon a digital tangle. You must stay here and continue to evince ignorance and anxiety. You must not crack, Victorine, and let your guard down. You must be convincingly anxious and steadfast in our own confidentiality. His parents will no doubt probe you for signs that you're playing a double game."

Victorine slid her Wayfarers onto the table and considered Caverlock with a flinty skepticism. "What evidence do you have for any of this? It's awfully farfetched."

Caverlock met her gaze and was momentarily lost in her green-brown eyes. "Yes, let's stipulate it is indeed farfetched, and the evidence is both meager and circumstantial. Perhaps this entire picture I've painted is nothing but brushstrokes of an overactive imagination."

He leaned forward and Victorine's eyes widened as his voice deepened into an authoritative tone. "But let's also stipulate that Drake's numerous excursions all over the planet are farfetched as well, as they do not align with his work: how do you explain Thailand, an obscure village in Japan and an equally remote village in the south of France? What possible explanation is there for all these destinations and for hiding them from you?"

Victorine did not have a ready reply, and Caverlock continued. "I will be the first to confess that the family connection to this web of travels is circumstantial, and I welcome your skepticism. I'll have JP forward you Carlito's database of Drake's father's links to these peculiarly well-connected but strangely inactive organizations, which are like fancy offices with impressive lettering stenciled in gold on the door but few desks and no visible employees. Isn't that a bit farfetched as well?"

Caverlock's mobile phone chirped, mimicking a bird's three-note warble, and he took the call with evident satisfaction. "Excellent, JP. Your womanly wiles are in high gear."

Turning to Victorine, he said, "Drake bought two tickets to Bangkok via Japan with cash at a Chinatown travel agency, and his companion was a young woman."

Despite her best efforts, Victorine blanched and Caverlock added, "Now please don't hold this against JP, but she reckoned from the first that the conventional explanation for Drake's convoluted travels and cover-ups was an affair—the Other Woman on a global scale."

Victorine's grim expression softened. "That was first on my list, too. I know women tend to be in denial about this sort of thing, but I honestly think Drake would break up with me rather than skulk around."

"I agree with your assessment, and I suspect there is another explanation for the female companion. She might be a colleague or someone involved in the murky business abroad."

Caverlock was struck with a thought and he made a call on his mobile phone. "JP, I've been remiss. Gather up photos of women Drake might have taken to the travel agency under innocent circumstances—colleagues from work, family friends and so on, and go back to the agency to see if they recognize Drake's companion." He paused to listen to JP and then replied, "Excellent, I'm not surprised."

Placing the phone on the table, Caverlock said, "JP is already assembling photos. Perhaps you can send her any photos you have of family gatherings, parties at Drake's employer, that sort of thing. Perhaps he went to lunch in Chinatown and the woman in question merely accompanied him to the travel agency by happenstance."

Victorine nodded and Caverlock raised his index fingers in a gesture of alarm. "I'm not thinking clearly. JP will not send you Carlito's database. It must be delivered in a thumb drive, and you must open it in a device that's never been connected to the Internet. It would be child's play to sniff out anything stored on your known devices, and Carlito's database will be highly flammable to those who understand its contents. Perhaps you can order a cheap tablet online and have it delivered to your workplace."

Victorine extracted a credit card from her purse to pay the tab and Caverlock lowered his voice. "We must also prepare for your travel overseas by sowing the seeds of misdirection. JP will show you the travel agency where you can buy a ticket for cash; as cover, we'll meet for lunch tomorrow in Chinatown. When the moment arrives, perhaps you can conjure up an excuse to travel to Los Angeles or some other hub airport, ostensibly for work or to visit friends, and then take your overseas flight."

Warming to the clandestine subject, he spoke with new urgency. "You must tell his parents about your travel plans to LA in an offhand fashion, and keep the real reason confidential from your employer and friends. You will want to stay close to home in case there's news of Drake, of course, and so only a weekend trip will not arouse suspicions. Do you reckon you can do this?"

Her green-brown eyes widened beneath her wide-brimmed hat and she laughed for the first time in their meeting. "You mean can I play Mata Hari? Yes, I think I can manage."

The towering waiter whisked the payment to the register and Caverlock gazed intently at Victorine. "There's one more delicate task you must accomplish. You are skeptical of the idea that Drake's family is keeping tabs on you. To confirm or deny this, we must reach into the classic playbook of espionage and drop some bit of information that triggers a reaction."

Victorine leaned forward to hear Caverlock's muted voice. "The U.S. Navy's codebreakers had broken the Imperial Japanese Navy's code in the early days of World War Two, a monumental task that collapsed the health of the lead codebreaker. The Navy suspected the Japanese were planning an invasion of Midway, a natural stepping stone to the main islands of Hawaii, and so they sent an uncoded message reporting that the water supply on Midway was threatened by an equipment malfunction. The Japanese dutifully reported this development, thereby revealing their code name for Midway."

"So I need to report something confidentially that they mention later in conversation?" Victorine asked.

"Yes, precisely. I will leave it up to you to choose the gambit. For example, if you distribute an email about traveling to Europe next week to look for Drake, and they ask you about your travel plans the following day, that would be evidence they're monitoring you."

Victorine's expression turned pensive and she put her sunglasses on.

"We're being forced to play multiple games of chess simultaneously and must keep our strategies well disguised," Caverlock said. "Now go home and plant your gambit to confirm you're being watched. Call his parents, or drop by if that's not too out of the ordinary. Express your growing anxiety, and ask about their private investigators' results. Keep a close eye on their reactions, but do so under the cover of being distracted by an all-consuming worry."

Victorine nodded slightly and Caverlock continued in a hushed voice. "Remember to download the photos we discussed earlier on a thumb drive--we'll exchange the goods tomorrow at lunch. Buy a tablet so you can review Carlito's database securely, and remember—disable the wireless. It must never be connected to any network—never never never. And lastly, compose an email to me bemoaning my failure to turn up anything and I shall respond by proposing lunch in Chinatown, as if I am an old fool leeching off the good graces of a winsomely worried young beauty. The game is most definitely afoot and we must guard our king and queen most carefully."

Chapter Seven

Pausing at the door of a café shoehorned into a narrow Chinatown alley, Caverlock and JP followed the gesture of an overworked waitress and threaded their way to a corner booth. Raising his voice above the noontime din, Caverlock half-shouted, "Forgive my curiosity, but what prompted you to set your jeans and shirt uniform aside today?"

JP tugged on the sleeve of her lace-trimmed café-au-lait colored dress and replied in a reprimanding voice. "Bosses shouldn't ask employees things like that."

Giving her an admiring gaze, Caverlock said, "I'm dining with an absolutely gorgeous model today. Lucky me."

JP self-consciously swept her long black hair over her shoulder and gave her employer a scrunched-face expression of disapproval before turning her attention to the plastic-clad menu. Caverlock's phone chirped and after listening for a moment, he turned to her with a wry grin. "Carlito is lost. You know his paranoid penchant for only using throwaway phones and turning off GPS. As a result, he's wandering aimlessly on Stockton by Jackson. You'll have to go fetch him."

JP's expression soured and she arose with an irritated sigh. "Don't worry," Caverlock shouted after her. "I won't order until you return."

As JP pushed her way toward the entrance, Victorine slipped past an arguing couple blocking the doorway and gazed uncertainly over the bedlam. JP graciously took her arm and pointed out the corner booth where Caverlock was valiantly attempting to make himself inconspicuous despite his battered fedora, lavender shirt and conspicuous bulk.

Spotting him in the corner booth, Victorine paused to survey the crowded restaurant. Though she cast a striking figure with her assured posture, dark hair coiled in a chignon and crisp white long-sleeved blouse tucked into black jeans, none of the customers gave her more than a passing glance.

As she took a seat on the worn red faux leather cushion beside Caverlock, he raised his voice above the raucous mix of Mandarin and Cantonese, and to those who knew local dialects, a table of Suzhou natives. "You undoubtedly noticed we're the only round-eyes here," Caverlock said in greeting. "It's still an undiscovered gem. I suspect the bilious green exterior turns away the uninitiated."

Two harried waitresses in apricot-colored smocks delivered four heaping platters to the table beside them, and the sweet-pungent scent of oyster sauce wafted over the corner booth. The noise level dropped as the diners focused on the aromatic dishes, and Caverlock lowered his voice to explain JP's absence to his client.

The younger waitress, her face damp from the heat of the kitchen and the fast pace of the lunchtime service, delivered a steel teapot as she swept past their table. Caverlock turned over two of the five sturdy white tea cups on the table and filled them with steaming jasmine tea.

Leaning over confidentially, Caverlock said, "Let's swap the thumb drives, shall we? While one of these Chinese *babushkas* might be keeping an eye on us, I think the odds are relatively low. Have a look at the menu."

Slipping the plastic device beneath a menu, Caverlock slid it over to Victorine and made a show of pointing out the twice-fried green beans. Victorine returned the menu with a similar gesture and Caverlock palmed her thumb drive. "Did you get a secure device to review Carlito's data base?"

"It arrives today."

"Marvelous. We now have your photos and you have Carlito's research." Taking a sip of the hot tea, Caverlock said, "I am keenly aware that you find my philosophizing irrelevant to the search for Drake, but we are not just seeking Drake, we are seeking the truth behind his disappearance. If we find the person but not the truth, we will have completed only half the task, and you will be standing on increasingly unsteady ground."

Victorine ran her finger around the rim of the tea cup, seemingly lost in thought, and Caverlock continued. "The essence of existentialism is that a commitment to a course of action generates purpose and meaning, even if knowledge is imperfect and a passion for the path is lacking. The initial commitment generates its own self-reinforcing dynamic, as the first step leads to the second and so on. The point here is that the commitment itself generates a direction that becomes source of purpose and meaning. The world may be chaotic or even absurd, completely devoid of any sustaining faith, but the action itself generates the purpose and meaning all humans need."

Caverlock sipped his tea again and his voice betrayed a gravely annoyance. "I realize you're juggling a variety of thoughts and emotions, but you hired me to solve this mystery and I must go about it in the only way I know how—and that requires you to understand the context."

Victorine turned and her green-brown eyes glittered harshly. "I'm listening."

"Thank you," Caverlock replied. "These are times that try our souls, and we must hold fast to our deeper understanding or we will surely lose our way."

The older waitress with blunt-cut black hair delivered another platter to the adjoining table and Caverlock exclaimed, "I am sorely tempted to snatch a serving of that eggplant with fungus ears." Victorine cupped her tea in her hands, unresponsive, and Caverlock said, "So purpose comes from action. But how do we choose which action to pursue? This brings us to Saint Augustine and the role of destiny in human life. Has God pre-ordained our fate, or is free will essential to faith? The Chinese of the Sung Dynasty attended to a god of destiny with a colorful name, something along the lines of *Emperor of the Eastern Infernal Regions,* and I wonder if Drake's crisis was destined."

"And what difference would it make if it was destiny?" Victorine asked, and her tone cut the air like a well-sharpened blade.

"An excellent question," Caverlock replied. "It matters because it would have happened at some point, and you are fortunate that crisis erupted before your marriage."

Victorine turned to meet The Consulting Philosopher's grave expression. "I suspect that Drake is predisposed to commit to a course of action wholeheartedly despite imperfect knowledge of what's he's getting into," he said. "This is an admirable trait in many ways but it has led him into deeper waters than he anticipated. Having pondered the consequences of his commitments, he may well be wondering if they were merely unwise or if they're metastasizing into disaster."

"How do you mean?" Victorine asked, and her irritation gave way to anxiety.

"Drake didn't disappear as a lark," he replied. "Your marriage has yet to occur, and so he could withdraw from that commitment, though I doubt he wants to. As for this murky business overseas, he is in too deep to back out, and so the one remaining option was vanishing. I doubt he has a plan for unvanishing."

"How can we possibly find him? He could be almost anywhere," Victorine said, and her despair was palpable.

"We'll come to that once JP and Carlito arrive," Caverlock replied. "I strongly suspect that his doubts about this murky business have cascaded into doubts about your marriage, for the two may be connected. If he feels his family obligations cannot be abrogated, he may conclude it would be unfair to place those burdens on you. Or he may feel he has failed his family by being unable to bring this business to a satisfactory end. He may feel unworthy of you, as I mentioned before. His character destined him to make these commitments all too readily, but he may be inadequate to the task of fulfilling them."

Victorine gulped her tea as if it were neat whiskey and Caverlock refilled her cup. "Victorine, your destiny is caught up in all this as well. If you were destined to fall in love with Drake, and you are predisposed to trusting intimates, as I believe you are, then this murky business would have ensnared you at some point. You should be grateful that the *Emperor of the Eastern Infernal Regions* arranged for this confluence to occur now, before you have more at stake—for example, children."

A sight blush colored Victorine's cheeks and she gripped her teacup tightly.

"You asked what destiny has to do with his disappearance, and the answer is everything," Caverlock said. Glancing at the door, he exclaimed, "Ah, JP has Carlito in tow. Excellent. We shall turn JP loose on the menu and stand in awe of the results." A wry smile brightened Caverlock's somber expression and he murmured to Victorine, "It seems you've inspired JP to break new ground. She's wearing a dress for the first time since I've known her, and it does her admirable justice."

JP's high-collar café-au-lait colored dress stood in stark contrast with Carlito's sartorial excesses; he wore a peaked Alpine hat suitable for a Swiss walkabout and an oversized long-sleeve shirt that combined all the colors of the Caribbean flags in one wild pastiche that clashed mightily with his blue-and-red striped trousers.

As the two took their seats, Caverlock said, "Carlito, this is Victorine, our client. Victorine, this is our resident digital wizard." Transfixed by Victorine's cool allure, Carlito mumbled his greeting and then switched his gaze to JP, newly enchanting in her clinging dress. Carlito's attention cycled between the two women, as if he could not make up his mind who was the more captivating, and Caverlock masked his amusement by handing JP a menu. Sweeping her long glossy hair over her shoulder, JP studied the menu with the intensity of a passenger reading the safety card in a sputtering aircraft.

"I'd like the eggplant with fungus ears, if I may, and something with oysters," he said. Addressing Carlito and Victorine, he asked, "Any requests, or shall we trust JP with the selection?"

In the gesture of a shy schoolboy Carlito removed his Alpine cap from his abundant mop of curly hair and nodded. Victorine asked for vegetables, and Caverlock said, "Splendid. Now I remind you all that we are likely being observed, but pay that no mind. We're here to enjoy a fine meal and share what we've found so far."

The young waitress with the pony tail approached to take JP's order, and a back-and-forth in Mandarin reflected JP's not-on-the-menu choices. The overworked waitress bee-lined to the kitchen and Caverlock lowered his booming voice. "JP, you'll find the photos to aid your search for the Woman of Mystery who accompanied Drake to the travel agency on the drive which I have placed on your lap."

JP withdrew her tablet from her handbag, surreptitiously inserted the drive and held the tablet in her lap while she scrolled through the images.

Turning to Carlito, Caverlock said, "Carlito, what can you tell us about this email account you found that's connected to Drake?"

"It came up on a dark web search," Carlito explained. "It's mostly short messages to other anonymous email addresses, 'funds received,' 'funds sent,' 'arriving tomorrow,' that sort of thing."

"How do you know this is Drake's account?" Victorine asked, and Carlito looked pained. "You know nothing on the web is ever truly secret, right? All secrecy is conditional—where it's stored, how it's encrypted, who has access to the server, the security of the server, all of that. This account can be traced back to IP addresses we know are his. Even better, it's configured to reveal each IP that email was sent from, so we can track his general movements."

"Or the movements of whomever is using the account," Caverlock observed.

"Of course. But the locations line up with the receipts JP found," Carlito countered. "I think all these people assume they're accounts are anonymous. So why would somebody use Drake's account when they think their own account is anonymous? Unless he's having someone else use his account to lead us astray."

"Precisely," Caverlock said. "Or alternatively, he knows the account can be traced to him and he's hoping it will lead us to him."

"Where did his last email come from?" Victorine asked, and Carlito met her anxious gaze with self-conscious hesitancy. "Bangkok, Thailand."

Victorine absorbed this without comment and Caverlock asked her, "How did his parents respond to your questions about their private investigations?"

"As I expected," she replied. "Not quite evasive, but guarded."

"And did your experiment get any results?"

Victorine's expression sharpened. "I followed your idea and sent several emails and texts about traveling overseas to look for Drake myself. His father did ask about my travel plans, and suggested I stay close to home in case their investigations turns up something new."

"That seems definitive," Caverlock said with evident satisfaction. "So they are tracking your communications."

"It might have been coincidence," Victorine replied, but without her usual confidence.

"No, they're monitoring you," Caverlock insisted. "Coincidence isn't an explanation, it's an excuse. They're terrified you might get to him before they do. The family is deeply involved in this murky business, you can count on that."

"They're guarded people," Victorine protested. "They may have nothing to do with all his trips. Maybe he has a secret life nobody knows about."

"Almost nobody," Caverlock replied. "Do you still share JP's suspicion that there's Another Woman at the root of all this?"

"I'd be a fool to dismiss it," Victorine replied.

"It would be useful to identify the Mystery Woman who accompanied Drake to the travel agency," Caverlock mused. "JP, after lunch make haste to show the photos to the travel agency clerks."

JP looked up from her tablet. "I already sent them, and they already recognized the woman. It was his sister Isabelle."

Victorine looked ashen and Caverlock said, "There you are. The family is involved, we don't yet know how intimately, but we can surmise it's at the very heart of this mystery. Thank you, JP, for your very timely work. It seems your Other Woman theory is now considerably less compelling. I have my own report, which is surprisingly brief."

Reaching for the teapot, he exclaimed, "I've been remiss as a host," and filled two tea cups for Carlito and JP. "In pondering Drake's many destinations, I sought some common thread. It's obvious enough: each of these places is a major exporter or consumer of an essential grain—wheat or rice. Consider the list: Ukraine, Canada, France, Thailand, Australia and the U.S. are exporters, Japan and China are major consumers. The links Carlito established to these shadow front organizations have a common interest in commodities and global trade, and so we have the outlines of a well-cloaked effort involving global grain, the very lifeblood of humanity."

Refilling his own cup with tea, he added, "Considering the care given to confidentiality, I think it's fair to assume the organizers are not planning a charitable campaign."

Victorine's eyes widened in dismay. "Are you saying that Drake and his family are involved in some scheme to influence grain prices?"

"No other theory covers all the facts," Caverlock replied sternly. "Yes, a scheme designed to enrich the organizers at the expense of grain consumers. If we keep digging, I'm confident we'll find links to financial institutions in some or all of the global money centers and a banking haven in the U.S. such as South Dakota. It takes money to tie up commodities such as grains, and the typical approach is to risk other peoples' money but keep the gains for the organizers. I suspect they've borrowed the money that is being gambled on the grain speculation, and it's very likely the sums are large."

"This is all speculation," Victorine declared with some heat. "You've no evidence for any of these accusations."

"They're not accusations," Caverlock reprimanded her. "They're theories assembled to explain the facts in hand. Please review the database we've provided and then we'll revisit the subject. In the meantime, let's sketch out a plan of action. We'll each lay out the piece of the puzzle and what can be done to find it. JP, you start."

JP leaned forward to speak in a confidential tone and her glossy mane of black hair spilled over her shoulder. "Carlito said Drake could have somebody else using his account in Thailand to lead us astray. Or maybe the boss of the operation ordered it. For all we know, Drake never left San Francisco. He could be hiding a few blocks away."

This possibility stunned Victorine and caused Caverlock to exclaim, "Remarkable deduction, JP, well done. This opens the door to a question at the heart of the mystery: is Drake in control of his disappearance, or is he acting on others' orders?"

"I think the most important job is to find Drake," JP continued. "Everything else will be answered once we find him."

"I reckon we all agree on that," Caverlock said, "but even if he is only three blocks away in a secure hidey-hole, we have no way to locate him."

Carlito folded his Alpine hat on the green Formica table top and spoke in a low voice. "So far nothing I've done is illegal. All I've done is search what's out there and correlate it to the receipts JP discovered. We could probably find more with hacking tools, but I never do anything illegal."

"And rightly so," Caverlock interjected.

Carlito's tentative shyness was replaced by a youthful animation. "Looking at how these guys operate, I think it's a safe bet they're keeping all the good stuff on devices that aren't connected to any network."

"Are you proposing Drake hid a backup drive somewhere?" Caverlock asked.

Carlito shrugged. "He's a smart guy, so the idea of keeping his own copy of the files probably occurred to him—you know, insurance, just in case."

"So we need to search his flat again," Caverlock concluded. Turning to Victorine, he asked, "Did Drake ever give you anything for safe-keeping? I don't mean a thumb drive—anything that a thumb drive could be hidden in."

Victorine pursed her lips and smoothed her dark brown hair with her right hand. "Not that I can recall."

The group was silent for a moment and Caverlock interrupted her reverie. "It's your turn, Victorine."

His youthful client looked down at her teacup and ran her finger slowly around the rim. "Nobody has any proof that he's still alive," she said quietly, and the other three pondered this truth. "I'd be happy just to know for a fact he's alive."

"That is the same as finding him," Caverlock said. "As we've just discussed, any account of his could be in the hands of others." Turning to Carlito, he said, "He must have a phone, even if it's a rental from an airport. Somebody must have his number."

"If he's being careful, he switches phones a lot and only turns it on for a few minutes at a time," Carlito said.

"You mean like you," Caverlock said with a grin, and Carlito mimicked The Consulting Philosopher's deep voice. "Precisely."

As he refilled Victorine's tea cup, Caverlock said, "I want to stipulate that I consider Drake innocent until proven otherwise. This entire affair strikes me as something that began as a favor but quickly metastasized into something altogether more dangerous than Drake anticipated."

"Thank you," Victorine said, and her icy reserve thawed.

"How about this as a plan of action?" Caverlock suggested. "One, we search his flat again. We arrive separately, of course, and use the rear entrance to the building. Two, Victorine, you speak to Drake's sister Isabelle and share your feeling that the family is hiding something from you. Study her reactions. The parents will maintain their stone wall, but Isabelle might reveal something of importance. Also, ponder where Drake might have hidden something of value. Where would he hide something that he wants you and you alone to find? Are you able to do these tasks?"

Victorine's lack of enthusiasm was evident but she nodded affirmatively.

Shifting his gaze to Carlito, Caverlock said, "Three, Carlito, search Drake's digital world again, from the point of view that he is smart, anxious to hide his tracks, comfortable with the basics of computer technology but not an expert. One thing that occurred to me is there might be some access to remote servers we missed on his laptop. He might have hidden file transfer programs in a seemingly insignificant script or list of expenses."

Shifting round to his assistant, he said, "Four, JP, put the physical addresses of each place you have a receipt for on a map so we can start identifying nearby hotels he might have stayed, offices the enterprise might have rented, specific places we can investigate."

His broad face suddenly sagged in fatigue. "I'll be frank with you, my last-ditch plan is hideously unlikely to succeed, as it is based solely on intuition and the odds that some bit of luck will come our way. If we find absolutely nothing else to go on, I propose moving the investigation to the neighborhoods he visited overseas. This absurd idea is based on two intuitions: one, that Drake is indeed alive and well, and likely exceedingly anxious to remain hidden, and two, he is on his own and has gone to ground where an amateur would reckon it safest: a distant place where he is unknown and where he can blend in."

JP's expression brightened, Victorine's skepticism blossomed anew, and Carlito blurted, "I'm too busy to waste time traveling."

"Yes, yes, we know you're essential to every client, but we need you most," Caverlock replied. "Now here is my thinking. The village in Japan and Pingyao, China are unlikely choices, as he would stand out as a foreigner. He could pass as a tourist for a time, of course, but he probably wants to avoid the stress of constantly being on the move. Thailand would provide good cover, as many *farangs* stay for months at a time. The village in the south of France might appeal to him as a remote place that he can stay as a tourist without question. Ukraine is less likely, as the language poses a challenge. He will likely avoid any place where he might be recognized."

Caverlock shifted his bulk on the cushion and continued in a hurried voice. "If he is still operating under orders, he would still be here, working under plausible cover. This is why I suspect he has gone off on his own."

Heaving a sigh, he concluded, "That is my logic, which is teleological, leaving our good friend Aristotle's dialectical reasoning in reserve."

The young waitress delivered a steaming tureen of hot-sour soup and began ladling it into bowls, and her older colleague arrived a moment later with plates of oysters fried with ginger, eggplant with fungus ears, and *bok choy* in a clear sauce.

"There's three more dishes coming, Boss," JP said, and Caverlock's sagging posture straightened. "I have eyes for nothing but fried oysters with ginger at the moment, though I will allow the possibility that the next round of dishes may prove irresistible."

Chapter Eight

"I'm afraid we've lost Victorine's cooperation," Caverlock said to JP as he closed the entry door to his office-apartment with a heavy click. JP proceeded to the kitchen with the white take-out containers of leftovers from the restaurant, and Caverlock followed her with a downcast expression. "It wouldn't surprise me in the least were she to fire me this very afternoon."

"Why would she do that?" JP asked, and Caverlock threw up his hands in a gesture of despair. "Quite honestly, I think she fears what we might discover about Drake and his secretive family. This murky business overseas is already revealing the family's lack of trust in her, and Drake's evident penchant for hiding rather than trusting Victorine with his entanglements. Would you want to marry into Drake's family after such shoddy treatment?"

"Is that a rhetorical question or a real question?" JP asked, and he said, "By golly, I jolly well need a drink." Shuffling to his liquor locker, Caverlock withdrew a bottle of port and filled a tea cup to the brim with the amber liquid. "Yes, the question is very real. Imagine you're in love with a good-looking, personable, ambitious lad like Drake, and you find the family holds secrets that they will not entrust to you."

"Of course I wouldn't marry into that kind of family. Being rich isn't everything."

"Trust is the real wealth," Caverlock said. "That and truth. Truth is our greatest treasure, and the more intimate the truth, the greater its value. And that, dear JP, is why dear Victorine may fire me, to retain doubt rather than certainty, for certainty may upend her marriage plans."

Taking a sip of the port, he said, "Imagine finding that your fiancé has not only gotten himself into a trackless swamp without a moral compass, but his first decision in crisis is to abandon you. That is searingly painful, and Victorine may project her negative emotions onto us rather than direct them at the source--dear Drake--lest he reject her for not trusting his lack of trust in her—if that makes sense."

"So are we giving up?" JP asked, and Caverlock flopped heavily onto the velvet draped divan. "No, our duty is to the well-being of our client, not to her wishes. If we cannot drag her along kicking and screaming, then we'll find Drake ourselves using our own resources."

"You'd spend your own money?"

Noting JP's incredulity, Caverlock replied, "Yes, if need be. We will see it through to the end, even if I have to sell my position in cocoa futures to fund our travel expenses. I reckon Victorine will remit our expenses once we've uncovered what Drake and his family want so desperately to remain secret."

"What are our chances of doing that?" JP asked. "As you said, he could be dead for all we know."

"Possibly, but Drake strikes me a survivor," Caverlock mused. "He is quick to commit and once committed, enthusiastic, but cautious once the storm swells arise. He'll have a back-up drive or some sort of documentation to protect himself should this murky business come apart."

Swirling the port slowly in the tea cup, Caverlock said, "Given what we know about him, he might have put this back-up within reach of Victorine, an innocent who is exceedingly unlikely to betray him. He entrusted his sister Isabelle with his ticket purchase, but he may fear she will succumb to family pressure and betray him to the parents for what she perceives as his own good."

"How can you know any of this? You're just making this up."

Caverlock chuckled at his assistant's objections. "Human nature follows well-worn trails," he explained. "As I ceaselessly endeavor to instruct you, philosophy must survive contact with the real world, that is to say, it must provide practical guidance and insight." Draining the last of the port, he asked, "Based on what we do know, do you disagree with any of my contentions?"

JP poured herself a glass of water from the pitcher on the dining table and sat down across from The Consulting Philosopher. "I think Victorine is torn. You're right about that."

With sudden fervor Caverlock said, "You know the great irony here? Victorine is torn between wanting to know the truth and fearing the truth might shatter her marriage plans. The irony is that her only hope of salvaging her marriage is to understand that the only solid foundation of a relationship is the truth—about herself, about Drake and his family and about this murky business overseas. Truth is priceless, yet she fears it."

"Nobody wants to hear painful truths," JP observed.

"You're quite right," he replied. "We avoid pain, but at a cost. We can suffer the sharp pain of pulling out a poisoned arrow, or leave the arrow embedded to work its foul magic. You may recall the Buddha used a similar analogy to describe the difference between practical and abstract philosophy."

Toying with the empty cup in his palm, Caverlock said, "I'm not saying Victorine prefers lies; it's more a willful absence of truth."

Setting his empty tea cup on the round teak coffee table, he added, "As Nagarjuna said so astutely, 'If you desire ease, forsake learning.' My fear is that Victorine desires the ease of wishful thinking over the truth, and this avoidance of pain, which she clasps more dearly than the truth, will be her downfall."

The Consulting Philosopher sat up as if struck with a live electrical wire. "You see, JP, here's the thing I wish I could communicate to Victorine. This crisis is a unique opportunity to get to the heart of what matters in life, an opportunity to advance her understanding of herself, of Drake and their bond. If it shatters under the strain, so be it, they will both be the better for it. And if their bond survives the storm, they will understand each other at a depth that would have been impossible to reach in untroubled times."

Caverlock fell into deep thought and JP arose to retrieve the manila envelope of receipts collected from Drake's home desk. Opening her laptop, she began entering the addresses of each establishment that had issued a receipt.

His booming voice rasped by frustration, Caverlock said, "It would be enough to simply narrow the options of where he went to ground. The man is too restless to stay cooped up in a dank cave or drafty barn alive with the clucks of chickens. He will affect some thin disguise and go out where we can spot him—if we know where he's gone to ground. He doesn't know us, and so we won't arouse his suspicions. I am confident he will avoid any place he might be recognized."

Arising from the divan, Caverlock paused by JP's chair and said, "I think it self-evident that I have failed to reassure Victorine that we only seek the truth, and the truth is her only hope. Perhaps she prefers being mired in doubt to an inglorious unraveling of this murky business overseas. But there may be some other source of her distancing herself from our efforts. Perhaps I have botched the management of my first client."

This rare ebb of self-confidence caused JP to look at her employer with consternation. "Therefore it falls to you, JP, to renew her confidence in our approach so she views us as allies rather than enemies. As you know, I avoid gender generalities, and so I am not appealing to your female intuition but to your sympathetic sensitivity to our client. Though you may have been wrong about Drake betraying her for Another Woman, you were not wrong about Drake's abandoning her. As I said earlier, he may be trying to keep her safely out of a maelstrom, and we must allow for a noble purpose behind his decision not to entrust her. But I must task you with arranging a frank but sympathetic conversation with Victorine. If she insists on sabotaging our search for the truth, then all our work will be for naught."

JP's alarm grew and she said, "I don't know what to say to her."

Caverlock heaved a sigh. "I suspect she reckons me an old fool who against all odds might just be right, and that frightens her. She views you as a neutral figure in this drama, and I believe she is more likely to respond positively to your sympathetic nature. In many ways, she holds Confucian values you find familiar."

JP absorbed this without comment and Caverlock said, "We must gather ourselves for the ransacking of Drake's flat. Carlito has his own digital ransacking to do, but Victorine will be there and she will undoubtedly be followed. For this reason I recommend swapping out your delightful dress for something more anonymous, as a means of lowering our profile. Toward the same goal, I will affect a trifling disguise."

*   *   *

"Boss, you look ridiculous," JP whispered, and Caverlock replied, "Excellent, I achieved my goal."

Caverlock, wearing paint-spattered blue jeans with torn knees, a faded denim shirt and a paint-stained white cap, was lugging a soiled olive-drab canvas tool bag up the alley to the rear entrance of an old wood-sided apartment building.

"You're not fooling anyone," JP exclaimed in a hushed voice, and Caverlock paused to catch his breath. "Yes, I know, but they might wonder what I'm planning to do with these tools. I earned these workman's clothes, you know. I painted my flat myself, including the faux finish walls in the bathroom."

Glancing at his assistant, he muttered, "Meanwhile, you are ridiculously charming in your absurdly fashionable fedora and long-sleeve surfer shirt. I doubt you've ever actually entered the sea, much less splashed about in shore-break waves."

Making a face at him under the brim of her gray fedora, she replied, "I'm waiting for you to show me."

"If that's an invitation, I accept," he said. "I have in mind a marvelous white-sand beach in Hawaii few have visited. If we bring this case to a satisfactory close, a working vacation is definitely in order. Now let's see if Victorine left the rear door open as promised." The building had recently been painted a light-green, and the door had a fresh coat of dark-green enamel. Caverlock turned the brass doorknob and the pair entered a service hallway.

Clambering up three flights of carpeted stairs, the pair knocked softly at the door of Drake's flat. Victorine opened the door a moment later, still in the black jeans and white shirt she'd worn to the restaurant. She'd rolled up her sleeves as if preparing to clean, revealing her pale forearms.

JP and Caverlock entered the apartment and Victorine closed the door behind them. The apartment was modest in size and furnishings, reflecting not just frugality but a studied lack of personal expression. The walls were barren of art and only the photos and mementos on the bookshelf in the living room were unique to the apartment's resident. The stale air smelled of disinfectant, and JP opened one of the living room windows looking out on the street below. Setting her stylish fedora on the brown leather sofa, JP looked expectantly at The Consulting Philosopher.

Caverlock removed his paint-spattered white cap and asked Victorine, "Any joy?"

"I just got here," she replied, and her lack of a greeting chilled the air as if the walls were made of ice.

Caverlock overlooked her cool reserve and modulated his voice to a businesslike tone. "We've all seen the same spy movies, so let's start with the obvious hiding places Drake might have borrowed from espionage: the backs of picture frames, the underside of drawers, hollow tchotchkes, dusty books and so on."

"He's cleverer than that," Victorine said, and Caverlock smiled at the implied superiority in her tone. "Yes, of course he is, but we must make the distinction between items he may have intended you to find and items he intended to remain known only to himself. Did you happen upon any hiding places that he might have chosen based on private knowledge known only to you?"

Victorine glanced around the compact living room and dining area and shrugged.

Responding to her evident lack of interest in the search, Caverlock asked, "Are you keeping us in the dark about something? Or have you given up because you've already searched his rooms?"

Victorine bridled at his accusation and replied, "No, I'm not keeping any secrets from you. I just don't think Drake hid little things for me to find. He's not like that. If he's still alive, he'll contact me once he's out of danger."

"Let's hope you're correct," Caverlock murmured dismissively. "But in the meantime, do you mind if I ask a few questions?" Caverlock examined the bookshelf topped with photos and asked, "Does he have a favorite photo of you two? What are his favorite books? Is there a memento you bought him?"

Victorine approached the bookshelf and examined the books and the framed photos on display. "I know he liked *The Little Prince* as a teen. He doesn't have much time to read for pleasure. The last books I saw on his nightstand were *The Enigma of Arrival* by Naipaul, and a history of agriculture, *Against the Grain*."

"And a favorite photo?" Caverlock asked.

Victorine gazed at the photos and picked one of Drake peering out of a hollow in an ancient redwood. "He liked this one, though I don't know if it's his favorite."

"May I?" Caverlock turned the frame over and carefully removed the cardboard backing. Between the photo and the backing lay a slip of paper on which was hand-printed a long string of letters and numerals, and another series of numbers that started with the international access code 011.

"It seems Drake is the sort to leave little things for someone to find," Caverlock commented. "At least when he's pushed to extremes. The first item looks to be a cryptocurrency wallet address, and the second appears to be an international phone number—but appearances can be deceiving. A quick web search will tell us if this is a real phone number or a code designed to look like a phone number. Is this Drake's writing?"

Victorine studied the slip of paper with a mix of surprise and consternation. "Yes, it's his. But why would he hide these numbers?"

"I think we can safely assume he hid them in plain sight, so to speak, so he could tell you where to find them should the need arise," Caverlock explained.

"I didn't even know he had a cryptocurrency account," she said, and her voice betrayed an internal struggle. "Could this be his overseas phone number?"

"Possibly," Caverlock replied. "That would simplify things, wouldn't it?"

Turning to the bookshelf, he scanned the titles and extracted a well-thumbed copy of *The Little Prince*. Opening the thin volume, he shook out another slip of paper. On it were written *D999, D39, D169, D347 LDC Church of the Cross*.

"The enigma of arrival, indeed," Caverlock murmured. "We have the enigmas but not yet the arrival."

Ignoring Victorine's perplexed expression, Caverlock turned to JP. "While we're making progress on the little things Drake left for Victorine to find, I'd like you to look for what he might have hidden as a form of insurance should he feel a noose tightening around his neck. Start with his desk."

Proceeding into the bedroom to Drake's desk and filing cabinet, Caverlock said, "Here is my reasoning. Drake is a clever boy, to be sure, but very likely hurried, as his decision to vanish appears to have been made in relative haste. He probably did not have time for elaborate schemes such as prying up floor boards or constructing false bottoms in cabinets. So he made do with hiding places that are overlooked. For example, pull out the bottom drawer of that dresser and you'll find a few inches of open space. The cartridge in a printer could be removed and something placed in its stead, or an empty cartridge could be pried open and something placed within it. Something non-conducting can be hidden inside a light switch. Just remove two little screws and voila, an instant hiding spot few will think to examine."

JP could not hide her surprise at this catalog, and Caverlock opened the filing cabinet. "I suspect Drake is adept at misdirection, and so putting myself in his shoes, I suggest looking through innocuous files, for example those labeled auto insurance, that sort of thing. Open every folded sheet in the files, especially those which appear innocuous."

JP blurted, "Boss, how do you know all these things?"

"You already know the answer is philosophy," Caverlock replied. "Curiosity about the real world, logic, *praxis*." Turning to Victorine, he said, "Let's continue our search for what he might have left for you, shall we?"

"But why leave me riddles?" she exclaimed.

"As I said, perhaps he intended these to be kept in reserve, information he would instruct you to find if the situation spun completely out of control. Perhaps they'll make more sense once we find the entire collection."

"There's more?"

"Probably," Caverlock replied. "As you just noted, what we have so far is enigmatic. He might have reckoned it a form of protection to scatter the bits so that only you could assemble them all. Remember that he likely acted hurriedly and under pressure."

Striding to the nightstand, Caverlock opened the Naipaul novel and shook it, but only a bookmark fell from the pages. "Well, it was worth a try," he said, bending down to retrieve the bookmark from the carpet. Examining the strip of heavy paper, He murmured, "On second thought, he might have left clues without consciously doing so. Here, have a look."

Victorine studied the bookmark and handed it back. "It's from Paris. We already know he went there for work."

"Yes, but notice the two-digit number in pencil that's been erased by the bookstore's address on Rue Mouffetard. Why write a number and then erase it? Don't you find that curious?"

Mulling the bookmark, Caverlock said, "James Joyce and Ernest Hemingway lived only a few doors from each other on the same street, Rue du Cardinale Lemoine, though not at the same time, as I recall. That's just a short walk from Rue Mouffetard."

"Do you know Paris well?" Victorine asked, and Caverlock answered with unaccustomed brevity. "Well enough. Now may I suggest you look carefully at any tchotchke you gave him, or that he kept from childhood?"

"Boss, I found something," JP announced, and Caverlock and Victorine joined her at the file cabinet. "This was in the *restaurant reviews* folder." Caverlock took the proffered Excel spreadsheet and studied it closely. "Excellent, JP. Do you know what this is?"

JP gazed at the rows and columns without comment and Victorine said, "Something financial?" Caverlock gave her a look of strained patience. "Yes, but specifically."

Victorine said, "Sorry, it's not my field."

"Fortunately it is one of my mine. This is a list of agricultural commodity exchange traded funds and related futures contracts," Caverlock explained. "This confirms that this murky business is related to the ownership of agricultural commodities. If this column is the number of contracts or shares held, the sums at stake are monumental—in the tens of millions."

JP peered at the spreadsheet with renewed interest, and Victorine blurted, "Drake would never get involved in some dubious financial scheme."

"To echo Galileo, *and yet it moves*," Caverlock murmured. "You are saying Drake is immoveable and yet here is proof he is circling a dark sun of immense financial speculation. I think it likely he didn't intend to enter this orbit, but the gravity was irresistible."

Visibly upset, Victorine withdrew to the living room.

Caverlock leaned close to JP and lowered his voice to a whisper. "Now is the moment to strike up a sympathetic conversation. Don't worry about the results, just get her to talk. She's stunned that Drake is mixed up in some sort of vast financial scheme, and no doubt wondering if she knows him at all. She is vulnerable right now and could use a trustworthy confidante. You already know everything, so she doesn't have to worry about revealing too much. Remember that this crisis is a unique opportunity for her to get to the heart of what matters in her life. You must help her do so."

JP looked at Caverlock uncertainly and then nodded. She entered the living room and closed the bedroom door behind her.

JP's voice was faintly audible through the door, but Caverlock showed no interest in attempting to monitor the conversation. Instead, he methodically went from one potential hiding place to the next: pulling out the bottom drawer of the dresser and checking the exposed floor, feeling beneath each drawer for any items that might have been taped to the underside, and then moving to the solid mahogany night stand, which he turned round to examine the back panel and then set beneath the ceiling light fixture. Climbing on the nightstand, he removed the light fixture's ornately etched glass globe and peered around the light bulb.

Putting the globe back in place, he looked beneath the wooden bed frame and lifted the mattress. Finding nothing, he returned the bed to its previous state and withdrew a small flashlight and Swiss Army knife from his left front pocket. Opening the knife's flat screwdriver, he removed every light switch and electrical outlet cover in the room and examined the interior wiring with the flashlight.

The living room was quiet for some time and then Victorine's voice could be heard through the closed door. Caverlock continued his search, examining the interior of the closet and Drake's clothing, removing the base of the desk lamp and then exploring the desk and filing cabinet.

Slumping in the desk chair, Caverlock looked about the room in evident frustration. JP interrupted his meditation by opening the bedroom door. "Boss, Victorine found something else."

Fairly leaping from the chair, The Consulting Philosopher followed his assistant into the living room, where Victorine was holding a pink and white piggy bank and a folded square of paper. Setting the ceramic piglet back on the bookshelf, she unfolded the paper as Caverlock looked over her shoulder.

"At least Drake retained his sense of humor," Caverlock noted dryly. "These look to be family trust bank accounts in South Dakota, the Cayman

Islands and Geneva, Switzerland. He's given you the keys to the kingdom, so to speak."

"These are just bank addresses and account numbers," Victorine protested. "I can't get any money out of them."

"That wasn't his intention," Caverlock replied. "It's enough that you know these accounts exist. The family's reach and wealth are now known to you. That was his intention."

"But why?"

"We can only speculate," Caverlock said. "Perhaps it's a form of leverage over his family, or a secret he no longer wanted held from you. Perhaps it's a confession, or a guilty burden now lifted. Or a mix of all these motivations."

Waving at the bedroom, Caverlock said, "My intuition has failed me. My search was fruitless."

JP entered the kitchen and surveyed the blue ceramic jars on the white-tiled counter and the knife rack on the wall beside the stove. Opening the refrigerator and freezer, she glanced at a single stick of butter and a forlorn package of frozen peas and closed the doors. Glancing round the compact space again, her gaze settled on a decorative wall clock in the shape of a red apple. The hands were frozen, evidence of a dead battery.

JP unhooked the clock from the mounting screw in the wall and examined the back panel's defunct battery and the adjacent clock mechanism. "Boss, can you hand me a small screwdriver?"

"Flat blade or Phillips tip?" he asked, and JP replied, "Phillips." Caverlock retrieved two thin screwdrivers from his soiled canvas bag and handed them to his assistant, who chose the smallest tip tool and removed the plastic ring securing the mechanism and battery case to the back of the clock.

Taking out the battery, she lifted the rectangular mechanism case from the mounting ring and withdrew a bright orange thumb drive.

"Well done," Caverlock marveled, and Victorine's somber expression darkened with this new exposure of her fiancé's secret life.

JP looked up with a modest grin. "I just followed your idea. The clock wasn't working, and so I thought maybe he took out the mechanism to hide something."

"Excellent," Caverlock enthused. "I confess that didn't occur to me. We'll deliver this treasure to Carlito and hope that there's some clues to Drake's location. At least he left these clues."

Turning to Victorine, he said, "As Marx observed, everything solid melts into air. I recognize that everything we've uncovered dislodges another piece of what you'd taken as reassuringly solid, but all will be well if you reconstruct your future with Drake on the foundation of truth, however difficult that might be."

Victorine's embarrassment was evident and Caverlock collected JP's gray fedora from the sofa. "One last question," Caverlock said to Victorine. "Did you speak with Isabelle?"

Victorine nodded, and Caverlock awaited elaboration. Reluctantly, Victorine said, "She's hiding something, or maybe everything."

"I think we can assume the latter," Caverlock murmured. "The family has closed ranks. I believe we're done all we can here, JP. There may be more bits Drake squirreled away, but we have to enough to set a new course."

Addressing his distraught client, Caverlock chose a tone of matter-of-fact optimism. "I shall report what Carlito finds on the thumb drive. Pack your travel kit so you can leave on a moment's notice, and remember we must keep our knowledge, however incomplete, strictly confidential. His parents must continue to hear only of your frustration that the mystery remains impervious to the slightest rays of illumination."

Victorine nodded slightly and Caverlock said, "One more thing. We need a private way to communicate. Your phone and email may no longer be secure, so please open a new anonymous email account and only use an incognito browser to access it. Send the new email to JP and no one else."

"I will," Victorine said, and Caverlock reached for the front door knob. "Excellent. We'll communicate via this private email from now on, except when we intend on misleading those monitoring us."

Closing the entry door behind them, Caverlock pulled the paint-splattered cap on his shaggy head and handed JP her hat. "Needless to say, I await your report of your conversation with Victorine with the utmost impatience," he said in a low voice as they proceeded down the carpeted steps. "But first I insist we celebrate your success in finding the data drive. We conducted the search as stoics, and now we shall celebrate as epicureans. Would you prefer take-out or shall we dine in? We have the fresh prawns and an excellent bottle of Anderson Valley champagne that's begging to be savored."

Chapter Nine

"I am blessed to have such fine companions on this great adventure," Caverlock said as he raised his champagne flute. "I salute you, JP and Carlito."

The Consulting Philosopher clinked his glass with those of his young associates and drained half the bubbly beverage. "I held my curiosity at bay during the preparation of the prawns and Chinese peas, but now I must have your reports. JP, were you able to comfort our distressed client?"

Carlito and Caverlock turned to their charming companion, and Carlito's obvious enchantment caused JP to self-consciously twirl her champagne flute. "You gave me an impossible job, Boss."

"Yes, yes, I know, but the effort was essential, as this old fool only arouses her skepticism. What was her reaction to your sympathy?"

"You know her," JP declared. "She's very private. I can't talk like you. You start talking, and women either fall in love with you or they can't stand you."

Caverlock was taken aback by this champagne-fueled burst of unvarnished reporting. "I take it Victorine doesn't fall into the first category."

JP took a sip of her champagne and said, "She doesn't hate you, but it annoys her that you've been right."

Caverlock refilled his glass and set it on the wooden table. "Ah, yes, well, we all hate that, don't we?"

The champagne reddened JP's creamy complexion, and she too drained her glass. "You're like a boss in China, you get your employees drunk."

"We're simply being convivial," Caverlock protested as he refilled all three flutes. "Here, have a few roasted cashews and almonds. Champagne on an empty stomach is far from ideal. Please continue."

JP chewed a few of the proffered nuts and continued. "I ran out of things to say so I just gave her a hug," JP continued. "Her eyes filled with tears and she had a good cry."

"Remarkable," Caverlock murmured. "My trust in you has been fully rewarded. That was precisely what would comfort Victorine most. We all need a good cry when everything we cherish is under assault." Holding up his flute to examine the rising trails of bubbles, Caverlock asked, "Were you able to say anything about the value of truth?"

"Not like you, but I told her, 'you need to know the truth before you marry him.'"

"Much more concise than my blather," Caverlock agreed. "That's it exactly."

Gazing at the bubbles in her own flute, JP struck a contemplative pose. "I think she's giving up."

Caverlock's mood nosedived. "Victorine? How do you mean?"

"I think she doesn't want to be part of this family any more, and doesn't want to be kept in the dark about Drake's secret life. That's why she burst into tears."

"I fear you may be right," Caverlock sighed. "There is still hope he too doesn't want to be part of this family any more, and the two of them can escape together."

"You're a romantic, Boss," JP said in a chiding tone. "You hope they'll somehow still get together."

Yes, you're right. I am a romantic in this circumstance, as I hope love wins out over what may well be a monstrous swindle."

Arising from his chair, he said, "I'll serve the meal while Carlito begins his report."

Carlito nervously ran his hand through his luxurious mop of dark curly hair. "OK, so just as you guessed, Mr. C., Drake had a file-transfer program nested in an innocent-looking Music folder. The login and passwords to two servers were stored in the program, one in Bangkok, Thailand and one in the south of France. Now of course we'd love to access these servers, but then the administrator would see our login and lock it all down."

Caverlock carefully lowered a platter of savory prawns and Chinese peas and a bowl of steamed rice on the table. "JP's twice-cooked green beans and my *namasu* are arriving shortly. So we have this tantalizing temptation to log in and pilfer the files, but that would trigger unknown consequences for Drake."

"Correct," Carlito confirmed. "They'll probably shut down the whole operation once it's been compromised."

"Obviously we don't want that," Caverlock said. "But can you locate these servers with any precision?"

"There are some geolocation tricks," Carlito replied. "We might be able to buy data from advertisers who shipped a product to a physical address associated with the IP. We also have his GPS data from his fitness monitor."

"And the receipts I entered in the database," JP added.

"Yes, the receipts and the GPS," Caverlock said. "If you can geolocate the servers, that would give us enough data points to identify his likely haunts. What did you find on the thumb drive JP retrieved from the kitchen clock?"

"Financial statements for Drake's family, including the Darcy family trust. They're not mega-rich, but they're rich enough."

"Please define rich and mega-rich," Caverlock requested.

"Mega-rich: private jets. Rich enough: multiple accounts and homes around the world. What's interesting is they seem to be managing all these accounts themselves. I don't see any wealth management companies."

Caverlock delivered the vegetable dishes and asked, "Any account in London?"

Carlito nodded. "London, Paris, Geneva, Singapore, South Dakota, some for the family trust, others for a holding company in the Cayman Islands."

"Are they active or just shell accounts?"

"Not very active but they have serious money on deposit in Geneva, the Cayman Islands and South Dakota."

As she served herself rice, prawns and green beans, JP said, "I think this was leverage over his parents if he decided Victorine needed it."

"Is there any leverage if she can't access the accounts?" Carlito asked.

"Drake is a clever boy," Caverlock observed. "It's probably enough to make his parents guess what else he might have revealed to her." Turning to JP with a wounded expression, he said, "Have you rejected my pickled cucumber and seaweed *namasu*? You liked it last time I made it."

"It's good, Boss, but I need some rice first."

"Ah, of course," Caverlock said in a relieved tone. Addressing his digital consultant, he said, "You must feed that capacious brain of yours, Carlito. If you find the prawns too lightly flavored, I have a variety of sauces on hand. But I did season it with *toban djan* chili bean sauce." Catching himself, he blurted, "That international phone number we found in Drake's flat—is it a valid number or a code in the form of a phone number?"

Carlito replied while serving himself rice and prawns. "It's a Japanese mobile phone in Hiroshima, but that could just be happenstance. If it's a code, the fact it's a working number is just coincidence."

"My Japanese is too rudimentary to be useful, but I could recruit a friend to call the number under some innocent pretext. I sincerely doubt that anyone answers. And I fear even calling the number might set off alarms."

"Don't call it, Boss," JP warned. "Everything we've done so far is passive. Nobody can tell we're snooping. But if we start calling phone numbers or logging onto servers—that's active."

"Correct," Carlito added. "Then the other side can trace it back to us."

"It's like sonar, isn't it?" Caverlock said. "In passive mode, nobody can tell you're quietly listening. But once you send out an active ping, you've alerted the other side to your presence and capabilities."

As his companions tucked into the meal, Caverlock began pacing the cramped kitchen.

"Suppose it's a code, but for what? The possibilities are too broad without some additional context. I think we've exhausted what we can do here and must decamp to Bangkok, which is Drake's last known location, according to the email Carlito traced to him."

"It might be Drake," Carlito interrupted.

"Yes, but as you said, combined with the receipts, fitness monitor GPS and server, it's the best lead we have at the moment. And there's another reason to visit Bangkok first. My commodities trading mentor retired there some years ago with his wife. Despite his relative youth, he is well positioned to deconstruct the mechanics of this commodity speculation for us."

"You said 'visit first,'" JP said between bites. "Are we going somewhere else, too?"

"Unless we locate Drake in Bangkok, then the answer is yes."

"I can't go to Thailand," Carlito protested. "I'm too busy."

"Balderdash," Caverlock retorted. "You're a *mobile creative*. You can wave your digital wand anywhere where there's an Internet connection. You can do your work in Bangkok as easily as from this table."

JP's evident excitement at the prospect of travel contrasted sharply with Carlito's look of a condemned man being shuffled off to the sampan bound for Devil's Island.

"You're a wee bit too comfortable here," Caverlock said. "Being a bit uncomfortable as a result of novel surroundings would do you good."

Carlito's gloom lifted and he replied, "Being a mobile creative cuts both ways, Mr. C. Whatever I could do in person there I can do here. JP, you know about Telnet and Secure Shell, right?"

"A little," JP replied.

"I can log into any server or computer from here with Telnet or SSH," Carlito explained to Caverlock. "Plus my passport hasn't arrived, so I can't go abroad anyway."

"Nonetheless, be prepared to travel the moment your passport does arrive," Caverlock warned. "There may be some circumstance that can't be resolved remotely. It's possible that Drake's freedom or safety could at some point rest on your presence."

"Boss, you're being overly dramatic," JP chided him.

Sitting down at the table, Caverlock spooned portions of each dish onto his plate. "Perhaps. But consider the outlines of this commodity speculation. We know the sums being gambled are large enough to have consequences, even for the wealthy."

Deftly delivering a prawn from his plate to his mouth with his chopsticks, Caverlock chewed the glistening morsel with evident pleasure. "Now suppose Drake has discovered this speculation is not just unsavory, but exploits the innocent. Would his life be in danger if he sabotaged the gamble? Even if the answer is 'unlikely,' we can imagine a number of ways those who are losing millions of dollars might exact some revenge on Drake or his family. Accidents happen with alarming regularity to those who stiff wealthy people with unsavory ties. The bag of tricks is large and diverse."

JP gave Caverlock a skeptical look. "Like what?"

"A drugged drink and salacious photos of the groom with another woman might derail marriage plans, for example. A wealthy family like the Darcy's might have political influence that withers once publicly exposed. If this is indeed a monstrous swindle, what better revenge than pinning it all on Drake and his family? Imagine Drake's agony if his sins come back to haunt his family."

Crunching on the pickled cucumber salad, Caverlock added, "We shouldn't dismiss the possibility that a disgruntled loser might wish Drake to suffer an accident, as a reminder of the cost of his betrayal. Even if the threat were hollow, how could Drake dismiss it? No wonder he has gone to ground. The demons he fears may be real or mere shadows, but he has no way to know. Once again we encounter the limits of knowledge."

"Everything you say could be shadows," JP said.

Caverlock chuckled. "You're ably representing our client, JP. Yes, I'm speculating. But Drake has gone to ground for some pressing reason. Please recall the peculiar shell structure of the Trans-Pacific Council and the Commodities Board of Governors, and their ties to government agencies and banking. These centers of power don't operate like the structures of everyday life, to borrow the title of Braudel's magnificent three-volume history of capitalism. Our knowledge of these power structures is limited."

"Talk about shadows," Carlito interjected. "That's all these organizations are."

"Precisely," Caverlock said. "But shadows that act. Ask yourself why Drake's family is so keen on tracking Victorine's every move—what are they afraid of? Ponder these shadow organizations and then consider the possibility they they're not afraid of Victorine stumbling upon the truth, but of who else might be tracking her. For all we know, the trackers are themselves being tracked. Given the resources being put at risk in this murky business, what better way to track down Drake than to follow not just his fiancée and his family, but the trackers hired by the family?"

JP and Carlito exchanged glances and Carlito shifted in his chair. "That makes sense. But where does that leave us?"

"In a state of caution," Caverlock replied. "We must weave a narrative of harmless incompetence but not so overtly that any watchers will become suspicious. We must plan our exit overseas very carefully. It might be useful for Victorine to fire us and JP's Aunty in Hangzhou to suffer some medical emergency that gives us an excuse to book a flight to Asia."

JP looked askance at this suggestion and Caverlock said, "We are fortunate JP is such a superb cook."

"Not as good as my Mom and Aunty," JP said dismissively.

The three ate in silence until Carlito's phone announced an incoming text. Carlito glanced at the message and arose from his chair. "Sorry, a client has a quasi-emergency. Thanks for dinner."

As Carlito rose from his chair, Caverlock instructed, "Buy whatever data you need from advertisers, we need an address associated with the IP in Bangkok. And put the GPS tracks and receipt addresses on a map of Bangkok."

Carlito gave the OK sign with his free hand and headed to the front door.

After Carlito let himself out, JP fell into a contemplative silence and Caverlock's expression took on an air of anxiety. "I didn't mean to sound jocular about your Aunty's health."

Shrugging off his concern, JP said, "I know what you mean, we might need an excuse to go to Asia."

Noting her uncharacteristically sober mood, Caverlock arose to do the dishes. "Would you like some tea?"

"No thanks," JP replied. "I should be going." Despite this statement, JP remained at the dining table until Caverlock finished the clean-up.

"Sorry I didn't help you," JP apologized as Caverlock accompanied her to the front door.

"*De rien*," he replied. "It's nothing. You have weighty things on your mind but hopefully not on your spirit."

Taking her coat from the hook by the front door, JP twisted her glossy black mane into a rough ponytail and hesitated. "Boss, there's something I've been meaning to ask you."

"Out with it, then, before I burst with anxiety."

Overcoming a great inner resistance, she blurted, "Could I stay in the guest room awhile?"

"Why of course," Caverlock replied in a tone of relief. "Has something happened?"

Her voice quavering slightly, she said, "The family I rent my room from told me they need the room back. I stayed at a friend's for a few nights but there's four girls living in the flat, it's crazy. The rents are so high here, I don't know what to do."

"You reached the right conclusion," Caverlock said in a reassuring tone. "You are welcome to stay here indefinitely."

The invisible weight lifted and JP impulsively gave Caverlock a hug. "I already eat most of my meals here," she murmured.

"Yes, and happily so for me," he said. JP withdrew her embrace in embarrassment, and Caverlock's bemusement steadied. "I suppose we should address the usual delicate topics now rather than later. You don't have any horrid habits such as playing loud videogames at 2 a.m., do you?"

"No of course not."

"Yes, well, as you know I am very circumspect about prying into your personal life, so I'm afraid we must ask direct questions of one another. Should I expect visits from your Significant Other, if you have one?"

Her blush deepened and JP shook her head. "You know I don't have a boyfriend."

"I know nothing of the kind," he protested. "You might have an S.O. that you've kept private, as is your right. And how about your possessions? The room is already furnished and rather small."

"I have a couple of boxes, that's all," she replied.

"That smooths the transition," he remarked. "Do you have what you need to stay tonight? I have a stock of new toothbrushes, and clean shirts that could serve as nightgowns in a pinch."

"I have my toiletry kit in my backpack," JP said. "I'll bring my clothes tomorrow."

"Well then, you can use whatever clean shirts of mine you want tonight." Clearing his throat, he said, "As you know, we will share the bathroom, and so I ask that you don't flush the toilet at night if possible as I am a light sleeper. I shower at night, a habit I gained early in life due to athletics and manual labor. If you are as tidy as I reckon you are, we shall get along swimmingly."

JP nodded and Caverlock added, "On occasion I am pondering some topic in the middle of the night, or suffering a visitation of Churchill's black dog of melancholy, and so I may warm a cup of milk and read a bit of Marcus Aurelius. I hope this won't disturb you, and of course you are welcome to make yourself a snack or read in the living room if you prefer it."

JP nodded again, and after a pause Caverlock said, "Well then I suppose you can hang your coat back up."

After returning the coat to the hook, JP turned and met Caverlock's gaze. "Thanks, Boss."

It was Caverlock's turn to stumble in embarrassment, and he murmured, "Yes, well, it's settled then, except for one last delicate topic." Looking distractedly at the coat on the hook, he said, "San Francisco is refreshingly carefree about living arrangements, but tongues may wag about our sharing the flat, and I want to make sure this possibility doesn't vex you. That is to say, do you feel everything is correct between us?"

Suppressing a grin, JP said, "Yes, Boss. It's fine. I'm not worried people will think we're girlfriend and boyfriend."

Shifting as if he were standing on a hot plate of iron, Caverlock exclaimed, "To put it bluntly, you know how precious you are to me, and I would be ashamed to cause you any discomfort."

Giving him a brief reassuring hug, JP said, "You worry too much, Boss."

Retrieving her backpack, she said, "Do you mind if I take a bath first?"

"No, by all means," he replied in a flustered tone. "I'll fetch you some clean shirts straightaway."

*   *   *

Pulling his dragon-emblazoned red robe close against the morning chill from the half-open window, Caverlock entered the kitchen and said, "To state the obvious, my shirt and sarong look much better on you than they do on me."

Her hair held in a loose chignon by a chopstick, JP sat at the table wearing a white button-down shirt and a blue-and-red paisley sarong. Not looking up from her tablet, JP said, "Good morning, Boss. Tea is ready and there's congee on the stove."

"Thoughtful of you to crack open the window against the dawn assault of pickled cabbage," he murmured. "Did you sleep well?"

"Very good."

"Excellent. Any developments worthy of note today?"

"Your wish came true," JP replied. "I think Victorine fired you."

"Ah, splendid," Caverlock said sardonically. "My wish was for a faux firing, not the real thing."

"Actually, it's hard to tell whether she's firing you or not," JP explained. "She says she no longer needs our services but asks us to keep her informed of any developments from the research we've already conducted."

"Now there's a puzzle worthy of Wittgenstein," Caverlock said as he filled his earthenware ceramic mug with tea. "What did she say exactly?"

"'Thank you for your efforts on my behalf,'" JP read aloud, "'but I no longer have need of your services. Please present an invoice and return any balance of my retainer that is due me. Please keep me informed of any developments that result from the research you've already performed.'"

Caverlock asked, "Was this from her new for-our-eyes-only email account or her public account?"

"Her public account."

Caverlock's mood lifted and he said, "That's actually rather perfect. I doubt I could better the ambiguity. I think she's caught on. She's basically telling us to stop reporting to her unless we have actionable intelligence on Drake's whereabouts. Meanwhile, her watchers will report we've been sacked. As Mao said, there is great disorder under the Heavens and the situation is excellent."

Sipping the hot tea, Caverlock went to the stove and lifted the lid on the pot of congee. "I fear we have a moral crisis on our hands," he said. "When I ask myself what narrative best explains Drake's disappearance, the answer is a morally repugnant task that he feels obligated to complete but cannot do so in good conscience. So he goes underground until he can resolve the conflict within him, but there is no clean resolution, as we cannot resolve good and evil."

JP looked up from her tablet. "You mean this commodities trade is a scam."

"Worse," Caverlock said. "From the outlines traced so far, it seems to be a vast gamble that can only be won at the expense of the innocent: those who buy grain to keep body and soul together rather than as a profitable speculation."

"And Drake is obligated because his family's involved."

"Precisely. Destroying the speculation may destroy his family's wealth, and might paint a target of retribution on the family."

"And he can't tell Victorine, as she will be really angry at him for getting into this, and angry at his family for obligating him."

"That's it in a nutshell. Drake can't bring himself to further a monstrous fraud, but he's afraid that in revealing it he will lose his family and his bride."

"That's a high price," JP concurred. "Is his moral standard really worth it?"

"Hurting others in the all-consuming pursuit of greed will haunt the person with a Kantian remorse to their deathbed. It's like a malefic ghost, you cannot escape your own conscience."

Warming to the topic, The Consulting Philosopher sat down across from his assistant. "Your countryman Mencius saw all humans as innately good until corrupted by society. The venerable Mo Tzu reckoned moral behavior was the Way of the Tao, as this restored order to a chaotic Universe. I daresay Drake is a decent fellow who doesn't appear to be ruled by greed, and so this speculation likely appalled him once he discovered its true nature. He may have intuited that completing this odious business would disorder everything he holds dear rather than restore order to his life."

Heaving a sigh, Caverlock said, "So he is trapped, and it is our task to somehow free the poor fellow, and in doing so, also free Victorine. But I confess to doubts that we can manage it. Our knowledge is so sketchy and the forces pressing this speculation wield a thousand times our feeble resources."

Noting JP's skeptical gaze, he added, "Yes, yes, I know this is all guesswork, nothing but shadows cast by a flickering fire. But if there is another story that accounts for everything we know, please tell me."

Gazing forlornly at the containers of pickled vegetables on the table, he muttered, "I know I'm worried, as I have no appetite."

"Stop feeling sorry for yourself, Boss. We have to do our best. Last night you said we had to go to Bangkok, as that was our best chance. I have my passport, and if we stay fewer than 30 days, we don't need a visa."

Caverlock took a gulp of tea and said, "It's true that I would be stricken by curiosity if we failed to go, and as Shakespeare reminds us in Macbeth and Richard III, timing is everything. Pack lightly for Bangkok, JP, as clothing is cheap there, but toss in what you need for Paris as well, in the event our search in Bangkok is fruitless."

Chapter Ten

"Boss, aren't you hot in that coat?"

Caverlock lowered his sunglasses to squint at JP, who wore a stylish woven sun hat, Wayfarers and a sleeved white cotton dress with a frilly knee-length hem that played in the light breeze wafting off Bangkok's turbid Chao Phraya River.

Smoothing the lapels of his straw-colored light jacket, he replied, "No, I'm absurdly cool despite the brutal tropic sun blasting me like some sort of alien weapon. Of course I'm hot, but that's the point. Professionals here wear a jacket despite the heat, as evidence of their obdurate refusal to bow to mere Nature. This light linen is the best possible solution for an old *farang* like me."

Observing a pair of elderly Thai ladies giving JP a lingering glance, Caverlock said, "While I must sweat buckets to maintain a minimal respectability, you are awarded high status by virtue of your fair skin, Chinese features and demure manners."

JP studiously ignored his commentary. "You're not that old. Wait until you're really old to complain."

One of the vendors pushing a cart through the kaleidoscope of scruffy backpackers, Thai school girls in uniforms of white blouses and stiff blue skirts and motor-scooter taxis awaiting a fare caught JP's attention and she intercepted the young woman to buy two fruit popsicles. Returning with a perplexed expression, she handed one to The Consulting Philosopher. "Thank you," he replied. "I would gladly buy one large enough to fill a backpack."

JP licked the frozen fruit-bar and commented, "Why does everyone speak Thai to me? Can't they tell I'm a Chinese tourist?"

Adjusting his battered fedora, Caverlock sucked on the iced treat. "They speak to you in Thai because everything about you says you're an educated high-status Thai Chinese," Caverlock explained. "Your fair skin means you don't work outside. The ethnic Chinese own most of the wealth here, as they do throughout the Chinese diaspora in Southeast Asia, so it's assumed you're well-to-do. And to top it off, your manner and body language is much more Thai than American."

Surveying the crowd of tourists and locals, he said, "When we get to Paris, we'll ride the Metro and I'll demonstrate my ability to distinguish between Asian-American tourists and Vietnamese-French young ladies without hearing either speak a word. Though their features are such that they could be cousins, their body language tells all. American women of all ethnicities carry themselves very differently from French women of all ethnicities."

Between licks of his frozen fruit treat, Caverlock gazed at his skeptical assistant. "Certain elements of your demeanor are similar to Japanese ladies, but you're quite tall and while your body language is uniquely Chinese, it is very close to Thai."

"So that's why you stare at all the young women," JP teased him.

"One of the reasons, yes," Caverlock replied. "The pleasures of beauty being another. Philosophers observe Nature closely and are attuned to Beauty in all its forms."

A thin man in a sweat-stained cotton shirt and bright pink shorts pushed a cart of fresh fruit through the crowd and Caverlock said with visible excitement, "Fresh pineapple spears. Hold my Popsicle while I get us two."

Returning with two water bottles and the glistening spears of pineapple on a skewer, Caverlock motioned to a recently vacated bench facing the river. After handing JP a bottle of water shedding flakes of ice and the pineapple, he took his fast-melting Popsicle from her and gestured across the river.

"That's where my trading mentor lives," he said. "We'll take a river ferry there once we complete our search of Banglamphu."

Retrieving a damp white handkerchief from his breast pocket, he wiped his forehead. "I've been in Bangkok many times, but the heat and humidity always surprise me."

"It's like Shanghai in summer," JP replied, and Caverlock exhaled loudly. "Yes, Shanghai in July, where I saw birds drop from sky, not merely expired but already roasted."

"You're exaggerating," JP berated him, and he replied, "In this case, not by much." Turning half-round on the bench, Caverlock said, "The River is of course our orientation reference. Behind us is busy Banglamphu, a traditional retail district overlaid with guesthouses and beer gardens serving the frugal backpacker trade. A bit further on, Old Chinatown begins. I hope my favorite tea house has not yet been sacrificed for yet another concrete tower."

Licking the sweet Popsicle drips from his fingertips, Caverlock continued. "The teeming mass of young Western tourists here provide excellent cover for Drake, a fact that he would not overlook, judging by his GPS track and the receipts you located. Those are useful but we can't stake out cafes and guest houses. We desperately need an address from Carlito to narrow our search. Did his plan of seeking an IP address connected to a package delivery bear any fruit?"

Dabbing her fingers with a dampened napkin, JP withdrew her mobile phone and held the screen under the shadow of her wide-brimmed woven hat. "He said he uploaded something on his server for us to download."

"Let's decamp to the room," Caverlock said. "I need respite from the heat and a nap to battle jet lag."

*   *   *

Yawning, Caverlock glanced at the supine figure of JP asleep on the other bed and arose to open the sliding door to the narrow lanai overlooking the river. The setting sun reddened the smoggy skyline, and the savory scent of grilled spicy chicken arose from the alley café three stories below.

"This is my favorite place to stay in Bangkok," he said, and his booming voice filled every square centimeter of the narrow room. "Yes, we could stay in a luxury hotel but they lack this view of the river and the cooling breezes."

JP stirred and Caverlock went to low dresser across from the beds and began peeling one of the mangosteens arrayed on the dark tropical hardwood top. "It's best to awaken now lest we toss and turn all night," he announced. "With the afternoon zephyrs, we can dispense with the air conditioning."

JP sat up, straightened her white dress and murmured, "I don't feel so good."

Retrieving a fresh bottle of water from the room's small refrigerator, Caverlock poured the water into a glass and handed it to her. "Jet-lag?"

"Hmm."

"That time of month?"

"Hmm."

"I have something that might help," he said solicitously, retrieving his toiletry kit from his worn black canvas bag. Handing her two capsules, he explained, "Here's an Ayurvedic tonic and a pain reliever if you have cramps." JP took both capsules and drained the water. Caverlock segmented the mangosteen and handed her half the succulent wedges. "Let's enjoy the bounty of tropical fruits while we're here."

Opening his laptop computer on his bed, Caverlock said, "It's a propitious time to go exploring, as the day's heat is fading but it's still light. Let's see what Carlito has for us."

"As we say in California, Eureka," Caverlock murmured, and JP sat beside him to look at the screen. "It seems a travel router ordered from the IP here was delivered to an address on Chakrabongse Road, just a few blocks away. I sent the map to your email, so we'll use your phone as our guide."

Closing the laptop, Caverlock donned his wheat-colored linen jacket and battered fedora. "I confess to butterflies at the prospect of finding our man," he said. "What if he takes off running like a banshee?"

"You'll think of something, Boss," JP reassured him. "We have surprise on our side."

"Let's hope he doesn't have an even greater surprise awaiting us," Caverlock murmured. Handing JP her woven hat, he ushered her into the hallway and softly closed the door.

Once they reached the pungently scented, *tuk-tuk*-clogged street, Caverlock said, "Do you reckon you will recognize Drake from his photos? He might have grown a beard and may use the usual devices of sunglasses and a hat."

"I don't know," JP said. "You know all *laowai* look alike."

Caverlock grinned at her deadpan humor. "Yes, all these wandering *farangs* do share certain characteristics. But Drake won't be able to hide his height or his nicely even teeth. That said, the odds of us spotting him in these crowds are near-zero—if he's even here. We cannot count on a chance miracle."

Stopping by an elderly female vendor in a hand-woven peasant's hat selling grilled chicken on skewers, Caverlock bought two and handed one to JP. When he thanked the vendor in Thai, her stolid nut-brown face creased in a smile, and Caverlock exchanged pleasantries with her in halting Thai.

"It's important to learn a few words of the local language," he said between bites of the savory chicken. "Thai will be easy for you as a native Mandarin speaker, as the tones are similar. Do you remember how to say *thank you* from our brief practice?"

"*Kap kun kaa*," JP said.

"Excellent. Use that frequently, along with the female gender *hello*, which is...?"

"*Sawadee kaa*," JP answered. Examining her skewer of marinated chicken, she asked, "Is street food safe here?"

"Positively yes," he assured her. "The Thais are quite careful with their ingredients and these are hot off the grill. I subsist almost exclusively on sidewalk fare here, though there is a corner café a few blocks away that serves the most delectable spicy greens."

As they approached Chakrabongse Road, Caverlock diverted JP to a side street, which was a hive of activity as daytime vendors folded up their tarps and cooking equipment and evening vendors set up stalls in their place.

"This is street-level economic vigor at its finest," Caverlock explained. "In the morning, one set of vendors serves Thai coffee and breakfast. Around mid-morning these vendors close up shop and a set of lunchtime vendors take their place. Now we're witnessing the third set of vendors set up for dinner and a night market of household goods and trinkets. Were we to stand in this one spot all day, we could buy breakfast, lunch, dinner and a sweet for dessert from three different vendors without moving more than two meters."

"How can they stay so thin if they eat so often?" JP marveled, and Caverlock said, "It's a mystery."

As they threaded their way through the press of youthful tourists and local residents, JP asked, "Boss, what brought you here in the first place?"

"An intense meditation exercise," Caverlock replied. "I was anxious to practice Buddhism after absorbing the principles in the classroom."

"Did you learn anything?"

"Of course. Every exercise is a learning opportunity. I learned that I fall asleep as soon as I quiet the cacophony of my monkey-mind. This has helped me sleep more soundly than I would have without the exercise. I glimpsed transcendence, and learned about detachment and the limits of my meditative ability."

"And what are your limits?"

"Such a sly humor you have," Caverlock said. "My limits are on parade this very moment."

Reaching an intersection, Caverlock announced, "Chakrabongse Road. I believe our destination is ahead. I confess anxiety has overwhelmed my clarity."

"He might not even be here," JP said. "Let's just take a look."

The address was a mildew-streaked two-story concrete building across from a bank and adjacent to a banyan tree adorned with offerings surrounded by a small court of stalls serving Pad Thai noodles and other street fare.

Pulling his hat lower despite the dusk, Caverlock passed the clothing shops on the ground floor and approached the entrance to the upstairs units. Removing her wide-brimmed hat, JP studied the signage by the glass entry door. "They're all offices," she said, and Caverlock nodded towards the lighted windows above them. "Yet somebody is still there after hours."

Pointing to a placard reading TPC, Caverlock asked, "What would you wager this is an outpost of the Trans-Pacific Council?"

Gazing uncertainly at the stairs visible through the glass door, JP asked "What's the plan, Boss?"

"Let's see if he answers the door."

Opening the entry for JP, the pair quietly climbed the bright-green painted concrete stairs and worked their way down the scuffed yellow linoleum of the dimly lit hallway to the mahogany door marked TPC. After exchanging nervous glances with JP, Caverlock knocked on the door lightly and paused expectantly. Receiving no response, he rapped the wood hard with his knuckles. "*Sawadee krup*, delivery," he said in a high voice.

Leaning his head lightly against the door, Caverlock listened intently for a few seconds and then whispered to JP, "I don't think anyone's inside. I'll leave noisily and then let's see if anyone emerges."

Banging on the door one last time, Caverlock spoke loudly in Thai as he retreated to the stairwell.

Crouching down on the top step, JP peered down the hall at the TPC door, and Caverlock leaned over her. Seconds turned into minutes and Caverlock sat down heavily beside JP. "It was too easy to find him here," he said. "Life is rarely that easy. I suspect there's nothing in that office but a modem, router and server."

"What about Drake?" JP asked.

"He could be a block away or 8,000 miles away," Caverlock replied in a defeated tone. "We must make a good-faith effort to search the places indicated by the receipts and GPS track, but at this point technology hands the baton to human contact. Our best hope is finding someone who has transacted some sort of repeat business with him: a guest house clerk, a waiter, someone who might remember him."

Standing up with an effort, Caverlock said, "I will pose as his uncle and you can pose as his anxious fiancée. But that can wait. First we must nourish ourselves."

The pair passed cafes and beer gardens filling with young tourists, and turned to cross a fetid canal, one of the few remaining *khlongs* that once connected much of the city to the river. A few drops of rain presaged a tropical downpour, and Caverlock pointed to their destination. As the rain pounding on sheet metal roofing drowned out the din of vehicles and human voices, The Consulting Philosopher and his lissome assistant ran toward a brightly illuminated corner café covered in tarps that gushed rain water onto the surrounding sidewalks.

The sweet smell of rain replaced the odor of decaying fruit discarded by the nearby fruit stalls, and the pair, thoroughly soaked despite the brevity of their run, ducked under the tarp and took a seat at one of the five small turquoise plastic tables shoehorned into a compact L around the propane-fired stove.

Catching her breath, JP set her damp hat on an empty chair and wiped the wet hair from her forehead. Her soaked cotton dress clung to her shoulders, outlining the straps of her bra, and Caverlock offered her his pocket handkerchief. "It's only slightly less damp than our clothing," he apologized as he peeled off his jacket. "It's actually quite refreshing, given the heat of the day."

A young Thai waiter with neatly trimmed hair in an NBA-emblazoned T-shirt and faded green cargo shorts delivered a spattered one-page menu and Caverlock indicated a large bottle of Elephant brand beer in the cooler.

Addressing JP, he asked, "And what sparks your appetite tonight, or perhaps it's our morning. Noodles? Fish? Prawns?"

Sagging tiredly in the plastic chair, JP said, "You order," and as Caverlock delivered the order in a mix of English and Thai, the waiter filled two glasses with cold beer.

Clinking glasses in a toast, Caverlock said, "*Chok dee, gunbei, cheers.* I've ordered us a splendid meal of spicy spinach, chicken curry with vegetables and noodles with mild seasoning."

Nursing her beer, JP gazed at her newly enlivened employer and observed, "You were depressed a little while ago. What changed?"

"We're hungry and about to eat a meal worthy of an 8,000 mile journey. That's one change. The second one is that I've admitted to myself that it's virtually impossible to find someone who has gone underground unless you discover their links to the above-ground world. Consider the immense but ineffectual FBI and police search for a handful of Weather Underground fugitives in the 1970s. Yes, we now have technology to aid us, but the solution for those living underground is to avoid the digital world and follow Carlito's lead in using throwaway phones and so on. Turn off you smart TV, remove the SIM card from your phone, stay offline, pay only in cash and move often, and technology is thwarted. Fortunately for us, Carlito knows to look for user errors, such as Drake leaving the GPS function of his fitness monitor on. But that only helps if Drake is using his fitness monitor, and it's been silent for days."

Draining the small glass of beer, JP said, "OK, so it's hopeless. And that cheered you up?"

"We would need a bit of random luck to find him," Caverlock replied, "but can't count on a bolt of luck. No, the key is Drake's link to the above-ground world, which I now believe is a single person he trusts implicitly: his sister Isabelle."

JP's tired gaze sharpened and Caverlock continued. "We had the essential evidence thanks to you but I overlooked its importance. Who was with Drake when he bought his ticket in the Chinatown travel agency? Isabelle. Who denied knowing anything when confronted by Victorine? Isabelle. Not because she's following her parents' orders, but because she can't trust Victorine not to give away Drake's whereabouts."

The waiter slid a bowl of steamed jasmine rice and the spinach, curry and noodle dishes between them and Caverlock spooned a portion of the curry into the two melamine bowls provided. Sliding one bowl to JP,

Caverlock said, "Use a spoon if you wish with the curry, it's perfectly acceptable here."

Sampling the noodles with his chopsticks, Caverlock expressed his pleasure with a broad gesture of wonderment. "Isn't this delightful? A chilled beer, sumptuous dining and a feast for the senses surrounding us."

Engaged in sampling each of the dishes, JP did not respond, and Caverlock resumed his discourse on Isabelle. "So how do we extract information from Isabelle? Our starting point is both moral and practical: Isabelle, as innately wise as she might be, is ill-prepared to extricate Drake from this vast swindle. So while she believes hiding his whereabouts is protecting him, she is unwittingly increasing his danger, as neither of them have the wherewithal to extricate him."

JP paused between spoonfuls of curry to ask, "And you do?"

"Perhaps not, but my mentor will. The net result, JP, is that we are morally bound to trick Isabelle into revealing Drake's location, as only we grasp the peril and his inability to extricate himself. Only we can extract him with a minimum of risk."

"So how do we trick her?"

Refilling their glasses with beer, Caverlock lowered his voice. "You will send Victorine an email to her new private account instructing her to confront Isabelle in person. Victorine must convince Isabelle that she knows Drake has been in Bangkok and that he left very recently."

"We don't know that," JP protested, and Caverlock theatrically cocked one eyebrow. "Of course we don't, but by claiming we know, Isabelle may be tricked into confirming or denying it. Then Victorine must persuade Isabelle that this swindle is about to blow up in Drake's face if we can't reach him in time. That will likely strike Isabelle as fulfilling Drake's greatest fear, for we can be relatively confident he's sketched out his anxieties to Isabelle. Victorine must tell Isabelle that there's a resource available who can save the day, referring obliquely to my commodity-trading mentor, but only if we can reach Drake soon. Victorine can honestly state that if Isabelle refuses to reveal Drake's location, her family's fortune and reputation will swirl down the sewer."

JP's voice expressed a renewed enthusiasm. "This might work. Isabelle wants to save her brother and her family. If Victorine convinces her this is the only way to save them, then how can Isabelle refuse?"

"Precisely," Caverlock replied. "The timing is perfect. If we send an email to Victorine within the hour, it will be 7 a.m. in San Francisco. She can act on our instructions while we grab a few hours of sleep."

Dividing the last of the noodles between their two plates, Caverlock said, "It's absolutely essential that Isabelle understands that warning Drake of our arrival will only send him fleeing straight off the cliff to his doom. We must impress this most forcefully upon Victorine."

"But what if Drake hasn't left Bangkok?" JP asked.

"That would be ideal, as we could reach him within an hour of receiving his location from Victorine, and my trading mentor is a mere half-hour boat ride and walk away."

"Yes, but why would Isabelle trust Victorine if she's wrong about Drake having left Bangkok?"

Heaving a sigh, Caverlock murmured, "I don't know. Victorine will have to improvise. But my sense of Drake is that staying in one place increases his anxiety. He is likely living by Andy Grove's dictum that *only the paranoid survive*. So the likelihood that he has left Bangkok is rather high in my view. Why else buy a travel router?"

Withdrawing baht from his wallet to pay the tab, Caverlock said, "Let's get back to the room so you can send the email. I think Victorine will respond positively to you. We'll stop by the night market in the hopes an elderly vendor I met last time is still making her splendid coconut-rice treats wrapped in banana leaves. That and a slice of fresh dragon fruit would yield the perfect dessert."

Chapter Eleven

Caverlock arose from the bed with a groan and made his way to the glass sliding doors overlooking the river. The early morning overcast was streaked with hazy light from the rising sun, and he went to the dresser to look at his watch. Brushing aside the folded banana leaf remains of their dessert, he announced, "6 a.m. in Bangkok is 4 p.m. in San Francisco."

JP stirred and half-opened her eyes. Focusing on Caverlock's dragon-emblazoned pajamas, she murmured, "Does everything you wear at night have dragons?"

Taken aback, Caverlock replied, "I've never considered it, but yes, a very high percentage of my pajamas have dragon motifs. I suppose I rest best with sleeping dragons."

Proceeding to the bathroom, Caverlock rinsed a washcloth in warm water and delivered it to JP, who dutifully wiped her face. "I'm sorry to awaken you, but I'm anxious to see if Victorine responded to your email."

Blinking at the morning brightness, JP sat up, straightened her lace-trimmed peach nightgown and entered the password for her phone. "Nothing yet."

"Perhaps Isabelle isn't available until after work," Caverlock said, but his attempt to hide his anxiety failed. Turning to his assistant, he asked, "Did you sleep well?"

"Not really," JP yawned.

"I had an atrocious night myself," Caverlock said. "Only by the most disciplined meditation was I able to drift off for a few hours of troubled sleep. I hope I didn't snore."

"I only heard you breathing," JP said. "And your nightmare. It didn't bother me."

"Nightmare? That's interesting, because I always remember nightmares, regardless of their size. Nightmares are scale-invariant."

"You talked in your sleep," JP explained. "I think it was French."

"Well now we are in trouble," Caverlock said with dark humor. "I only dream in French when I'm truly struggling." Exhaling loudly, he said, "But there's nothing to be done but press on. Bertrand Russell believed that thinking deeply about a problem in the conscious realm triggered the subconscious mind to work out the problem in our sleep. Perhaps my agitated dream in French was part of that process."

Caverlock walked to the closet to feel his wheat-colored linen jacket. "Perfectly dry. The downpour washed out the sweat. Excellent. Let's get breakfast in the street market, and proceed straightaway to my mentor's house across the river."

JP scurried into the bathroom with an armful of clothing and Caverlock performed his Tai Chi routine in front of the glass doors.

JP emerged some time later in a long-sleeve white blouse with lace openings at the sleeves and elbows, and a matching frilly knee-length skirt.

As she combed her glossy black tresses, Caverlock gazed at her fresh adorability and then turned his eyes to the river. "Is that outfit from last night's shopping haul at the street market?"

"Yes," she said with evident satisfaction. "Everything is so reasonable here."

"I'm delighted you found a cartload of things you like," Caverlock said as he headed for the bathroom. "You looked positively local as you flitted from stall to stall like a bee pollinating flowers. Do you think your multiple purchases will fit in your suitcase?"

Glancing at herself in the mirror, she bound her hair in a ponytail and said, "I noticed yours has plenty of room."

"Yes, you would notice that," he replied. "I shall hurry my toiletry and we can be on our way."

*   *   *

"Fish sauce was the foundation of the Roman Empire as well as the Thai empire," Caverlock said as JP scanned the many options for breakfast arrayed on the morning market's tables. "Full of nutrients and just the thing to flavor bland food."

Despite the early hour, the street market was thronged with local residents and a smattering of expats and tourists. "If you favor congee, there are several stalls over yonder," Caverlock said, his voice rising over the din. "I am heading to the Thai coffee stalls at the end of the street. Would you like a sweet, strong coffee?"

"No thank you, I'll buy a tea," JP replied, half-shouting to be heard in the cacophony of voices.

Caverlock scanned the busy street and touched JP's elbow to gain her attention. "I want you to observe the morning ritual of offering food to the monks of the nearby temples." Withdrawing baht bills, Caverlock bought two plastic bags filled with various vegetarian dishes and condiments in smaller bags sealed with rubber bands.

"Here," he said, handing one of the bags to JP. "Choose a monk to donate a daily meal to. Don't worry which one, they take everything back to the temple to share. And put your hands together and bow slightly after he accepts the offering. That gesture of respect is called a *wai*. Here, I'll show you."

Caverlock approached a young monk in saffron robes with a newly shorn scalp who stood uncomfortably amidst his older colleagues. Removing his battered fedora, Caverlock approached the youthful aspirant and handed him the bagged meal. As the monk accepted the offering, Caverlock placed his hands together and dipped in a slight bow.

The monk smiled in embarrassment at the sign of respect from the graying *farang*, and Caverlock motioned JP to make her offering. After considering each of the nearby monks, she approached a grizzled elder monk, slipped off her floppy woven hat and handed him the bag. He accepted the offering and looked on stolidly as she made a hurried *wai*.

"We both gained a bit of merit," Caverlock announced. "Every Thai male is duty-bound to become a monk, even if only for a few weeks. Some men do their service right out of school, while others wait until they retire. Hence the young and old men. The middle-aged monks tend to be ordained reverends attached to one of the local temples. My meditation exercise was held at one such local temple."

"What about women?" JP asked, and Caverlock nodded toward the center stalls of the crowded street. "You see the pair of Buddhist nuns? They're present, but not in the same numbers as the men due to the tradition of sending one boy of the family to the temple. That is no longer the case, but the duty to serve once in your life remains. Is anyone in your family religious?"

JP ignored the question and said, "You'd make a good monk, Boss."

"I would welcome the discipline but chafe at the hierarchy. But Thai coffee calls. I'll meet you back here in twenty minutes."

At the appointed time, Caverlock threaded his way through the sea of pedestrians and met up with JP. "And what did you select for breakfast?" he asked.

"Noodles," JP replied, and Caverlock exclaimed, "Me, too. Thin rice noodles with a prawn or two." Glancing at his watch, he asked, "Still no email from Victorine?"

JP Shook her head. "No, I just checked."

"The cross-river ferry dock is that way," Caverlock indicated. "My mentor will meet us on the dock."

The morning heat raised beads of sweat on the faces of The Consulting Philosopher and his assistant as they made their way to the ferry dock. The pair waited while the dock filled and emptied with passengers from the larger river taxis that plied the more populated shore. A short time later Caverlock pointed to the approaching cross-river ferry, a smaller craft with fewer passengers.

"You don't want to be splashed with this water," Caverlock warned in a soft voice. "Better to sit toward the center, and hold onto your hat. The breeze can get rather blustery mid-river."

Not a single tourist boarded, and Thai passengers, many clutching bags of produce from the morning markets, filled every seat on the craft. The ferry motored briskly across the churning brown water of the great river, rising and falling with the waves trailing the slow-moving freight barges that kept to the center channel.

Caverlock let the other passengers disembark, murmuring to JP, "As you can see, this is the non-tourist side of the city."

A single road led inland, devoid of traffic other than passengers arriving or departing from the ferry. A once majestic but now abandoned villa surrounded by a decaying wall of peeling plaster occupied the riverfront beyond the concrete quay; a forlorn sheet-metal refreshment stand beside a sheltering tree was the sole enterprise other than the handful of motorbike taxis and *tuk-tuks* that awaited passengers seeking transport.

Those departing passengers who didn't flag one of the motorbike taxis walked past the refreshment stand and on down the quiet road, while the few people waiting to cross the river boarded the ferry, leaving Caverlock and JP alone on the quay.

Wiping the sweat from his forehead, Caverlock said, "It's not like him to be tardy." A moment later a brightly decorated *tuk-tuk* taxi roared up to the quay and screeched to a halt by the refreshment stall. A lithe dark-skinned man in a faded flowered short-sleeved shirt and tan shorts wearing a frayed baseball cap leaped from the vehicle and waved at Caverlock.

"Is your friend Thai?" JP asked.

"No, Filipino-Hawaiian-Portuguese," Caverlock replied. "But he blends in rather well, doesn't he?"

"Oliver, you're looking well for an old rascal," the man said as he embraced The Consulting Philosopher, who stood a half-head taller than his friend.

Caverlock turned and said, "Ben, my assistant, JP. JP, this is my trading mentor, Ben." JP politely extended her hand and Ben grasped it warmly. He had large, expressive eyes, and his face seemed perpetually animated by a new bit of humor awaiting release. "I don't need to tell you how bothersome he can be."

JP giggled despite her reserve, and Caverlock motioned to the waiting *tuk-tuk*. "I am sure you two can amuse yourselves at my expense until lunchtime, if not dinner, but times presses and we have much to cover."

"I'm sorry I was late," Ben said as they clambered into the tricycle-wheeled taxi. "My favorite driver, Choo-Choo here, had another fare."

The passengers ducked beneath the gold-fringed red fabric canopy and squeezed into the seat, with JP between the men. Caverlock and JP removed their hats as Choo-Choo revved the engine and turned to head down the access road.

"Ben was a helicopter pilot in the U.S. Army," Caverlock said to JP in a voice loud enough to be heard over the engine. "We met during a brief foray into conventional employment in San Francisco trading options and futures. I noticed that Ben was rarely flustered, even by losses that would have dismembered other traders, and so I became his avid apprentice. It was difficult to tell whether he was winning or losing, but he was winning 75% of the time and limiting his losses on the remaining 25%."

Bracing himself on the vertical stanchion, Ben turned so his guests could hear his reply. "Oliver here was not the only guy who claimed to see the Tao in trading, but he was the only guy who turned that crazy idea into successful trades."

Shouting over the engine and wind, JP addressed Ben. "I hear all about the Tao but never how to make money like he does. I hope to learn something useful from you."

"The trick is to understand there's risk and apparent risk," Ben said. "They're not the same. If you can somehow measure the difference and relate it to price, then you can trade that edge."

"You see?" Caverlock interjected. "Clear as mud."

The tuk-tuk careened around a corner into a narrow alley barely wide enough for the vehicle and after a few more turns slowed to a stop by a low wall pierced by a wooden gate with a curved headpiece between the posts. A small ornately decorated wood replica of a house bedecked with fresh flower garlands occupied a platform held aloft by four short stout posts beside the gate, and as they disembarked, Caverlock observed JP studying the garlanded miniature structure and the offerings of bananas, figurines and garlands surrounding it.

"It's a Spirit House," Caverlock explained. "Ben can enlighten you further, of course, but the core idea is the resident spirits of the land occupy this house, and if you are respectful and generous to them then good fortune will be yours."

Ben paid the driver and patted him on the shoulder, and then turned with half-smile to JP. "He can really talk, can't he?"

JP did a poor job of hiding her amusement, and Caverlock said, "JP told me that women either fall in love with me or loathe me as a result of my loquaciousness. It seems our client is leaning toward the latter option."

Opening the gate with a creak of old hinges, Ben commented, "If we save her fiancée's bacon, you might at least win her respect." Their host led them past the courtyard's banana trees, their leaves drooping in the windless morning heat, and announced their arrival.

A slim Thai woman in a white blouse and red sarong greeted them at the door of the wooden house; her hair was not quite as long as JP's, and her white shirt set off her deeply tanned face and arms.

Ben led them to the steps and then addressed his wife. "Winnie, you remember Oliver; this is his assistant JP. They arrived yesterday from San Francisco." Winnie hugged The Consulting Philosopher and then took JP's hand warmly. "I hope you brought a cold fog with you," she said with a smile, and Caverlock said to JP, "Winnie lived in Hong Kong and San Francisco as an au pair in her youth." Turning to his host and hostess, he asked, "And how are the kids?"

"Very well," Winnie answered. "I'm afraid you'll miss them today, as they have lessons after school."

"Perhaps on our next visit," Caverlock said, and then placed his hand on Ben's shoulder. "I'm afraid we need your expertise on the delicate matter I described."

Motioning them into the shutter-darkened living room cooled by ceiling fans, Ben said, "Let's get to it." JP and Caverlock sat down on the low-slung divan, and Ben pulled a cushioned chair around to face them. Behind him, the wood-paneled wall was adorned with a gold-framed poster of a bright-red cluster of lychee fruit being held in a child's hand. "This is in the style of a traditional Thai home," Caverlock explained to JP. "Dark wood paneling and minimal furniture, with a few modern touches like fans and air conditioning. Ben and Winnie have a high-rise *pied-a-terre* across the river, but this is their true home. They could live anywhere, but choose to live here."

Winnie delivered bowls of salty Thai snacks, Japanese *arare* crackers and cold water to the coffee table, and Caverlock handed JP a bottle of water and opened one for himself. "Given what we know, what do you reckon is the master plan in which Drake is playing a part?"

Ben frowned and then leaned forward, his elbows resting on his knees. "I think the plan here is to exploit the global grain trade by buying enough futures contracts to push the market higher. Once price skyrockets, they unload their futures contracts for a huge profit. It's like the Hunt brothers trying to corner the silver market in the 1980s."

Caverlock drained half his bottle of water and said, "Explain how you'd manage this."

"Ok, remember what I said earlier about risk and apparent risk? If the market's perception of the risk that prices will rise goes from low to high, price responds. So the trick here is to change the market perception with the least leverage possible."

"And how do you do that?" JP asked.

Ben crunched a salty cracker and took a gulp of water. "First, you place big bets on a price rise. Big money, enough to make people notice. Everyone will assume the buyers know something, so you've primed the perception that the risk is to the upside. This is only apparent risk, unless the buyers can take ownership of enough grain to actually change global supply."

Turning to JP, Ben explained, "A commodity contract is the right to buy or sell a certain amount of oil, rice, wheat, whatever, at a specific price. The owner of the contract doesn't actually own any oil or grain, he just owns the right to buy or sell a certain amount of oil or grain at a specified price. But if the owner of the contract exercises the contract, they take actual physical ownership of the commodity, and that means they have to buy the stuff and pay to store it somewhere in the real world. That costs money, so very few speculators take ownership."

Sitting up, he said, "So the ideal situation is to own only the contracts, and move the market up to increase the value of the contracts, and then sell for a profit without having to actually take possession and store the underlying commodity."

"The trick is to move the price in the direction you want," Caverlock said. "But these are enormous markets, and not easy to push around."

"True," Ben said, "but remember it's the marginal buyers who set the price."

JP gave him a quizzical look and Ben held up a bottle of water. "Let's say the price of this is one dollar. Now if there's a shortage of drinkable water, maybe because of a natural disaster, people in the affected area might happily pay two dollars for a bottle. So these buyers on the margin of the market can push the price of all bottled water higher. Why sell water for one dollar here if I can move it to where people are paying two dollars?"

JP still looked puzzled, and so Ben moved to another example. "Take a neighborhood with 100 houses. How many are bought and sold every year? Maybe five houses. Now if buyers are willing to bid up the price of these five houses, the price of the other 95 houses goes up, too. It only took five buyers to push up prices across the entire market. Those marginal buyers set the price."

JP nodded and Caverlock stood up and began pacing the hardwood floor. "So you push prices higher by placing big, obvious bets on future price increases. Nobody bets millions of dollars without knowing something, that's the assumption of all participants. So simply making the bets creates the illusion of inside knowledge."

"That's right," Ben confirmed. "And a rumor machine would add fuel to the fire. A rumor of supply disruption, for example. Then traders will say, aha, that's why somebody's betting so big on price going up. Other traders will join the bet and their bets will push the price higher. That starts a feedback loop, where the higher the price goes, the more traders jump in to bet on higher prices, and their buying pushes prices higher."

"But isn't spreading false rumors illegal?" JP asked.

"It's called 'psychographic microtargeting,'" Ben explained. "You target influencers in the industry with reports of shortages and supply disruptions, and you make it out to be more than it is. You don't lie, you manage perceptions of which way the market is heading. That's leverage, because modifying the influencers' perception of price direction will change the entire market."

"Now I see how this works," Caverlock said. "The information itself is the leverage. Once traders believe prices will rise, someone who owns grain will decide to hold it off market to get a higher price in the future, and that restriction of supply creates a real shortage."

"Yup," Ben said, "that's how it works."

"It's a mind game," JP concluded, and Ben nodded. "But with real-world consequences. Rice and wheat go up in price and millions of people pay more for food."

"Precisely," Caverlock exclaimed. "JP, I want you to understand a key distinction here. When Ben or I speculate in options or contracts, we have no inside knowledge. If we make money, it's at the expense of other speculators, not the end consumers. What the people behind this speculation are doing is different: they're manipulating the prices of staple grains higher, taking money out of the pockets of millions of people, as a means of reaping millions of dollars in profits."

JP nodded and Caverlock turned to Ben. "So how could Drake stop this monumental swindle?"

"Sell," Ben said. "Sell big and sell fast. Traders would assume new information meant the price rise was no longer likely and they would sell, too."

"And how could Drake protect his position from enormous losses?"

"You know how a hedge works," Ben said. "Drake would have to buy bets on the other side of the trade, bets that price would fall."

JP's phone chirped and Caverlock froze. "Please tell me that's Victorine reporting Drake's location."

JP retrieved her phone from her maroon purse and opened the message. "Isabelle broke down," JP said. "Drake flew to France. Isabelle isn't sure where."

"She's still protecting him, the poor deluded girl, but no matter, we know where he'll be," Caverlock said excitedly, "because Drake told us in the GPS track, the receipt you found and in the coded message left in his flat: Saint Martin du Fort."

Taking his water and battered fedora from the table, Caverlock said, "Ben, you've painted the picture for us with a few deft strokes. I cannot thank you enough. Now time is of the essence, as we must snuff this swindle before it's completed. I will consult you further from France. Come JP, we must collect our bags and head straight to the airport. Email Victorine to launch her campaign of misdirection and meet us in Paris. Our first stop will be the Rue Mouffetard. We have a partially erased address to visit and a mystery to solve."

Chapter Twelve

Following JP out the hotel's door onto Rue Cardinale Lemoine, Caverlock asked, "Do you need a tea or coffee, or is the excitement of being in Paris sufficient stimulation for now?"

Gazing up the street, JP replied, "Maybe we can stop for tea later."

"I have no idea what meal my poor stomach expects," Caverlock said. "Breakfast, lunch or dinner, but it expects some sustenance soon. We were fortunate that my favorite little two-star hotel here in the 5th had a room with two beds."

"The lift is like a closet," JP observed, and Caverlock replied, "Yes, but imagine the difficulty in adding elevators to old buildings with no allowance for modern contrivances. It's the same in all the old hotels here."

A high overcast dampened the May morning sun, and JP had pulled a light cashmere sweater over her café-au-lait colored dress. Glancing down at his assistant's black flats, Caverlock said, "I hope your shoes are comfortable, as we have quite a bit of walking ahead of us."

"You worry too much, Boss," JP said. "I'll be fine."

Tilting the brim of his fedora up at a jaunty angle, Caverlock swung his arms energetically. "You must forgive my anxiety. This frenetic schedule has played havoc with our body clocks, and I am nervous about meeting whomever is associated with this address on Rue Mouffetard that Drake erased."

Stopping abruptly in front of a building with an understated stone facade, Caverlock exclaimed, "Here is where Hemingway lived for a time, and there is where James Joyce hung his hat. The city is littered with literary, musical and philosophic history. If we happen to reach the other side of the river and the 9th arrondissement, we may pass the flat where Proust wrote, usually in bed. In the 18th, there's Eric Satie's *petite chamber* on the Rue Cartot, just below the magnificent *Sacre-Coeur* cathedral."

Resuming their brisk pace, Caverlock asked, "Any confirmation yet from Victorine?"

"Not yet," JP replied.

"That's another worry of mine," Caverlock said. "I feel obligated to include her in this final phase, but I fear she might disrupt what promises to be a delicate operation."

"I think she'll be a big help," JP countered. "If Drake really loves her."

Exhaling loudly, Caverlock said, "We may end up in a crisis where he must prove that one way or the other. Ah, here is the famed Latin Quarter and Rue Descartes, which leads straight to Rue Mouffetard. It's all terribly touristy here of course, but there is a community that lives and works here beneath the tourist trade. One of my academic friends who happens to live on Rue Descartes rarely leaves the 5th and 6th arrondissements, and views a trip across the river to the 11th as visiting Mongolia."

The sun broke through the overcast and JP shed her sweater. "Don't be surprised if people speak to you in French and are dismayed by your incomprehension," Caverlock said, "as many will assume you're French-Vietnamese."

At the next intersection Caverlock turned, explaining, "Rue Mouffetard is best enjoyed from the pedestrian-only length that starts by the *eglise*, the church. I know time presses on us, but this detour is worth the sacrifice."

Once the pair reached the square fronting the church, Caverlock pointed to a bookstore adjacent to a flower shop and fruit seller. "Drake obtained his bookmark there. We are retracing his footsteps."

As they approached the open-air fruit and flower shops, Caverlock turned to JP. "Would you do me a favor? Pick some flowers you favor to brighten our room."

JP scanned the array of reds, pinks, purples and golds and pointed to a bunch of yellow tulips. "Lovely," Caverlock enthused as he paid for the bouquet. "Now let me take a photo of you holding the tulips."

JP's smile faded as Caverlock repeatedly shifted his position, squinting at the phone screen. "Hurry up, Boss. It's just a snapshot."

"No, it's you on your first visit to Paris. There. Got it. You only look slightly annoyed."

Caverlock trailed JP, snapping photos of her as she wandered up the cobblestoned pedestrian street, stopping by each shop regardless of its offerings—patisserie, curios or clothing. When they reached Rue Arbelete, he caught up and directed her to turn right. "It's a bit early for lunch, but my favorite café in this neighborhood is nearby. It's a short distance in meters but a world away from this touristy artifice. The waiters don't speak English, the customers are mostly locals, and the food is a notch above the usual bistro fare."

The cafe's outside tables were already occupied by customers nursing cappuccinos, so Caverlock removed his well-worn fedora and ushered JP into the interior, where the pair were guided to a table that looked out on the sidewalk tables through a low open window.

Setting the bundle of tulips on the table, Caverlock engaged the waiter in French, and expressed jovial astonishment at the waiter's good-humored banter. "He doesn't remember me from my last visit here a few years ago, but he remembers my hat," he explained to JP once the waiter had left. "Remarkable. It's a small insight into human memory. He said he was delighted that I still have the hat and that I've eaten well in the intervening years. A sideways compliment, *n'est pas?* Scan the menu and I'll provide a poor translation. Would you like an aperitif, a glass of wine or a fizzy drink? I'm having a glass of sparkling wine, I simply can't resist. It is after all, your first day in Paris and our first visit together."

While JP studied the single-sheet menu, Caverlock motioned the waiter over and ordered aperitifs. "I took the liberty of ordering a champagne for you as well." Gazing out the open window at the street beyond, Caverlock mused, "I envy you your first experience of Paris, JP. It's a truism that regardless of the year or era, a great city dazzles the newcomer. It's all exciting and interesting. Then, a dozen visits and 20 years later, the traveler sees decay and roughening edges, and is convinced the city has been going downhill since their first visit. And so it seems to me that Paris has grown colder, a reflection perhaps of the entire world becoming coarser and colder."

JP glanced up from the menu and said, "I envy you all the cities you've visited and lived in."

"Ah, well, that is just a matter of time. My first visit here required 300 bag lunches and 300 bicycle rides to work to save the necessary money."

JP's eyes wandered to nearby tables, and a young man in a tailored blue suit with tousled hair and an air of amiable confidence met her lingering gaze and smiled at her. JP quickly returned her attention to the menu, and Caverlock murmured, "He fancies you, too."

JP's cheeks flushed, and she protested, "You're not supposed to notice that kind of thing, Boss."

"I'm sorry," Caverlock apologized. "I want you to go out on dates with other young people and have fun—*sanuk* in Thai. I won't be offended if you leave me moldering in the hotel room, and I say that very sincerely."

"Thanks, Boss, but I don't need any dates right now."

A wistful expression softened Caverlock's craggy features, and he said, "We have something other than envying each other in common, JP. We both fear loneliness."

JP looked over the menu at The Consulting Philosopher with unguarded expressive eyes, and he smiled in reassurance. "I know we're here on serious business, but I can't resist enjoying this rare moment together."

The two glasses of sparkling wine arrived and the pair clinked glasses. "*A santé,*" Caverlock said with a self-conscious grin. "To your health, to your first visit to Paris, and to a successful conclusion of our mission."

JP tasted the sparkling wine and looked down at the white tablecloth. "Thanks, Boss, for bringing me along. I could never do this alone."

"Ah, well, me neither," Caverlock said. "I harbor all the trepidations and anxieties due those who tread on uncertain paths. You steady me, JP, in every way, and I thank you for accompanying me. It makes the task ahead much less daunting."

Peering closely at his youthful companion, Caverlock said, "I've never really appreciated your faint freckles before; it must be this springtime light. Do freckles run in your family lineage? Perhaps it reflects some Western Chinese heritage."

"You have the weirdest interests, Boss," JP said dismissively. "Nobody's ever mentioned my freckles."

"Well, they're very fetching," Caverlock commented. "A truth not lost on the young gentleman there who's hoping to catch your eye again."

"Boss," JP said disapprovingly, and Caverlock quickly turned his attention to the menu. "The salmon is undoubtedly worthy, and the *moules et frites* and the cassoulet are classics. But who can resist roast duck or ravioli with mushrooms?"

JP settled on the cassoulet, her first taste of the traditional bean-meat stew, and Caverlock ordered the ravioli and a glass of red wine. JP was mopping up the last of her cassoulet with a piece of bread when her phone chirped with an incoming text. "It's Victorine," JP exclaimed. "She just landed. What do I tell her?"

Handing her the business card of their hotel, he replied, "Instruct her to meet us at our hotel. If they have no rooms available, there are other hotels within two blocks."

Retrieving his own phone, Caverlock called the hotel. "They had a cancellation, so I booked Victorine a room," he reported some moments later. "Tell her to check herself in. I want to explore the mystery of this address on Rue Mouffetard before we meet. I think it best not to involve her in what could be a dead end."

Draining the last of his red wine, Caverlock said, "Ask her if she reckons her travel artifice succeeded, and she got clean away."

JP complied, and a moment later read Victorine's message in reply. "She says she bought a round-trip flight to L.A., and that she's confident nobody tracked her cash purchase of the flight to Paris."

"Let's hope she's right," Caverlock murmured. After paying the bill, the pair returned to Rue Mouffetard and proceeded up the cobblestoned street at a brisk pace. Clutching the tulips in one hand, Caverlock apologized, "I am sorry to hurry you past such delightful shops, but we have to follow this lead before we meet Victorine."

The pair exited the retail district and entered a stretch of five-story residential buildings; a shuttered second-hand shop and a Chinese restaurant occupied the nearby ground floor commercial spaces. The address belonged to a narrow building faced by yellow brick, and Caverlock took off his fedora and looked up at the tall narrow windows and ornate wrought-iron railings of the flats above. Turning his attention to the names on the building's security-entrance panel, he murmured, "I confess I haven't any idea which of these flats is the one we seek." Withdrawing Drake's bookmark, he examined it in the sun and turned it to maximize the faint dimpled shadow left by the erased pencil marks.

"Do you discern a third numeral or letter?" As JP peered at the bookmark, Caverlock gazed in frustration at the locked entry door.

"Could it be a G?" JP wondered aloud, and at the moment the security door opened and a petite woman in a scarlet scarf scented with lavender exited. Murmuring *merci*, Caverlock held the door open and he and JP entered a passage that led past an elevator to a small brick-paved inner courtyard. The entrance to a second three-story brick-faced building opened onto the courtyard, and Caverlock approached the doorway to examine the six names on the placard. "Interesting," he murmured. "You reckon that Drake might have visited G?"

"Maybe," JP said, re-examining the bookmark in her hand. "But I can't tell for sure."

Withdrawing his phone, Caverlock entered one of the names in a search window and scrolled through the results. Caverlock gave JP a pensive look and murmured, "G might be our man."

Finding the security door ajar, he led JP up a narrow stone staircase to the second floor.

Each floor had only two flats, and as the pair looked uncertainly between the two faded blue doors marked G and H, the door to flat G suddenly swung open and a middle-aged man with tangled blond locks falling to his shoulders came out and hurriedly closed the door behind him. His dark tailored coat and the soft leather briefcase he was clutching were conventionally bourgeois, but his long unkempt hair, unshaven visage and penetrating feral stare were alarmingly unconventional.

"*Excusez moi*, a friend of ours recently visited you," Caverlock said in a polite voice.

Observing the yellow tulips in Caverlock's hand, the man gave Caverlock a flinty glare and darted down the stairs. Caverlock and JP gave chase, and Caverlock shouted, "Our friend is in danger," and repeated the phrase in French for good measure.

The man forcefully pushed the security door open and muttered in accented English, "It is not my concern."

Matching the man's rapid pace step for step across the brick courtyard, Caverlock said, "Perhaps, but is it a concern that your work is being used to cheat people of their daily bread?"

The man stopped abruptly and turned his unblinking gaze on Caverlock. "What do you know of my work?"

"I know it's being misused by the few to cheat the many," Caverlock replied in an even voice.

"And how do you know this?" the man demanded.

Glancing around the narrow brick courtyard, Caverlock asked, "Is this the proper place for our conversation?"

The man hesitated, clearly torn between fleeing and engaging this troublesome stranger. With a reluctance so violent that he seemed to suffer a spasm of physical pain, the man angrily stormed across the courtyard and up the stone stairs to his flat. A few steps behind him, Caverlock whispered to JP, "It's uncanny, Monsieur Gerard looks just like Descartes, or perhaps Moliere."

Fumbling with his key, Gerard muttered, "I don't receive many visitors." Opening the door, he let his visitors in with a sour expression. Every window in the flat was wide open, and the faded white curtains rippled as if alive in the light breeze. The cramped living room was stacked with books and journals; a grand piano served as a tabletop, and the piano bench supported stacks of bound notebooks. An enormous long-haired black cat with a white patch on its chest occupied an overstuffed high-backed chair as if it were a throne; at the sight of the strangers, it leaped as if its cushion had been electrified, and ran for cover behind the piano.

"I'm terribly sorry we startled your remarkable cat," Caverlock said, and the apology only seemed to increase their host's irritability. Gerard led them thru a doorway to a small square table covered in oil cloth at one end of the cramped kitchen. A round loaf of bread cut to a semi-circle on a well-used cutting board and a cube of butter lay on the table; their reluctant host motioned them to take the two chairs and snapped, "Now tell me what this is about."

Setting the bouquet of tulips on the table, Caverlock complied, first introducing himself and JP and then sketching out the speculation and the reason for Drake's visit.

"They wanted to use your work to introduce a cascading narrative into the grain commodity community with the least effort possible," Caverlock explained. "The handsome consulting fee they undoubtedly paid you was a mere trifle compared to their expected profits, which I conservatively estimate could run into the tens of millions."

Gerard gave a Gallic shrug of resignation. "Junior academics make almost nothing. As you see, I cannot afford a grand life. I had no idea he intended to use my work for this horrible exploitation." Taking a serrated bread knife from the white-tiled kitchen counter, Gerard sawed off two lengths of the bread and cut each in two. Taking one piece, he slathered the coarse bread with butter and motioned his guests to help themselves.

Between bites of bread, Gerard asked, "How is it that you are familiar with my work? Very few people know of it, even within my field."

Caverlock tore a piece of the bread in half and chewed the crust absent-mindedly. "This is quite good," he remarked. "Chewy and flavorful. Is it from that acclaimed *boulangerie* in the 10th?"

"I have no idea," Gerard answered. "A friend gave it to me."

"I have an abiding interest in cascading cultural, social and political changes, and so your work is of intense interest to me."

"Really?" Gerard said, and his annoyance slipped a notch.

"*Vraiment*," Caverlock said. "Consider the rapid rise of radical Left-inspired domestic bombings in the United States circa 1970. This social phenomenon peaked in just a few years, a period in which hundreds of bombs were detonated by underground groups, and then just as rapidly, the violence dissipated and the movement lost all popular appeal. How can we explain that without your model that unifies network effects, the critical dynamic of key influencers, the appeal of new narratives and the manipulation of social networks?"

Gerard made a gesture of modesty with his free hand, and Caverlock continued. "Unfortunately, some ruthless speculators discovered your work and saw how it could be used to create a cascading narrative of impending shortages of grain. Other speculators would naturally place bets to profit from this rise, and those purchases would cascade through the system, just as your mathematical model predicts, pushing prices higher with each new wave of buying. This speculation would be harmless if it was only taking money from other speculators, but this will take money from everyone buying bread and rice to feed their families."

Handing JP a piece of the bread, Caverlock concluded, "It's fallen from fashion, but I refer to Sartre's *Critique de la Raison Dialectique* for our starting point: *besoin*, or need. The people need grain to live, and the speculators do not need to profit from the misery caused by sharply higher grain prices."

Gerard raised his hands in a gesture of futility and said, "And how will you stop them?"

"We will need your help, but you will be compensated if we succeed. How much did Drake pay you for your help?"

Gerard hesitated and then relented. "Ten thousand euros."

Caverlock nodded. "A princely sum. We shall pay you five times that sum if you help us plan a counter-campaign that negates the campaign they have already launched."

"That's two year's salary for an average worker," he exclaimed.

"I've told you the sums at stake are formidable, in the tens of millions, and that might be only one slice of a much larger loaf," Caverlock said. Gazing at their reluctant host, he added, "Monsieur Gerard, do you happen to have any *vin ordinaire* that we might share to toast our arrangement?"

Twitching one hand as if rotating a faulty light bulb, their host frowned. "I have a very poor quality bottle, two euros."

"Splendid," Caverlock replied in a booming voice. "The two-euro bottles often beat the ten euro ones."

Gerard brought the bottle to the table and Caverlock examined the label. "It's from Languedoc, perfectly drinkable, possibly excellent. Monsieur Gerard, may I bother you for three cups? Anything will do."

Opening the cabinet above the sink, their host withdrew three dusty wine glasses, which he hastily rinsed. "My friends call me Nico," he said as he set them to the table, and Caverlock grabbed a roll of paper towels from the window sill. "Here, JP, let's dry them."

As JP wiped each glass and set it back on the table, Caverlock splashed a slug of the red wine into each one. Standing up, he handed a glass to Gerard, and said, "*A santé.*" The three sampled the red wine in unison, and Caverlock said, "Very nice. Now I want to be quite clear here, Nico. If we fail to stop this vast speculation, I cannot pay you anything. We can only pay you the 50,000 euros if we succeed in reversing this foul exploitation."

"*Je comprend*," Gerard said.

"We must first find the fellow who visited you," Caverlock said, "and win his cooperation. If we accomplish that, we will contact you to set the counter-cascade in motion."

"*D'accord*," Gerard replied. "It won't be easy if they have invested substantial money in their campaign."

"*Je comprend*," Caverlock replied. "But we must do our best."

Caverlock poured more wine for himself and Gerard; JP declined and the host and guests drained their glasses. After a brief pause, Caverlock collected the bundle of tulips and said, "I'm afraid we must be off."

As they walked to the entry, JP said, "I'm sorry we scared your cat," and Gerard replied in a reassuring voice, "*C'est pas grave*. He's fine." To her surprise, Gerard lightly kissed JP on both cheeks and repeated the farewell with Caverlock.

Once the pair had crossed the brick courtyard and reached the sidewalk, JP rubbed her cheeks. "He was scratchy."

"Yes, in more ways than one," Caverlock agreed.

"He smelled better than I guessed he would," JP said, and Caverlock laughed. "Yes, we feared the worst when he saw the shambles. His flat reminded me of Satie's; it's remarkable, right down to the grand piano serving as a tabletop. Only Satie did him one better; he had two grands, one stacked upon the other."

Walking down Rue Mouffetard, Caverlock exclaimed, "Did you notice his long nose and thin lips? With his flowing hair, I felt as if I was meeting an ill-tempered Descartes in the flesh. A phenomenal resemblance."

Halfway down the cobblestoned street, Caverlock touched JP's elbow. "We were deprived of dessert by the rush of events," he said. "I insist you select a patisserie to enjoy in our room, and choose one for Victorine as well. This opera cake looks divine, the *Jesuite* makes my mouth water, and the *Paris-Brest* would make a hardened man weep, but I will take a *Religieuse*, and savor every morsel. If you can't decide, buy one of each and we'll share the bounty."

Chapter Thirteen

The pair turned onto Rue Cardinale Lemoine and JP said in a scolding tone, "Boss, you were crazy to offer him 50,000 euros. He would have done it for 20,000."

"Possibly, but I needed absolute certainty he will do his very best."

"And where are you going to get the 50,000?" JP asked in a tone of exasperation. "Victorine doesn't have that much cash."

"We shall speculate ourselves," Caverlock replied. "I will bet we will succeed, and hedge that bet in the event the scoundrels succeed. If Nico fails, my speculation yields nothing, but then we owe him nothing. If he succeeds, then we will net far more than 50,000."

"It's too risky," JP declared, and Caverlock hastened to explain. "If you're confident the market will rise, then you place most of your money on that wager. But to cover the possibility the market moves against you, you place some of your money on a bet that the market will decline."

"You bet against yourself?" JP asked.

"In a way, yes. There are ways to leverage such a hedge so that it only pays off if you're horrendously wrong. But thanks to your hedge, the gains reaped by the bet against yourself will cover your losses."

"And if you win your main bet?"

Then you lose the money you bet against yourself, but since it's only a fraction of your winnings, it's the cost of doing business, like an insurance policy."

JP mulled this and then changed topics. "Did you really know of Gerard's work?"

"For all of a minute, yes."

"You mean you looked up his name, scanned the search results and learned enough to fool him into thinking you're an expert on his work?"

"Knowledge is about filling in the blanks," Caverlock explained. "The more you know, the easier it is to connect key words and concepts. I am in fact deeply interested in cascading social trends, and since this is a key dynamic of this vast swindle, I've pondered how it might work. So it wasn't difficult; just repeat the key concepts gathered from a summary of his most important research papers, conjure up a plausible sounding example, express my profound admiration for his insights, and voila."

JP shook her head in grudging admiration. "And he fell for it. You really know how to talk, Boss."

His voice taking on a wounded tone, Caverlock said, "JP, you act as if I cheated him. I gave him a great gift—sincere admiration."

"From one minute reading about his research?" she asked dubiously.

"Yes," he replied. "It was enough. Now let's discuss our battle plan. Let's keep the payment to Gerard and my speculation confidential, shall we? There's no point in burdening Victorine with complexities that are extraneous to the search for Drake."

Carefully holding the bright yellow tulips by his side, Caverlock came to a halt in front of a lingerie shop and turned to JP with a serious expression. "We're almost at our hotel, and I need to explain something before we meet Victorine. You must arrange to have time alone with her, not to say or do anything in particular, but just to be present if she wants to talk to someone she trusts. The potential burden is that if she tells you something in confidence that could jeopardize Drake or our mission, then you must share the outlines with me lest confidentiality destroys all we hope to accomplish. Can you do that?"

"Yes, Boss," JP said soberly. Glancing at the skimpy underthings in the display window, her serious expression melted into an impish grin. "Did you stop here to buy me something?"

Caverlock's grave expression gave way to craggy embarrassment. "It was mere coincidence, but by all means, go ahead and enjoy melting me into a helpless puddle of befuddlement."

Gazing down the sidewalk, he said with evident relief, "I see Victorine is waiting for us."

Their client wore a striking midnight-blue dress of wrinkled crepe with a high collar, a small chic gray felt hat with a gold-colored hat pin, a pearl necklace and heeled sandals. "Like a movie star, indeed," Caverlock murmured to JP as they approached. "I'm afraid I must split the tulips between our rooms, lest we look ungenerous."

Giving his reserved client the local greeting of a light kiss on each cheek, Caverlock enthused, "We're delighted that you arrived safe and sound." Giving Victorine a brief hug, JP asked, "Are you OK?"

Victorine nodded but her smile was perfunctory rather than reassuring.

"You look *formidable*," Caverlock said. "May I ask the designer of your dress?"

"Constance Lafayette," Victorine responded.

"Clearly a tremendous talent," Caverlock remarked. "JP, if you ever fancy anything from this line, it's my treat. You would stun the room in such attire."

JP gave Caverlock a look of disapproval and Victorine hastened to add, "It's *pret-a-porter*, of course, I can't afford designer clothing."

"*Pret-a-porter* is very pretty," Caverlock mused, "if you'll pardon my alliteration. Shall we go up to our room? I want to show you a map and book our seats for tomorrow morning's TGV train to Nimes."

Stopping by the front desk to ask for two flower vases, Caverlock proceeded up the narrow stairs to their third floor room. Throwing open the tall casement windows to the afternoon warmth, he divided the tulips between the two vases and set them on the night stand. "One of these is for your room, Victorine," he said, and then withdrew his laptop and a heavily creased paper map from his bag.

Opening the folded map of Southern France on JP's bed, he called up a map of the Cevennes district on his computer. As Victorine and JP bent down to look at the maps, Caverlock addressed his client. "As you recall from the database assembled by JP and Carlito, café receipts and GPS data from Drake's fitness monitor point to the village of Saint Martin du Fort, which is reached via the string of country roads listed on the slip pf paper Drake left for you in his flat: D999, D39, D169, D347. There is some confusion between LDC, which we can see on the digital map must be *L'Eglise de Cros*, the local church of the hamlet of Cros. Drake's translation, *Church of the Cross*, likely resulted from his assuming *Cros* is the French word for *Cross*, while the correct word is *croix*, with an X."

Pulling the well-worn paper map forward for better viewing, he traced the route from Paris to Nimes with his finger. "We'll take the fast train to Nimes tomorrow morning, and pick up a car there. I dread driving the tangle of local roads, but there is no other way for us to reach Saint Martin du Fort. We should book a bed and breakfast near but not in the village."

Victorine studied the map with a pensive expression. "I understand the evidence, but what if he's not there?"

"Then we'll regroup," Caverlock replied. "My concern is that he might be hiding in a farmhouse a kilometer away from the village, and we will assume he's not there because we didn't spot him in the village. This region is littered with isolated *hameaux* and farmhouses tucked away in valleys served by one-lane roads."

Standing up, Caverlock said, "My other concern is that the sudden appearance of Americans in the village might reach Drake and cause him to flee the moment he receives a report of our arrival. Wouldn't you hire a friendly local as a lookout? I would."

Victorine frowned. "How can three strangers find him if he's in a remote farmhouse? It would take pure luck."

"That's an excellent point, which is why I've recruited some local help," Caverlock said. "Yes, luck plays a part in any search for someone seeking to remain hidden. But luck is rarely blind, and some locals will know where Drake is staying. No stranger can remain hidden for long in such places."

Giving Victorine a penetrating glace, he asked, "How comfortable are you with children?"

Taken aback, Victorine answered, "I babysat kids when I was a teenager. Why do you ask?"

"We must cloak your presence in some way," Caverlock said. "If you're with children, you won't be seen as someone to be monitored."

In a voice betraying skepticism, Victorine said, "So you'll borrow some children for me? It's awfully elaborate, given we don't even know if he's even there."

"The children and the local informant are a package deal," Caverlock explained. "I have an old acquaintance in Marseilles who has generously recruited his daughter and son-in-law who live in Montpellier for this weekend." Smiling to himself, Caverlock mused, "We go way back, my Marseilles friend and I. Our adventures include a harrowing encounter with the giant rats of Sumatra, but that is a tale for another time."

"Why should Victorine disguise herself?" JP asked. "Why would Drake run away from her?"

"Out of fear of who's behind her," Caverlock replied. "Given the care he's invested in hiding, he won't believe she found him on her own. He will anticipate that someone brought Victorine to draw him out."

Suppressing her emotions behind a rigid mask, Victorine remained silent, and Caverlock spoke in a calming tone. "I know that sounds terribly cynical, but keep in mind that Drake hid those clues for you in his flat, but he has yet to contact you, much less direct you to the clues. For whatever reason, he fears you discovering his whereabouts, perhaps because it increases his own risk and possibly because he fears it places you in jeopardy."

In a vexed tone, JP murmured, "He should trust you."

"We must reserve judgment until we know the entire situation," Caverlock said. "Entrusting Victorine with too much information would burden her, and perhaps he feared it would tempt her into a reckless search for him that would endanger them both. What seems correct is not always effectual in a nuanced situation such as this one. We must consider the entire gestalt, and this is why our precautions must be as elaborate as those cloaking this speculation."

Fixing her gaze on the map, Victorine said, "I understand what you're saying about burdens and risks, but I have to agree with JP. He should have trusted me."

Caverlock shrugged and said, "I am not defending Drake, I am merely suggesting we keep an open mind. Now we have a busy day tomorrow, and should fortify ourselves with a decent dinner."

"There's a bistro nearby that I read about," Victorine ventured. "Could we go there?"

"Of course," Caverlock exclaimed. "We'd be delighted to join you."

Victorine pulled up the address on her phone and handed it to Caverlock. "It's in the 6th, a pleasant walk from here," he announced. "JP and I will freshen up and meet you downstairs in a half hour." Retrieving one vase of yellow tulips from the night stand, Caverlock handed the flowers to Victorine and said, "For beauty, love and luck."

Chapter Fourteen

Pausing beneath the building's imposing stone archway, Caverlock held the door open and Victorine and JP entered the cavernous splendor of the *Gare de Lyon* train station. Gazing at the high glass ceilings and clerestory windows, JP exclaimed, "It's just like in the movies."

Removing his faded fedora, Caverlock surveyed the crowded station, noting the flow of passengers to and from the ticket counters and the doorways to the tracks, and then gave an appraising glance at his wards: JP was wearing blue jeans and a mannish button-down white long-sleeved blouse, and Victorine wore loose khaki trousers and a white and blue striped shirt with whimsical cloth ties on the sleeves. Both appeared distracted, JP by the grand building and Victorine by an inner turmoil.

Raising his voice enough to be heard above the ambient noise, Caverlock addressed his companions. "Speaking of movies, I recommend studying Bresson's wonderful film *Pickpocket* for the legerdemain available to the experienced thief. This is one of my favorite train stations, but like all such bustling nodes, it's also ideal for pickpockets, so hold your bags and purses tightly."

"Boss, you're making me paranoid," JP complained, and Caverlock tightened his grip on his worn canvas bag. "If everything is contingent, as the Postmodernists hold, then paranoia in a setting such as this is mere prudence."

In contrast to JP's wide-eyed wonderment, Victorine's focus was entirely internal; bag and purse in hand, she followed Caverlock's lead and glanced at other passengers only to avoid collisions. Caverlock absorbed her unseeing gaze and spoke quietly to JP. "I'm worried about our client. She seems stretched to the snapping point."

JP shot a glance at Victorine and gave Caverlock a surreptitious nod of acknowledgement.

Pausing at the list of trains and destinations, Caverlock studied the board and referred to their tickets. A musical tone presaged a public announcement, and after listening intently, Caverlock pointed the way to their track. Leaning close to JP, he said, "Speaking of paranoia, it wouldn't surprise me if we were being followed. No, don't look around; there's no way to spot surveillance in this crowd. I awoke from a troubled sleep last night and realized Monsieur Gerard might be a person of interest to those seeking Drake. We might have attracted a tail by visiting him."

JP's straight brows knitted in worry and Caverlock said, "On the other hand, perhaps I'm spinning circles within circles."

After guiding his companions to the first class car of the TGV train to Nimes, Caverlock took the aisle seat so his companions could have the window seat views. Once the train left the station and reached its cruising speed, the overcast of Paris gave way to bright spring sunshine. Victorine gazed pensively at the lush green fields and passing village church spires for a time and then fell into a deep sleep.

A nearby passenger began playing pop music on a boom box, a violation that soon drew a conductor reprimand. In the absence of the blaring low-fidelity music, the train's steady hum and vibration was a soothing background to the subdued conversation between The Consulting Philosopher and his assistant.

Gazing at the slumped rag-doll form of his sleeping client, Caverlock half-turned to address JP in a stage whisper. "I doubt she slept a wink last night. I suspect she's as afraid of finding Drake as of not finding him."

JP shifted her attention from the lush farmland and quaint villages to Victorine. "You mean she's afraid of what happens if we find him?"

"Yes," Caverlock replied in a low voice. "Regardless of what transpires, her world has been shattered. I suspect she fears having to make a terrible decision: let go of Drake and the marriage or recommit to what is now an uncertain relationship and future."

Cupping her hand to shield the sound of her voice from Victorine, JP said, "I would dump him. Even if she loves him, look at his family. Who wants to be part of that?"

"You're so right, we don't marry just the individual; we marry the family. But Drake might be realizing the same choice confronts him: he must choose between his family's secrets or Victorine."

"Boss, you're a romantic," JP chided.

"True," Caverlock agreed, "but if Drake was unreservedly delighted by his family's participation in this vast swindle, he wouldn't have disappeared."

JP absorbed this and Caverlock continued. "Here's what kept me awake: is Drake letting the swindle run, or is he trying to stop it? We have no evidence one way or the other. If I put myself in his shoes, I suspect he is frozen between the two options: he no longer wants to be part of the swindle, but he is hesitant to stop it, out of fear of the consequences to himself and his family."

Victorine shifted slightly, and Caverlock paused until she returned to fitful slumber. "We humans are a peculiar animal, JP," he mused. "We reckon that if we trigger a train wreck, our responsibility is lessened if we don't look at the wreckage. That may be Drake's mindset. By disappearing to wring his hands over what he has wrought, he feels he has withdrawn his approval without endangering his family fortune. We all seek what he seeks, a morally defensible position without risk or cost. But as the full weight of moral philosophy from East and West alike has shown, there is no morally defensible position that doesn't exact a price. Drake's discount morality fails to impress."

Keeping his voice in a confidential tone, he continued. "Our job is complicated by his apparent ambivalence. If he is leaning toward disrupting the swindle, our job is to nudge him into action. If he is resistant to actually torpedoing the swindle, we must neutralize his defense and torpedo it ourselves."

"Can we stop it?" JP asked, and Caverlock gave a barely discernable shrug. "With Gerard's help, perhaps. But perhaps not. It may be beyond stopping at this point."

Gesturing toward the supine figure of Victorine, Caverlock whispered, "I wish I knew how to encourage her to help us, but I confess I am at a loss. I am sorry to burden you with the task, but it's up to you to recruit Victorine to the cause of stopping the swindle, regardless of her feelings for Drake."

JP ran her fingers through her long black tresses. "You worry too much, Boss."

"I worry about what I don't know and what I don't control, which is essentially everything of importance at this point," Caverlock said darkly, and JP's expression betrayed her own doubts.

"I can't stop Victorine from cracking," JP whispered, and Caverlock made a Gallic gesture of resignation. "Of course you can't, dear girl. It's out of our hands. We can only hope she doesn't add to our burdens by shattering into pieces or impulsively diving into some reckless misadventure that throws all our work to the wind."

Caverlock's phone chirped and he glanced at the display. "It's Gerard. I want you to hear everything, lest a fog descend on my memory."

His expression telegraphing alarm, Caverlock arose and JP followed him into the lounge between cars reserved for phone conversations. Redialing the number, Caverlock placed his phone on speaker and huddled close to JP.

"It's not good," Gerard reported. "I offered my 10,000 fee for a counter-operation, but my contact refused. The other side paid them a quarter-million."

Caverlock glanced at JP and shook his head. "I was afraid of that," he replied. "How about the moral darkness of plundering hungry children?"

The pair could almost hear Gerard's disgusted shrug. "It's just business."

"Yes, I was afraid of that, too," Caverlock said. "*Ecoutez attentivement*, Gerard. I've studied your last paper. Isn't it possible to leap ahead of the conventional narrative cascade? To use a chess analog, to castle when the opponent expects us to advance a pawn?"

Gerard's pause was long enough for Caverlock to doubt the connection. Gerard finally responded in French and Caverlock struggled to reply in kind and then surrendered, as had Gerard, to his native tongue. JP listened to this two-language conversation with a perplexed expression, and Caverlock offered a brief precis. "The strength of the conventional network effect is based on the number of users and connections in the network," he explained. "But in Gerard's model, it's the quality of the information being disseminated through the network that triggers cascading narratives."

"*Exactement*," Gerard confirmed.

"This includes the novelty of a new narrative and its appeal to our base emotions of greed, fear and fairness," Caverlock continued. "Our opponents are relying solely on greed, but we might be able to fashion a campaign that combines novelty, greed and an appeal to fairness."

"Yes," Gerard cautioned. "If we had a week, and a quarter million."

"But alas, we only have hours and a budget of peanuts," Caverlock said with a renewed urgency. "Just as a thought experiment, why don't you design a model for an avalanche rather than a cascade, an avalanche with three parts? By claiming the swindle has hidden vast stores of grain that are soon to hit the market, we spark moral outrage and the novelty of exposing a great swindle, while speculators will seize on the opportunity to profit by betting grain prices will plummet."

Gerard's skepticism crackled through his rapid-fire French, and Caverlock interrupted him. "I will send you funds via cryptocurrency."

"You must find Drake," Gerard implored, and Caverlock offered a booming reply. "That is our sole goal, Gerard. But I need you to sketch out the most effective sabotage."

Caverlock rung off and JP studied the Consulting Philosopher's grave expression. "Boss, what funds are you sending him?"

"My own, of course," Caverlock replied in a low voice. "As moral beings, we have no choice. If we stand aside, we become part of the swindle. No, JP, we must throw everything we have into this conflict. We cannot let the swindlers win as a result of an enfeebled, half-hearted response."

"But Boss—"

"Yes, yes, I know. We enter the battle too late, with too few resources and too little knowledge. But we have several weapons in our quiver which the other side does not possess. Nothing ignites quite like the moral outrage sparked by a violation of fair play that exploits the innocent. That is one weapon. Surprise is another. We know the outlines of their plan but they don't yet know ours. Even if they have shadowed us and eavesdropped on Gerard, they don't yet know what we know. We have a third weapon, greed. Greed and fear pivot with remarkable ease, and their reliance on greed makes them vulnerable to a change in greed's polarity. Those betting on grain's sudden rise will just as happily switch their bet to grain's decline. And then there's our fourth weapon: Ben."

JP's alarm grew. "How much of your own money are you putting in?"

"A good chunk of it," Caverlock admitted. "To be entirely honest, I feel a sense of impending doom, a fear that I am throwing away a small fortune on a vain and gallant gesture. But I am with Kierkegaard on this, JP; we are nothing but the quality of what we believe to be good and true."

The two returned to their seats and fell into their own thoughts until the train slowed on its approach to Nimes. The deceleration roused Victorine, and Caverlock briefed his companions on the logistics of their search for Drake: his friend's daughter and son-in-law Yvette and Michel had arranged to borrow a local car for their use, and secured rooms in an aunt's farmhouse. Victorine would accompany Yvette and Michel and their two young children while Caverlock and JP would travel separately in the borrowed car to Saint Martin du Fort. The two parties would conduct their search independently, with Yvette and Michel making discreet inquiries of local residents while Victorine kept the children company. They would then meet up at the farmhouse and compare notes in the evening. Victorine would make a special effort to thank Yvette and Michel for taking time out of their busy lives to help in the search for her missing fiancé.

Revived by her sleep, Victorine listened attentively to Caverlock's briefing and followed his instructions to tie her hair into a chignon to modify her appearance from a distance.

The trio exited the arched façade of the Nimes station, luggage in hand, into the bright southern sunshine, and paused by the fountain, some distance from a squalling baby who would not be comforted. As Caverlock pensively scanned the street and square, he masked his anxiety with an absent-minded soliloquy addressed as much to himself as to Victorine and JP.

"It's a pity we can't tarry a bit here. The Romans favored Nimes, and the ruins of their extensive baths remain immensely charming. This playful fountain is but a small taste of the waterworks here." Inhaling deeply, he murmured, "Perhaps it's a trick of the imagination, but I detect the scent of history in the air. Then there's the exquisite Nimes Amphitheatre, a smaller version of the Coliseum in Rome. Do you know why it's so well preserved? People fashioned an extensive shantytown inside it for much of the Middle Ages, so it wasn't disassembled for building materials like so many other Roman structures."

A tall young woman in a flat-brimmed hat, flax-colored work shirt and billowing green-striped trousers approached the fountain and after a brief hesitation, waved to Caverlock. A scruffy young man with a mop of dark curly hair wearing denim overalls was towing two children behind the young woman, and Caverlock's expression brightened. "There they are," he exclaimed. Hurrying forward, he dropped his canvas bag and embraced the young woman, dislodging her hat in his enthusiasm. Apologizing profusely, Caverlock retrieved the hat and gazed appreciatively at her fair features and shoulder-length strawberry-blond hair. "The last time I saw you," he said in his booming voice, "you were a surly teenager with pink-dyed hair who thought your father and I were among the most annoying creatures on the planet."

Yvette's grin masked her embarrassment, and she replied in charmingly accented English. "So you remember a horrible girl."

"No, I remember a teen," Caverlock said, "so all is forgiven. What I treasure is my memories of you as a nine-year old rascal. Do you remember mixing up dreadfully tasting 'cocktails' of vinegar and cumin and Lord knows what for me to drink?"

Recalling her mischief, Yvette giggled and Caverlock turned to the young man in faded overalls sporting a week's beard. Clasping the man's shoulders, Caverlock exclaimed, "*Enchanté*, Michel. A great pleasure to meet you." "*Moi aussi*," Michel replied, and having taken Caverlock's measure, he gazed with evident curiosity at Victorine and JP. Caverlock motioned the pair forward and after Caverlock's introduction, Yvette and Michel greeted them with kisses on each cheek.

While the adults exchanged awkward pleasantries, Caverlock bent down to address the young boy and girl. Ceremoniously extending his hand in greeting to the boy, he said, "*Je suis* Caverlock. *Pardon, mon français est pauvre.*"

The boy, dressed in blue denim overalls to match his father's, took Caverlock's extended hand with an expression suitable to a serious 9-year old. Smoothing his mop of straight dark hair, he said, "*C'est pas grave. Je suis* Jules."

"A fine name, Jules. Reminiscent of Truffaut. *Vous comprend Englais, n'est pas?*"

"*Un peu*," the boy replied diffidently, and then gazed up at JP and Victorine. Caverlock turned his attention to the shy 6-year old girl, whose curly gold-tinged blond locks touched the shoulders of her checked blue and white smock. *"Vous êtes très jolie, mademoiselle,"* Caverlock exclaimed, and the girl bravely blurted, *"Je suis* Juliette."

"Bravo," Caverlock replied. "A most excellent name."

At their father's urging, each child welcomed JP with a kiss on each cheek; as Victorine kneeled with her signature reserve to accept their greeting, Caverlock studied each child's response to his client with anxious interest. Juliette dutifully offered Victorine a kiss on each cheek, but Jules first gazed into her green-brown eyes and then planted a firm kiss on her mouth with a deliberation far beyond his tender years. As Victorine's eyes widened in surprise, Jules declared, *"Je veux t'épouser."*

Victorine glanced up at Yvette for a translation, and Yvette suppressed a smile. "He said he wants to marry you."

Victorine met the boy's serious gaze and smiled, not in derision but whimsy. "I will wait for you," she replied. "Do you understand?"

Jules nodded gravely, and as Victorine stood up, he took her hand, and as she swung their hands playfully, Jules allowed himself a grin of happiness.

"Extraordinary," Caverlock marveled, and JP's cautious expression broke into a dimpled smile.

"He's strong that way," Michel offered in accented English, and Caverlock nodded agreeably as he collected Victorine's luggage and his own worn canvas bag.

Ignoring Victorine's lack of comprehension, Jules began describing the day's plans in French to his new amour as he led her to the family's white Renault sedan, pausing occasionally to insert a few words in English for her benefit.

Lowering his voice, Caverlock addressed JP. "Needless to say, I'm relieved. I was worried she wouldn't take to the children, as delightful as they are."

"I hope she does wait for Jules," JP replied, and Caverlock was taken aback. "Let's give poor Drake one last chance to redeem himself," he murmured.

After the men loaded the trio's luggage in the trunk, the five adults and two children piled into the compact car, with Jules pressing close to Victorine while Juliette sat on her mom's lap in the front seat. A short drive took them to the borrowed vehicle, a faded-blue Citroën 2CV *Deux Chevaux* with a dented grey fender.

"Splendid," Caverlock enthused. "It reminds me of your father's old green *Deux Chevaux*. We shall blend in like natives."

"They're not common these days," Yvette commented, and Caverlock gave a Gallic shrug. "Better to be dismissed as a harmless eccentric than identified as a nosy American. Who is the owner?"

"Michel's aunt," Yvette replied. "It's been stored at the farmhouse where we'll stay tonight."

"Michel's aunt has our eternal gratitude, "Caverlock declared. "My memory is a bit rusty, but I am guessing this is an early 1970s model."

JP gave the flat-sided old car a skeptical glance and murmured, "Is it safe?"

"Utterly reliable," Caverlock assured her as he tossed their bags in the back seat. Caverlock slid the vehicle's folding canvas top open with some difficulty, and JP's skepticism morphed into alarm. "It's like a tin can."

"You're prescient," Caverlock replied. "It was known as the 'tin snail.' It's basically an enclosed motorcycle with four wheels."

Touching the folded canvas, JP asked, "What if it rains?"

"You worry too much," Caverlock declared, and JP playfully punched his shoulder. "I'm serious, Boss," she hissed. "This is an accident waiting to happen."

Michel opened the front door and slid behind the wheel. "I learned to drive in this car," he said fondly, and then addressed Caverlock. "I don't know why, but to start, you must do this three times. I know it's crazy, but it works." Michel tapped the underside of the front panel three times with his fingers, and then turned the ignition key. The air-cooled engine coughed and then started, maintaining a noisy rhythm that rattled the entire vehicle.

Michel got out and opened the passenger door for JP. "I changed the oil this morning," Michel said over the racket, and Caverlock nodded as he eased his bulk into the driver's seat. JP gingerly took the passenger's seat and fastened the lap seatbelt as Michel closed the door.

"Refresh my memory of the gear shift," Caverlock said in his booming voice, and Michel complied, tracing the unusual pattern in the air with his hand gripping an imaginary shifting handle.

"It's coming back to me," Caverlock said, but his tone betrayed uncertainty. As Michel headed back to his own car, Caverlock said, "I'll follow you at a distance. We must appear to arrive separately." Michel waved to acknowledge the instruction and returned to his Renault.

JP leaned forward to examine the Spartan dashboard controls and exclaimed, "The seat's as hard as a wood box."

"I told you we would take the Stoics path to conserve Victorine's money," he reminded her. "And here we are, in the adventurous Stoic's vehicle of choice."

Caverlock gingerly pressed the gear handle and the ancient vehicle lurched forward.

"Ah, success," he declared, and JP braced herself in anticipation of a rough transition to second gear.

Michel and Yvette's Renault sped away and Caverlock's attempts to reach third failed in a grinding of gears. "Blast," he muttered. "I should have practiced a bit." The transmission recalcitrantly entered third gear and Caverlock pressed the accelerator.

Trying to catch up to the white Renault, Caverlock negotiated a corner at speed and as the 2CV leaned precariously into its soft suspension, JP clutched the window frame with a gasp. "Boss, not so fast. We're going to tip over."

"It's just the way this car corners," he assured her. "You'll get used to it."

"I won't," she protested. "Can't you slow down?"

"We're falling behind," he replied. "Would you prefer we navigate there on our own pace?"

"Yes."

"Well then, call Victorine and inform them we'll be taking a leisurely route, and activate your navigation tools. It's all country roads."

JP complied, and Caverlock drove at a leisurely pace. The pair soon reached the two-lane road D999. "Voila," Caverlock said. "Do you remember the series left by Drake? D999, D39, D169 and D347. Those are the roads we'll take to the village."

"You memorized them?"

"I reckoned we might need a mental map, so I turned to mnemonics: D39 reminds me of Pier 39, D169 reminds me of the typical screen aspect ratio, 16 to 9, and D347 reminds me that three plus four equals seven."

JP gave her employer an appraising look. "That's a good trick."

"Technique, not trick," he corrected her.

The underpowered *Deux Chevaux* struggled valiantly as the road wound into the hills, and a battered farm truck carrying three goats in rusted steel cages passed them with ease.

"The goats are going faster than we are," JP said disparagingly.

"As well they should," Caverlock replied. "The farmer is in a hurry."

The narrow road passed a recently mowed field, and Caverlock inhaled deeply. "There's little more gratifying than the scent of freshly cut hay."

Gazing out at the hilly terrain of sundried grass and clusters of weathered trees with dark-green foliage, JP blurted, "Boss, we won't blend in."

"We don't have to look local, we simply have to pass for French," he replied. "There are plenty of Asians in Paris. If you don't speak, people will assume you're French-Vietnamese."

"Boss, you don't look French."

Caverlock's expression was one of dismay. "I'm wounded," he said. "If don't look French, why are people always asking me for directions in Paris?"

JP shook her head. "Your body language isn't French."

"Body language? I wore blue jeans and this yellow shirt because I bought it here last trip. And I've been told my accent isn't half-bad for a foreigner."

JP remained silent and Caverlock gave her a deflated look. "OK, *je comprend*. I'm too big around the middle to be French."

"Sorry, Boss. A big guy and a Chinese girl. We'll stick out."

"Yes, we will," Caverlock conceded. "There's no getting around we're not local, or French, so we must embrace being eccentrics. Nobody would hire eccentrics as investigators. The very fact we stick out is evidence we can't possibly be skulking about spying on people. We must make a show of our eccentricity. We must drive up in our magnificently ancient *Deux Chevaux* and stick out with a flourish."

JP's skepticism morphed into anxiety. "I'm afraid Drake will spot us before we spot him."

After a moment's consideration, Caverlock said, "You may be right. So what can we do to allay his suspicion, or the suspicion of his local watcher? I think our first step should be avoid speaking English at all costs. If I speak only French, and you speak only Mandarin, he will have very little to be suspicious about. His French is minimal—recall his error about cross and *croix*—so as long as my accent is passable, I could speak complete gibberish and he couldn't tell."

"But how do we communicate?" JP asked. "You don't speak Mandarin, and I don't understand French."

"I know a few words of Mandarin from my time in Hangzhou," he replied. "For example, *buyao* and *meiyou*. We must act as if we understand each other; nod when I speak French, and say *zhege* when you want to call my attention to something."

JP's tense expression telegraphed her doubts, but she kept them to herself. Pulling off the pavement to let a string of vehicles pass, Caverlock turned onto D347 and heaved a sigh. "JP, I confess the low odds of finding Drake and reversing this foul swindle are wearing on my confidence. I must remind myself of Winston Churchill's dictum that success is proceeding from failure to failure without loss of enthusiasm."

""We made it this far, Boss," JP said. "We're so close."

"It may be the Marcus Aurelius in me, but I loathe being reduced to relying on luck."

"Didn't you tell me we make our own luck?" JP replied.

"Yes, and that is intertwined with destiny: If it's meant to be, it is already done. That said, we are at the frayed end of a long and tenuous string of suppositions."

An ancient stone church came into view and Caverlock exclaimed, "*L'Eglise de Cros.* You're right, we are close. It would settle my nerves if Carlito had some confirmation of Drake's location. Any developments on that front?"

JP shook her head. "He says the networks are all inactive."

Caverlock's voice took on an ominous tone. "That may mean the swindle is about to bear its repugnant fruit."

Caverlock steered the old car over a narrow bridge and the village of Saint Martin du Fort came into view. Glancing at the fields below the village church, Caverlock exclaimed, "Look, the orange wildflowers are just like California poppies."

Downshifting to second, Caverlock slowed the 2CV to a leisurely crawl as they passed a one-story yellow-brick elementary school and entered the village square, much of which was sheltered by the canopy of a magnificent old tree whose roots had rippled the nearby pavement. Inhaling deeply, Caverlock said, "Ah, the scent of fresh bread. This village has a bakery, a school, an *eglise* and I see a sign for a post office; not many villages have all four essentials nowadays. Sadly, those that don't fade away."

Picking up her phone, JP said, "I'll call Victorine. They must already be here."

Two streets exited the square, and Caverlock pulled the Deux Chevaux to the curb in front of a busy French-windowed patisserie while JP listened to Victorine's instructions. "They're at the farmer's market. Take the left road, it's just around the curve."

JP ended the call and Caverlock remarked, "It's an excellent place for Yvette and Michel to gather information about Drake. At this point, that's our best hope."

"What are we going to do?" JP asked.

"Be conspicuously eccentric," Caverlock replied. "There is little we can do other than familiarize ourselves with the village and look for evidence of an outpost of the Trans-Pacific Council or the Commodities Board of Governors, though I doubt they would be clumsy enough to advertise their presence."

"I thought Drake was hiding from those guys," JP said.

"That's been my assumption, but my initial suspicion that his disappearance was part of the operation's deep cover came back to me last night. Perhaps this village was selected as a suitably remote place for Drake to do his work."

"You mean maybe he hasn't run away?"

"Precisely," Caverlock confirmed. "As I said at the time, his sudden disappearance could have been a well-planned contrivance. I've been skeptical of his expertise in such matters from the beginning. But we have no way of knowing until we run him to ground."

JP's response was tinged with exasperation. "So we'll just wander around town?"

"We have nothing else unless Carlito identifies Drake's location with some precision or Yvette and Michel turn up some leads from locals."

The street led to the parking area for the bustling farmer's market and Caverlock swung the Deux Chevaux into a narrow opening between a silver Mercedes and a red Fiat sedan. Caverlock turned off the clattering engine and said, "We might as well enjoy the farmer's market first. Remember, ignore Victorine if we see her and speak Mandarin. If you must tell me something in English, whisper in my ear. Meanwhile, I'll ramble cheerfully in garbled French."

The engine creaked as it cooled and Caverlock withdrew euro notes from his travel wallet. Handing the money to JP, he said, "We'll appear purposeful if we buy a few things. I wish I'd thought to borrow two shopping bags from Yvette, but alas, one can't think of everything. I'm ravenous, and don't think well when I'm hungry. Aren't you famished?"

JP glanced at the busy covered stalls of the outdoor market. "A little. Boss, what happens if someone in the village has seen Drake?"

"I imagine we'll stake out his routes and try to locate his living quarters," Caverlock replied. "Once we've tracked down his lair, we'll unleash Victorine and hope his guard will drop in the shock of being confronted by his fiancée."

"Then what?"

Setting his well-worn fedora firmly on his head, Caverlock said, "We attempt to persuade him to help us torpedo the swindle. Failing that, we try to extract enough information from him to attempt the reversal ourselves."

The Consulting Philosopher rubbed his eyes and his voice, normally so robust, faltered. "I feel like Cervantes' foolish make-believe knight, mistaking windmills for giants I must slay, inventing noble causes out of mere mischance. At this point, the swindle is still conjecture. We can discern its mass, but who's to say if it's a gigantic machine that must be destroyed or a common windmill, spinning slowly in the breeze?"

Removing her Wayfarer sunglasses from her maroon purse, JP twisted her long hair into a ponytail and placed her stylish cream-colored hat lightly on her head. "Boss, you're losing faith right when we're close. Drake is here."

"How can you know that?" Caverlock challenged her.

With renewed exasperation, JP said, "You're always talking about intuition."

"Yes, in a Jungian sense of perceiving truth unconsciously, or in a Buddhistic sense of a faculty unavailable to rational thought. Which is it?"

Putting on her sunglasses, JP opened the passenger door. "Boss, let's get something to eat."

"I agree wholeheartedly," Caverlock replied, carefully opening the driver's door until it touched the adjacent vehicle. "Now let's see if I can squeeze past the Mercedes without tipping the Deux Chevaux onto the hapless Fiat."

Chapter Fifteen

The weekend market's stalls were arranged in a rough oval on a slightly sloping unpaved square, with charcuterie and cheese vendor trucks anchoring the upper end and a string of white-tarped vegetable and fruit vendors lining the square on one side and clothing and sundry vendors on the other. At the opposite end, a fishmonger was selling his fresh trout from a fiberglass tank on his truck.

Caverlock gravitated to the bakery stall, and JP followed from a distance, surreptitiously scanning the crowd while making a show of browsing the summer blouses fluttering on vendors' hangers in the early-summer breeze. Spotting Victorine and the children by the fishmonger, she made her way to the baked goods and touched Caverlock's elbow as he was completing the purchase of a baguette and *pain au levain*.

Taking the round loaf of crusted sourdough from him, she said, "*Zhege*," and then leaned over to whisper, "Victorine."

"*Merci, Mon Cherie*," Caverlock replied in his booming voice, and turned to follow her gaze. Victorine was being pulled in two directions by the children, and Caverlock tugged JP toward the cheese vendor's truck, muttering about *les Amis du fromage*.

While JP kept an eye on Victorine and the children, Caverlock selected three wedges of cheese, one each of cow, goat and sheep origin. Holding the baguette under one arm, he carved off a rough slice of *chevre* with his pen knife and then tore off the end of the baguette to complete a primitive but satisfying meal.

Gesturing to JP to join him in the movable feast, Caverlock offered her the baguette. With some difficulty she twisted off a small piece of the chewy bread, and foregoing the proffered cheese, headed toward the line of produce sellers. Caverlock followed, clutching his purchases while devouring the last of his bread and cheese.

While JP selected containers of cherries, apricots and strawberries, Caverlock busied himself with buying a bright green shopping bag large enough to hold the day's purchases. Once JP paid the vendor, Caverlock opened the bag and carefully placed the fruit on top of the *pain de levain* and brown-paper-wrapped cheeses.

JP glanced at Caverlock and then turned her attention to the next vendor's array of lettuces, zucchini and green beans. As if hit by an electric shock, she froze in mid-step. Recovering, she grabbed Caverlock's wrist and spoke in an urgent whisper. "That's Drake, in the blue baseball cap."

Caverlock focused on the tall slim unshaven young man in black jeans and a white T-shirt stacking produce boxes in the adjoining stall and whispered, "The fellow with the two-week beard? Are you sure? How can you tell?"

"It's him," JP insisted. "I saw his face. Look how he keeps his head down, avoiding the customers. I noticed his body language right away."

"Don't stare at him," Caverlock warned, pulling JP around. "He'll feel your eyes on him."

JP obeyed and whispered, "What do we do now?"

"Go get Victorine," Caverlock replied in a low voice. "Tell her we need her. Don't mention Drake. You'll have to watch the children until we fetch Yvette. I'll stay close to make sure he doesn't get away. Go, go, go."

JP slipped through the crowd of shoppers and Caverlock spent anxious minutes masking his bulk behind other customers, keeping the young man in the baseball cap in his line of sight while making a show of browsing the produce.

Caverlock was so focused on the young man that JP's voice startled him. "Boss, we're here."

Though her hat and sunglasses obscured her features, Victorine's anxiety charged the air like an electromagnetic field. Facing his client, Caverlock said, "There's a person of interest working in the back of the next stall. Take a good look at the fellow in the blue baseball cap, but don't alert him."

Encumbered by Jules and Juliette holding her hands, Victorine shifted forward to improve her view. Straightening a stack of empty produce boxes, the young man swept his gaze over the crowd and then tugged his baseball cap lower. In that instant, Victorine gasped. "That's Drake."

Kneeling down to address the children, Caverlock quickly explained in French that Victorine just recognized a friend from America working in the market. Shouldering his green shopping bag, he arose and gazed appraisingly at Victorine. "Are you ready?"

"I don't know," she replied.

"Don't worry, we'll seize the moment and respond accordingly," Caverlock said. "Take the children and JP round back to Drake's stall, and I'll meet you from the other side."

As Victorine led the children through the crowd, Caverlock instructed JP, "Focus on the children, don't let them wander off." JP nodded and started after Victorine.

Hurriedly working his way through the crowd, Caverlock rounded the line of stalls and threaded his way past the delivery vans of the vendors. He reached the rear of the target stall just as Victorine and the two children slipped between the stacks of produce boxes to confront Drake.

JP arrived and Caverlock ushered her into the confines of the stall ahead of him.

Still holding the hands of the children, Victorine approached her fiancé from behind and said in a clear voice, "Drake?"

The young man spun round and the turbulent emotions of fight or flight played out in his expression. When his initial shock wore off, he said in a querulous voice, "How did you get here?"

Releasing the children's hands, she replied, "Shouldn't I be asking you that?"

The realization that this was the moment of decision finally bored through his disorientation, and Drake rushed forward to embrace Victorine. "I'm sorry," he murmured, and while Jules eyed the interloper with raw jealousy, Caverlock leaned close to JP and whispered, "Those were the only two words he could have said that give him a fighting chance."

Releasing Victorine from his embrace, Drake took notice of his fiancée's companions for the first time with renewed alarm. "Who are these people?"

"We're with Victorine and Isabelle," Caverlock replied, and his booming voice alerted the other two youthful male workers of the drama playing out behind them.

Drake's tone darkened with explosive suspicion. "Who are you really with?"

"That's our only affiliation," Caverlock replied evenly. "Isabelle sent us to save you. She told us nothing but we know everything."

These statements completely destabilized whatever assumptions Drake had entertained the moment before, and he struggled for words. "What do you mean, everything?"

"The commodity swindle, Gerard, your family's involvement, your lies, everything."

"What lies?" Drake demanded.

"Withholding the truth from Victorine is like a lie," JP replied hotly, and the suppressed outrage in her voice crushed Drake's nascent defense.

Victorine seemed to waver between sympathy for her fiancé and the high dudgeon of a lovers' trust violated, and Caverlock pushed the conversation past the emotional whirlpool. "We have very little time to set things right," he said. "It may too late, but we must try. Now lead me to your lair straightaway and we'll get to work. Gerard is crafting a counter-strategy, but we need to know what you've done."

Drake's tanned face turned ashen. "It can't be undone."

"You mean it can't be undone without ruining your family and the other speculators," Caverlock corrected him. "There is a way to undo it and not ruin you, but we must be quick about it."

The possibility of redemption was clearly a revelation, and Drake turned to Victorine. "Do you trust this man?"

"Yes," Victorine replied, and the certainty in her tone moved what a moment before had been immovable. "I hired him, and he found you with no help from anyone."

"OK," Drake said uncertainly, and as Caverlock attempted to satisfy the acute curiosity of the other two workers in his simplified French, Jules stepped forward with a more entertaining explanation.

"*Merci*, Jules," Caverlock said to cut the conversation short, and then commanded Drake, "Let's go."

Jules possessively took Victorine's hand, to her amusement and Drake's consternation, and the party followed Drake out past the farmers' parked vehicles to the cobblestoned streets of the village.

The early afternoon heat radiated off the stone buildings and pavement, and Caverlock removed his hat to wipe his brow. Jules gestured to various points of interest—a shaded fountain of pure spring water, an old silk weaving factory--and provided a commentary in French that was lost on his companion, while Juliette was content to hold JP's hand and follow in her brother's footsteps.

Drake led them down a narrow curving brick-paved street lined with venerable two-story buildings painted in pastels of apricot, lemon and gold. An occasional small shop indicated the model of living above the family enterprise still existed, albeit precariously; most of the entrances were residential, and a few were empty or under renovation.

A workman was plastering the thick stone walls of the doorway in an ancient house that was being updated—bags of plaster and sand were visible through the doorway, and the upstairs windows had been removed—and Drake stopped to greet the worker by name. A delivery van entered the street and Drake waited until it had turned onto another lane before stepping over the worn stone threshold into the low-ceilinged first floor. The workman paused until everyone had entered the dim interior, and Drake led the way past stacks of lumber smelling of fresh sawdust to a poorly lit hallway and a solid oak-plank door with a gleaming new brass-plated lock. The cool interior was a welcome relief from the early summer heat and the adults removed their hats.

"A very clever location," Caverlock observed. "I commend you."

Unfamiliar with The Consulting Philosopher's manner of speech, Drake responded with a look of rank annoyance.

Drake opened the door and entered a small freshly whitewashed room with a double glass door facing an enclosed stone-paved courtyard shared by the adjoining houses. A heavily pruned peach tree in a massive blue ceramic pot by the rear door of the opposite house offered the only shade. The room was bare other than a laptop computer and yellow legal pad on a simple black laminate desk, an empty wicker trash basket, a fake-leather office chair and a modem and router on the floor whose lights cast an eerie green glow on the terracotta floor tiles. The space smelled of cement dust and wood stain, and Victorine released the children's hands to open the door to the courtyard.

Drake folded his arms in a gesture of recalcitrance and Caverlock addressed him in a commanding voice. "I'm assuming you favor honesty, and so I'll start by observing that you don't particularly like that your swindle has been unwrapped in front of Victorine, and as a result you don't particularly like me or our plan to reverse your swindle."

"It's not a swindle," Drake protested, and Caverlock slammed his fist on the desk, startling everyone; even Jules' eyes widened. "It is most definitively a swindle of the poor and powerless, and the sooner you stop rationalizing it the sooner you can escape the abyss you've fallen into."

Drake was sullenly silent and Caverlock continued. "Given your family fortune is at stake, your perverse loyalty to the scheme is understandable. But you too have sought some way to sabotage the scheme, and failing that, you retreated here, to the eye of the hurricane you've unleashed."

Victorine's gaze was locked on her fiancé, while JP's attention shifted between The Consulting Philosopher and Drake.

The children's interest in the drama playing out in a foreign tongue faded and they slipped into the courtyard to amuse themselves.

"Deservedly or not, you have won Victorine's undivided loyalty," Caverlock said. "Her commitment to finding you has been unrelenting, and she accepted the unpleasant realities of your participation in this wretched scheme with admirably pained dignity. She has paid our expenses without complaint and done everything asked of her. You could not ask for a finer, more devoted fiancée, and yet you have kept her outside your circle of trust lest she disapprove of your naive enthusiasm for the scheme or your self-justifications."

Drake recoiled as if struck by a whip, and his haughty resistance crumbled. Victorine went to his aid, extending a comforting arm around his waist.

"Your sister Isabelle protected you, far more than you deserved," Caverlock said. "We only extracted your probable whereabouts from her by artifice. As for the clues you left in your flat—had you trusted Victorine, we might have arrived early enough to reverse the damage with relatively little capital and effort. But as a direct result of your choice of secrecy over trust, we are left with faint hope of saving you or your family."

JP nodded her approval of this scathing indictment, and Caverlock began pacing the room in his signature figure-eight pattern.

"You now have a very simple but profound choice. You entrust Victorine with the absolute, unvarnished truth, holding nothing back, no matter how poorly it reflects on your judgment or character, or you hold back what you calculate can be held back without harm. If you choose the latter path of filtering what you reveal through a self-serving sieve, you will lose everything: Victorine, your family's admiration, your inheritance and perhaps most precious of all, your self-respect. Make your choice now, so I know whether to alert the authorities or attempt the reversal."

"I'll tell you everything," Drake replied, and his surrender, however reluctant, radiated sincerity.

Caverlock gave him a stern look of appraisal. "Making a clean breast of it requires sacrificing your ego, but it opens the door to a very freeing moral tranquility." The children's laughter in the courtyard seeped through the door into the silence of the makeshift office, and Caverlock stretched his arms above his head and set his palms on the desk. "Let's start with what you employed Gerard to do," Caverlock commanded.

Drake complied by sitting down and opening the laptop. As Victorine looked over his shoulder, he said, "It's faster to show you rather than describe it."

As Drake opened the relevant files, JP pulled Caverlock aside and whispered, "You really know how to talk, Boss." Nonplussed by her admiration, Caverlock shrugged and murmured, "Go get our computers from the Deux Chevaux. We need a conference call with Gerard, and then I'll call Ben. It's probably an ungodly hour in Bangkok, but we must act within the hour." Lowering his voice to a whisper, he added, "Take Victorine with you, she mustn't feel left out."

JP nodded and Caverlock turned to the pair at the desk. "Victorine, do you mind taking the children back to the farmer's market? JP will collect our gear from the Deux Chevaux. Perhaps you can call Yvette and meet her by our car."

Victorine glanced at the children playing a hop-and-skip game in the courtyard and shook her head in flustered self-recrimination. "I completely forgot about Yvette and Michel. They must be wondering where we disappeared to."

"Yes, we know the feeling," Caverlock said dryly, indirectly indicting Drake. "Time is of the essence, so hurry back with our gear. If you forgot the route back to the market, I'm sure Jules knows the way. "

Stepping to the open door, Caverlock announced the plan to Jules and Juliette, and after a brief show of reluctance they obeyed, with Juliette accepting JP's hand and Jules grasping Victorine's with a dagger look of rivalry at Drake.

Caverlock accompanied them to the entry and returned with three empty plastic construction buckets coated with cement dust and paint spatters. Turning the buckets upside down, he wiped the bottom of each one with a worker's discarded rag and positioned one by the desk as his informal chair.

Drake eyed him with active suspicion. "Tell me the truth. Who helped you find me?"

The Consulting Philosopher responded with a mirthless chuckle. "I suppose your skepticism is fair enough, but given the hell you've put Victorine through, your use of the word 'truth' is a bit rich. The truth is we found you without anyone's aid, other than Isabelle's confirmation of what we already suspected and the clues you left hidden in your flat but failed to mention to Victorine. Our success was entirely based on inference and meta-analyses."

"What meta-analyses?" Drake demanded, and Caverlock shook his head. "You've done nothing to deserve that knowledge. I suggest you focus on earning back Victorine's trust and on undoing some of the damage you've wrought."

Drake absorbed this rebuke but maintained his simmering resistance, and Caverlock's prodigious patience crumbled. "You epitomize everything that's rotten and venal in this era," he said, and his deep voice reverberated off the plastered stone walls. "You obsess over maintaining the *appearance* of trustworthiness rather than striving to *be* trustworthy. You are arrogant about your callow intellectual abilities and unashamed by your moral turpitude. You are quick to rush into questionable ventures and cowardly when things predictably go wrong. Your disposable ethical standards, your short-term expediency and your cheap strutting self-importance represent everything I loathe and fear, for it is people like you who destroy everyone and everything of value around you in your remorseless drive to impress. You exploit your unearned privileges and create nothing durable or valuable. What should be indispensable is mere pretense. You are nothing but a jumble of artifice and vanity."

Drake's simmer heated to a boil and Caverlock eyed him with disdain. "You've already destroyed your relationship with Victorine and are poised to destroy your family's wealth and reputation. By all means, continue on."

This dressing-down set Drake back, but he managed a dismissive shrug. "It can't be undone."

"You mean you don't want it undone," Caverlock corrected him.

"No, I mean it can't be undone," Drake insisted. "The money's all been invested. There's nothing left to spend on undoing it."

Arising from his overturned-bucket chair, Caverlock went to the open glass door and gazed out at the sun-drenched courtyard. "That may be, but the way of the Tao is reversal."

With visible annoyance, Drake glanced disparagingly at The Consulting Philosopher. "And what's that tidbit of wisdom supposed to mean?"

Wheeling round to meet Drake's sarcasm-soaked gaze, Caverlock replied, "It means all sorts of extremes reverse in the natural order of things. We can anticipate this or be snapped in two like a dead, brittle twig."

Issuing a sigh of depleted resignation, Caverlock began pacing out a figure-eight on the dusty floor tiles. "One of the great ironies here is the lengths I've gone to defending your honorable intentions," he said. "As every discovery further blackened your character, I resolutely reminded Victorine to give you the benefit of the doubt until all the facts were known. Now that the facts are largely in hand, your intrigues and duplicity exceed Victorine's worst fears by a country mile. And to add insult to injury, you treat me as an enemy instead of an ally who has defended you with precious little evidence in your favor and absolutely zero reward."

Drake's sarcastic disdain faded to dour recalcitrance and Caverlock said, "Nonetheless, we must put all that behind us and press on. No doubt you'd dearly love to destroy everything just to insure my defeat, but I'm hoping some faint flicker of your native intelligence and affection for Victorine is still alive beneath the ashes of your grand plan."

The opening bars of Mendelssohn's violin concerto wafted through the courtyard door from the adjoining stone house and Caverlock murmured, "Ah, E minor, the perfect key for our present distemper. Just as Mendelssohn snatched melodies from the air in Italy, so we must snatch strategies from the blue skies of *Sud de la France*."

Against his will, Drake absorbed Caverlock's musical musings, and the first faint cracks in his sullen demeanor opened. "What do you have in mind?"

Pausing his pacing, Caverlock said, "You're well acquainted with margin accounts, of course."

"Sure. You borrow against the securities in your account to buy more securities. But if your account drops in value, you get a margin call and have to sell something to pay off the loan."

"Just so," Caverlock replied. "So borrow a couple of million against the securities in the account, and use that capital to place bets on a decline in grain futures."

Startled, Drake exclaimed, "Why would I make a bet I'm sure to lose?"

"Unless a reversal occurs, in which case that will be your winning bet," Caverlock explained. "The strategy here is to place a big enough bet on grains declining that you'll be able to pay off your investors in full should their bet be lost in a crash of grain prices."

"And if the bet that grain prices skyrocket pays off?"

With a shrug, Caverlock replied, "Then your gains will far exceed the sum borrowed to hedge the original bet. If any of your investors question your hedge, your response is that prudence demanded a hedge."

Drake gazed at the computer screen of Gerard's campaign to boost grain prices and said, "Why would grain prices fall when Gerard's plan is working so beautifully?"

"What Gerard can do, Gerard can undo," Caverlock replied. Returning to his overturned-bucket seat, Caverlock studied the screen. "Since you've met Gerard, you will have noticed his uncanny resemblance to Descartes, not just his facial features but his avocations. Though few students who plow through his work are aware of this, Descartes was a big-stakes gambler. Indeed, we can surmise that he considered it his primary career interest early on."

Warming to the subject, Caverlock arose from his informal chair and resumed his pacing. "Gerard is in many ways a philosopher of social influence," he said, and his commanding voice filled every cranny of the room. "I reckon it's fair to say he implicitly shares Descartes' interest in wagers, or more accurately, an interest in wagers based on crowd behavior."

Resigning himself to Caverlock's soliloquy, Drake tore off a sheet from the yellow legal pad and crumpled it into a ball.

"We can profitably consider Descartes' distinction between the concrete and the essential," Caverlock continued, "which he explored in the example of candle wax. In this case, the essence of the wager is not identical with the concrete wager."

His voice expressing a dry skepticism, Drake asked, "And how does this help us?"

"An excellent question," Caverlock responded. "The concrete wager is one of momentum. Traders see the price of grain rising, and buy in to profit from the continuing surge higher. Gerard's campaign weds momentum buying to a plausible narrative, in this case, of grain scarcities. Never mind the story is fiction; the narrative and momentum effectively steer crowd behavior."

Stopping to face Drake, he lowered his voice. "The essence of the trade is greed untethered from real-world consequence and morality. Profits are the sole measure. That is the essence of the wager."

Drake was unimpressed. "And of every other trade."

"Not quite every trade," Caverlock replied. "Even the most unfeeling trader recognizes that much higher grain prices will cause suffering among those with very little money. Even if they feel zero remorse themselves, they recognize others may act on the moral repugnance of profiting from the suffering of others. That's an entirely different wager from bets placed at a table of gamblers who know the game and the odds, a game that only affects those who choose to play."

Tossing the crumpled paper ball into the air, Drake deftly caught it with one hand. "And so?"

Caverlock allowed himself a judicious pause and then resumed his pacing. "The rats scurry onto the ship to gorge on juicy profits and scramble off in a panic once it starts sinking. Since the way of the Tao is reversal, we'll reverse the polarity of the trade from greed to fear."

Rolling his chair away from the desk, Drake tossed the crumpled paper ball into the wicker basket. "With what money?"

"My own, of course."

Drake masked his surprise with a question. "How much?"

"Enough to buy a house anywhere but the most exclusive enclaves. It's not much compared to the millions at your disposal, but it might be enough to unleash an avalanche."

Drake gave Caverlock a supercilious smirk. "Willing to bet your inheritance, huh?"

"I have no inheritance," Caverlock snapped. "All of this money was earned via trading. So let's turn your queries on their source. How much of your own money is at stake? Not your family's money—your own money, money that you earned."

Drake's smugness faded and Caverlock said, "As I suspected, zero. And how much of your wealth resulted from trading? Also zero, n'est pas?"

Striding to Drake's chair, Caverlock spun it round so Drake was looking up at his formidably stern visage. "Justice would best be served by you, your family and all your investors being wiped out, but to serve the interests of my client, Victorine, I'm seeking an exit that will return your family and investors' original capital."

Drake tried to turn the chair to face the desk but Caverlock grabbed the chair arm, locking it with his firm grasp. "It will likely go badly for you if your investors lose their capital."

Drake's eyes widened in alarm and Caverlock said, "Let's settle two issues. Which matters more to you, thwarting my plan because you detest me, or salvaging what's left of your love for Victorine? Choose wisely because you can't have both."

Drake made no reply and Caverlock said, "Good. I would choose Victorine over a petty victory, too. Now to the second issue: do you want to reverse the swindle or would you rather see it succeed as proof of your loyalty and sage superiority? Please answer honestly."

Caverlock's description of the two options did not sit well with Drake, and Caverlock said, "Put another way, would you rather please your father and his peers or would you rather sabotage a heartless exploitation?"

A tense moment passed slowly and Drake looked out at the sunny courtyard. "Sink it."

"There can be no half-measures, for there is no middle ground," Caverlock warned. "You have grown accustomed to finessing everyone around you to appear blameless. There is no way to muddle through and please both sides. You must sell when directed. If you don't, things will go very badly for you, and I don't mean in an abstract fashion. There will be no victory, no marriage to Victorine, and no praise for loyalty from your father. You must stay the course and face your father with the confidence of moral certitude."

Releasing the chair arm, Caverlock's voice dropped to a gravelly sobriety. "I'm sorry it's come to this, Drake, and I say that with utter sincerity. You must choose between your father and Victorine. I do not know your father, but I have come to know Victorine in trying circumstances, and she is worthy of whatever sacrifice you could possibly make."

A chatter of voices in the entry signaled the return of JP and Victorine, and Caverlock went to the green grocery bag to retrieve the half-consumed baguette. As he tore off a piece of the bread, he murmured, "We shall soon see whose grasp of the way of the Tao is superior, ours or the swindlers."

Chapter Sixteen

Victorine and JP entered the room, took in Drake's glum visage and waited expectantly for an update. JP had rolled up the sleeves of her white blouse to her elbows, for the afternoon heat left her face as flushed as Victorine's. Victorine handed Drake and Caverlock cold bottles of water, and kneeled anxiously by her fiancé. In his sweat-stained T-shirt and scruffy beard, Drake's slumping posture sketched a portrait of disorientation.

Drake absent-mindedly loosened one of the cloth ties on Victorine's blue and white striped shirt sleeve, and then forced a wan smile of reassurance that only heightened Victorine's distress.

With the piece of baguette in hand, Caverlock gestured to the courtyard and said, "Ladies, the Fates have blessed us with Mendelssohn's violin concerto in E minor via the neighbor's open window, a piece that's lively, sweet, dark and dramatic by turns, a fitting match for the task ahead. JP, would you please set up a conference call with Gerard? I believe he's expecting us."

Opening one of the laptops, JP coolly conferred with Drake on the Internet access password and a few moments later Gerard's hawk-like eyes and long unkempt locks appeared on the screen.

"*Bonjour,* Gerard," Caverlock said in his booming voice. "I am sorry to impose on you during the weekend."

Gerard's voice was raspy with impatience. "Let's begin. The first phase is to introduce the idea that the sudden rise in the cost of grain is speculation *seulement,* that is to say, the sole result of speculator greed. The second phase is to arouse moral outrage at this exploitation of the innocent. I've activated social-media networks that focus on financial exploitation by a handful of inside operators. Fortunately for us, this kind of moral outrage spreads very easily in anti-capitalist and anti-Establishment circles. A number of influential alternative-media writers will be encouraged to inflame the outrage."

As Gerard referred to his notes spread before him on his dining table, his enormous black cat walked serenely across the sheets of paper, and JP suppressed a laugh as Gerard gently shooed the curious creature from his work.

"The third phase is to identify grain surpluses and distribute this news to the financial media. Though this is not my expertise, I have identified some potential candidates."

Referring to his notes, He added, "The initial sell should be very large, and executed in a period of illiquidity to maximize its effect. This initial sell should be completed before the news of grain surpluses reaches the media, so it will gain the influential veracity of insider knowledge."

"Brilliant," Caverlock enthused. "You are a worthy successor to Descartes. You have distilled the essence of the trade into pure praxis."

Gerard made a Gallic gesture of refusing the praise, and said, "Let's see if the work is successful first. I will need the *l'argent* we discussed."

"Yes of course," Caverlock replied. Withdrawing his phone, he tapped on the screen and announced a moment later, "The money is now available to you. Our appreciation of your work is boundless."

"Be ready to execute the initial trade Monday morning," Gerard said, and his voice betrayed his frayed nerves.

"We will be ready," Caverlock assured him, and ended the call. Glancing at the slumped figure of Drake, he said, "You've done an admirable job of misdirection regarding your location and intentions, but if we found you, others with much greater resources may have tracked you by means unavailable to us. Or, despite our best efforts, we may have been followed. I had the distinctly unnerving impression that Gerard's flat was being watched, and we might have picked up a tail there."

"Then why did you go there?" Drake demanded, and Caverlock snapped, "You left us no choice."

The ensuing silence was broken by Caverlock. "This location might yet be secure but prudence demands we minimize coming and going. Drake, is there a functioning toilet and water tap here?"

Drake nodded. "A bathroom on this floor and a half-finished kitchen upstairs."

"Excellent," Caverlock said. "I'll impose upon Yvette and Michel to scrounge up sleeping mats. In this weather, our bedding needs will be light." Caverlock paused to compose a text and then continued. "I noticed an auberge and a bistro on the way to the farmer's market, and I suggest Drake and Victorine obtain dinner first. Or if you prefer, we'll go first. In any event, we must first talk to Ben about the hedge and our trading plan."

"You go first," Victorine offered, and Caverlock said, "Thank you. We haven't eaten a proper meal all day. JP, would you mind setting up the call to Ben? I'm sorry to ask but I'm not at my best."

"No problem, Boss," JP replied, and her expression telegraphed her anxiety as her employer's energy faded.

His inner fuel seemingly drained, Caverlock sat down heavily on one of the overturned buckets and closed his eyes. "Drake, I know it's been a difficult day, but it's essential that you understand the trading plan."

Victorine took Drake's hand, and he met her anxious gaze with the look of someone struggling to emerge from a dense thicket of thorns.

The video call connected and JP said, "Hi, Ben. Sorry to call you after 8 PM."

Sitting on his divan with the open shutters of the living room visible behind him, Ben smiled broadly. "It is past my bedtime, but I won't tell if you don't."

"Ben, I'm afraid we're relying very heavily on you," Caverlock said in his loud voice. "We're all a bit worn here and can follow orders but not think it through ourselves."

"No worries, my friend," Ben replied. "I'll send you the plan. Just execute the trades."

"I feel an immense relief that you have it in hand," Caverlock. "Needless to say, the odds are very much against us, our capital is insufficient and our enemies will not surrender easily. I have grave misgivings about the entire enterprise, on which I have staked everything I own that's liquid other than the cash in the tin box at home."

JP's eyes flashed alarm and Ben said reassuringly, "We'll hedge to protect the initial capital. On the positive side, this could be a really good trade, and there's a pool of major players who are extremely interested in joining us should the trade start going our way."

This piqued Drake's interest and he asked, "How major?"

"Eight figures if things go our way."

"That means ten million, right?" JP asked, and Ben nodded. "Small change in the global picture."

"But enough to matter in this trade," Caverlock said. "Walk us through your plan, and we'll try to keep up."

Ben proceeded through a series of slides detailing each trade and hedge, a mix of both long and short futures contracts and out-of-the-money options. Drake had shaken off enough of his discontent to take an interest in the plan's potential gains, and while Drake asked questions of Ben, Caverlock turned to JP and said in a whisper, "Interesting how Drake is enthused by the profit potential of betting against his investors, isn't it?"

JP nodded and asked in a low voice, "Can I join the trade with my little account?"

"Of course, but you must follow Ben to the letter. You must buy a hedge, even if you're convinced it's throwing your money away. This could all go terribly against us. Sometimes Ben only wins because he bet against himself."

Caverlock waited for Ben to answer Drake's question and said, "Ben, please reassure me you won't risk your own money in this. We're only asking for advice on risking my funds and Drake's margin account."

The computer screen reverted to live video and Ben's serious expression softened to wry amusement. "You're all too transparent, you sly dog," he exclaimed. "You're trying to hog the trade by scaring me off. If your scheme starts working, I'll be the first to follow you in."

"That will likely be the trade that tips the scales," Caverlock said in a muted tone.

"Remember my favorite saying," Ben said. "*He who will not risk cannot win.* John Paul Jones."

"I'll up the ante with Douglas MacArthur," Caverlock replied. "*There is no security on this Earth, only opportunity.*"

"I'll raise you a Pasteur," Ben retorted. "*Chance favors the prepared mind.*"

"I'll call your Pasteur and lay down a Churchill: *success is going from failure to failure without loss of enthusiasm.*"

Ben chuckled and Caverlock's spirits lifted. "By Jupiter, I'm delighted you're on our side of the trade rather than the swindlers."

"Nothing is sweeter than swindling the swindlers," Ben said. "Add that to the pot of aphorisms."

Ben ended the call and Caverlock's phone chirped with an incoming text. "It's Michel and Yvette. They're sorry we won't be able to enjoy the hospitality of his Aunt's farmhouse, and will check the farmhouse for bedding."

Turning to Drake, he said, "Judging by the silence in the front room, the craftsman has gone home. Perhaps we should turn on a light to avoid alarming the neighbors with our presence tonight. They'll reckon the work crew left the light on."

"I slept here the first few nights," Drake replied. "I hung a tarp over the door to the courtyard so the neighbors couldn't see me. The walls are thick so we won't be heard. No one can see lights in the back half of the house from the street, I've checked. Also, we should come and go through the courtyard. There's a passage between the houses that back up to the courtyard. The gate is latched but not locked."

"A wise precaution," Caverlock noted. "I assume you two would prefer to bed down here." His voice was tinged with caution, and the pair picked up his implication. "I won't let him abscond in the night," Victorine said with a rare amusement.

"Excellent," Caverlock said without enthusiasm. "And where do you suggest we sleep?"

"There's a room off the kitchen upstairs that's clean and out of sight from the street," Drake replied.

"Originally a maid's quarters, I imagine," Caverlock said. "Is there no room downstairs?"

"They either face the street or are full of construction supplies."

Exchanging a skeptical glance with JP, Caverlock said, "Then we'll make do with the maid's room."

Checking his watch, he added, "I'll explain to Michel and Yvette that they should deliver whatever bedding they've found as quickly as possible. JP and I will slip away to dinner, and if you're as starving as we are, there's fruit, bread and cheese in the green bag."

The pair waited in awkward anticipation as Caverlock and JP exited through the glass door to the courtyard, and as they eased through the narrow passageway to the rear street, Caverlock glanced at JP with a wry look. "I think the lovebirds are starved for something other than nourishment, or perhaps I should say another form of nourishment."

JP blushed at the implication and Caverlock added, "Meanwhile, I'll gladly settle for fresh trout or an equivalent delicacy at the local auberge, which comes highly rated."

*   *   *

Caverlock and JP returned two hours later to an empty office and voices emanating from the entry. Navigating the dim hallway, they emerged into the front room and found Drake and Victorine sorting through a disorderly pile of foam mats, sheets, blankets and pillows on a plastic tarp.

"Michel just left," Victorine explained. "He also dropped off my luggage."

"Take what you need and we'll make do with what's left," Caverlock said. "Before you leave for dinner, we need to discuss our individual duties."

Handing Drake two mats and pillows, Victorine gathered up sheets and a blanket and the foursome returned to the office. Setting the bedding down in a corner, Victorine took the office chair and Drake sat next to her on an overturned bucket. JP declined a seat and Caverlock stood uneasily by the courtyard door. The sun had set and dusk tinted the courtyard with fading pastels of gold and orange.

"As I'm sure you all know, complex systems tend to change abruptly, that is to say, non-linearly, as opposed to smooth transitions," Caverlock began. "An avalanche is an excellent example. All appears stable until some small perturbation triggers a phase change in the snow pack, and it suddenly tumbles down the mountain."

Warming to the topic, Caverlock began his usual pacing. "A pile of sand illustrates the same principle. Adding sand grains enlarges the pile, until a single additional grain triggers an avalanche and the collapse of the pile. This is the model of our task."

Caverlock paused by the heavy wood door to the hallway and gazed at his three companions. "Imagine a pile of sand, and Gerard's campaign as adding sand in the hopes of triggering a collapse. Since it's impossible to detect the level of instability, we can't tell how many more grains of sand are needed to trigger a phase change. Now imagine that Gerard's campaign increases the instability to the point that three additional grains would trigger the collapse of the swindle. Yet if those three grains are not added, nothing happens—the swindle continues on unchanged. We must do whatever we can to add those last essential grains of sand. It may well boil down to whatever modest perturbations we can generate as individuals."

"What do you propose?" Victorine asked.

His voice intensifying, Caverlock said, "We must each spread Gerard's campaign in our own networks. Drake, you must have contacts in finance. Alert key traders of the opportunity to profit when the recent surge in grain prices reverses. Victorine, you must have contacts with large social networks. Contact them and explain why this swindle matters. JP, when things go viral in China's social media, the media takes notice. Contact anyone you know who lives and breathes social media. I will of course do the same, but given the paltry size of my network, your efforts will be much more likely to bear fruit."

Caverlock returned to the courtyard door to gaze pensively at the day's last light. "The plan is to sell a large block of futures when it will make the largest splash, before the European markets open Monday morning. By the time American markets open six hours later, we'll know if we've succeeded or failed. Until then, we should beaver away at spreading the message. That said, it's been a long day and I will be useless tomorrow if I don't take a sponge bath and collapse in a heap on whatever bedding is available."

No one in the captive audience of three protested, and Victorine and Drake left for dinner, quietly crossing the courtyard and disappearing in the shadows of the passageway.

Retrieving his travel bag from the floor, Caverlock made his way to the bathroom and when he emerged in his dragon-pajamas, he found JP ferrying their bedding up the stairs to the maid's room with the aid of her mobile phone light. "Watch out for the pipes on the floor," she warned, referring to lengths of electrical conduit beside the staircase.

Following JP up the steps, Caverlock surveyed the small room as JP laid the mats on the hardwood floor, positioning them a few feet apart beneath the half-open skylight that dimly illuminated the room with moonlight.

"At least the floor's been swept," Caverlock noted. Kneeling next to the bedding, he said, "Take whatever is most comfortable. What with the long day and the wine with dinner, I could sleep quite blissfully on a piece of cardboard."

"Both mats are thin," JP said.

"Take them both," Caverlock said solicitously. "You've weathered enough today."

With a depleted sigh, JP said, "I need a sponge bath, too." Turning her mobile phone light on the doorway, she descended the stairs with her travel bag in hand.

When she returned in her lace-trimmed peach nightgown, modestly clutching her bag to her chest, she was surprised to find Caverlock straightening the curling edges of a carpet he'd unrolled beneath their bedding, which had been pushed together to benefit from a thick rectangle of foam the size of a queen mattress.

"The rug was rolled up and is clean. I'm not sure where the foam came from, but in any event it increases our comfort greatly, if you don't mind sharing it."

JP briefly pondered the prospect of sleeping beside Caverlock and then flopped onto the makeshift bed, pulling one of the sheets around her and positioning a pillow beneath her head.

"I just hope you don't have another nightmare in French," she said in a tone of exaggerated grumpiness, and Caverlock chuckled. "No worries on that front, my nightmare is in my waking hours until we know the results of our plan. I shall also endeavor not to snore, or wander from my side of the bed."

Caverlock carefully positioned himself on the impromptu bed as far from JP as possible, and then sighed. "It's rather comfortable, isn't it?"

JP offered an "hmmm" in confirmation, and in a low voice Caverlock murmured, "If anyone ever asks if I've slept with my assistant, I can honestly answer yes."

JP turned to face him. "Don't even joke about that, Boss," she growled, and he protested, "It's a purely private gest."

JP fumed, "Only guys think that's funny," and then turned her back to her bedmate. Gazing up at the faint light of the crescent moon in the skylight, Caverlock said, "I apologize for finding it amusing."

"Boss, I'm tired, let's go to sleep."

"Of course," Caverlock murmured. "But not before I congratulate you on spotting Drake. That was extremely observant of you. I am a mere Watson to your Holmes. But tell me—did you have an intuition that he might be at the farmer's market?"

KP shifted slightly. "Maybe."

"I reckon you did," Caverlock said. "That's why you were especially alert to Drake's wariness."

JP remained motionless and after an interlude Caverlock exclaimed, "Look, JP, the moon is visible through the skylight."

JP made no response, and Caverlock continued in a low voice. "Here we are, busy little ants looking up at the moon, worrying about money, scheming to make more of it even when we have more than enough, like Drake's parents. But what is money, anyway? Nobody seems to ask, as if it's too obvious for words. Yet the obvious is precisely what demands the closest examination."

JP was quiet and Caverlock said, "JP, my confidence in this entire project is at low ebb. I don't even care that much about money, other than as a tracking mechanism for my trading progress, and yet here I am, committing my own fortune to a foolish bet with little chance of success, to prove what? That I don't care about the money, or that I'm virtuous for bravely sacrificing all in a vain attempt to stop a vast swindle? I am riddled with misgivings, and fear I won't sleep a wink."

JP turned to face him again. "Boss, you can't change who you are. You'd be miserable if you couldn't make this bet. We've done our best, there's nothing more we can do. If it fails, we can still be proud of our effort. Look how much we accomplished already. Everyone is amazed we found him."

Caverlock pondered her words and replied in a sheepish voice. "For all my pretensions, you are wiser than I am, and have more insight into my foibles than I have into yours."

JP shifted onto her back to look up at the night sky, and her eyes glistened in the moonlight. "Sometimes you know me better than anybody. I've told you almost nothing about myself, and yet everything you say about me is so true."

"Is that really true?"

Overcoming her hesitancy, she responded in a soft voice. "You're the only one who's made me cry, not because you're being mean but because you say things nobody else even knows."

Uncharacteristically, Caverlock had no reply and JP said, "Boss, let's go to sleep."

"Of course." After a brief pause, he added, "Thank you, JP. You are my one true treasure."

JP was silent, and a moment later she murmured, "If anybody asks if I slept with my boss, I'll say yes, because he made me."

Caverlock chuckled. "You mean he made the bed and you fell gratefully into it."

*   *   *

"Bonjour, you two," Victorine said, and her morning smile was affectionately knowing. Wearing shimmering silk pajamas, she held a box with two *café au laits* in paper cups, two croissants and a baguette cut in half, with a dollop of raspberry jam on a chipped saucer.

Her long hair tousled most fetchingly, JP sat up with alarm and straightened the spaghetti straps of her lacy nightgown. "It's not what you think," JP said in a voice hoarse with sleep.

Caverlock rolled over and his eyes flickered open. "It's exactly what you think," he muttered. "Two friends sharing a bed out of necessity."

In a teasing tone, Victorine asked, "How many years apart are you?"

JP's eyes widened in dismay and Caverlock played along, answering, "Eighteen. JP is 26 and I am ancient, old enough to be her father had I been wild enough to wed at such a rambunctious age."

"Boss," JP threatened, and Victorine tittered delightedly, something that was new to both JP and Caverlock.

"Lots of 26-year olds find happiness with 44-year olds," Victorine declared with mock seriousness. "Men come into their own in their 40s."

"You take him, and I'll take Drake," JP said grumpily, and her pout was so delicious that both Victorine and Caverlock suppressed giggles.

"I may take you up on that," Victorine replied, tugging playfully on Caverlock's untidy locks. "It's hard to find a man this trustworthy and considerate."

JP pursed her lips and said, "Boss, did you put her up to this?"

"What a dreadfully cynical suspicion," Caverlock murmured, "especially for someone in the flower of her youth." Gazing up at Victorine, resplendent in silk and the warm glow of amusement, he added, "You have three smitten suitors now, Miss V.: handsome, dashing Drake, the irrepressible young Jules, and the aging but trustworthy and considerate Consulting Philosopher."

"Every girl should be so lucky," Victorine said, and flashed JP a conspirator's grin. "Can't I have all three?"

"It seems you have all three well in hand," Caverlock replied.

Still pouting, JP said, "I would wait for Jules."

Turning to his charmingly disheveled assistant, Caverlock replied, "An admirable choice, though he does lean a bit to the possessive."

Sitting up to receive the box from Victorine, he said, "How thoughtful to bring us breakfast."

"Drake went to the bakery, as they already know him," she said. "He thought it less likely to raise eyebrows than if we all went."

"It's best to be cautious," Caverlock assented, "though interested parties might have spotted us together in the farmers market yesterday." Handing a coffee to JP, he set the box between them. Taking a croissant, he said, "This village is fortunate to have a bakery. Nowadays not many people are willing to awaken in the middle of the night to start the dough."

As JP sipped the coffee and crunched on the crisp end of the croissant, her mood brightened, and Victorine knelt down to hug her affectionately. Arising, Victorine said, "I'll see you downstairs."

Gazing at the skylight's shaft of morning sun brightening the freshly painted wall, Caverlock said, "A sound night's sleep, a sunny morning in the south of France, a café au lait and croissant—this would soften the heart of even the flintiest stoic, and delight the most jaded epicurean."

Smearing some of the raspberry jam on a piece of baguette, JP stole a glance at her bedmate and said, "You really know how to talk, Boss. That's why women fall in love with you."

"Or come to loathe me, as you so sagely observed," Caverlock replied wryly. "No, Victorine has it right. Intimates who are trustworthy, considerate and loyal are scarce. The jury is still out on Drake, but considering Victorine's radiant good humor this morning, it's clear there's still chemistry there, or pixey dust, if you prefer."

Running her fingers through her long black hair, JP said, "I don't trust him."

"Me, neither, but fortunately we don't have to," Caverlock said. "Our duty is to Victorine and her interests, and we've satisfied the terms of our contract by finding Drake. Technically speaking, whether the swindle succeeds or fails is none of our business, but Victorine's moral sensibilities impose a higher-order demand on Drake. As he is discovering, love is not just chemistry. I'm not sure if this comes from Stendhal or another source, but love requires not just hope and beauty but admiration. There is little to admire should Drake let the swindle run to avoid a conflict with his father."

JP drained the last of her café au lait and contemplated the remaining chunk of baguette. "I wonder if he's up to challenging his father."

"There's something inevitable in that," Caverlock mused. "The controlling parent views any independence in his children as a betrayal punishable by ostracism, which we now know activates the same circuits of the brain as physical pain. Drake's independence will likely cost him dearly, emotionally and financially. No wonder he hesitates to torpedo the swindle."

"But if he obeys his father, what will he lose?" JP asked.

"Precisely," Caverlock replied. "He will lose his self-respect and Victorine, if not at once then over time. In quantum terms, love and the swindle are now entangled. Regardless of distance, they cannot be disentangled."

Taking the last piece of bread, JP chewed on it contemplatively. Caverlock observed her for a time and then said, "The parent who abandons their child leaves scars, but so does the dictatorial parent. You and I bear the first sort of scars, but not the second. Who can say which hurts more?"

Arising with a groan, Caverlock went to his worn travel bag and extracted a rumpled gray turtleneck pullover. "I suppose the dread hour has arrived," he muttered. "We must chip away at the granite mountain of this swindle and hope we can transform it into dust with our tiny hammers and chisels."

*   *   *

JP had just finished brushing her teeth in the kitchen sink when a loud knock on the front door downstairs disturbed the Sunday morning quiet. Picking her way past boxes of ceramic tile and cardboard-wrapped cabinet shelving awaiting installation, she met Caverlock on the landing where they exchanged anxious looks. Caverlock was in his black jeans and gray pullover, and JP, still in her nightgown, hovered behind him.

From their perch, they watched Drake, clad in khaki shorts and a coarse wheat-colored peasant shirt cautiously approach the door and crack it open. Victorine, now in the floral-print sundress that she'd worn when meeting Caverlock at the waterfront café in San Francisco, watched from the hallway.

Jules and Juliette, dressed in matching striped blue T-shirts, slipped through the half-open door, followed by Yvette and Michel carrying boxes. Jules made a beeline past Drake straight to Victorine, hopping agilely over a stack of lumber, and hugged her tightly, murmuring his private farewell in French.

Not be outdone, Juliette shyly approached Drake and waited for him to bend down to receive her one-kiss-per-cheek sendoff. She then hugged him, much to her parents' amusement and to his befuddlement.

Caverlock descended the stairs to accept the gift boxes while JP scurried back into their room to pull on blue jeans and an embroidered white cotton smock.

Lifting the heavy cast-iron lid of a pot in the first box, Caverlock exclaimed, "Cassoulet, we are blessed beyond words. Who must we thank?"

"My aunt," Michel replied. "She is sorry you could not visit her, but she wants you to taste her cooking."

"*Encroyable*," Caverlock marveled. "And in the other box, bottles of water, a *pain au levain*, a bottle of rosé from Provence and a hearty red from Languedoc. Splendid, we cannot thank her enough, her generosity is measureless."

"There are bowls, silverware and glasses," Yvette explained, "and four patisserie. We are sorry we cannot stay, but we must return to Nimes."

"Of course," Caverlock said. "I cannot thank you enough, and your aunt, for helping us so unstintingly and on such short notice. I shall arrange to return the bedding, crockery and the Deux Chevaux to your aunt once the crisis is resolved tomorrow. We are deeply in your debt, and shall endeavor to repay you."

JP descended the stairs in time to exchange good-byes, and the family left in a flurry of hugs. Drake closed the door, and the four fell into a sobering silence: their only allies had left, and a project with little chance of success awaited them.

Attempting to dispel the dour mood, Caverlock spoke in an upbeat tone. "With the fruit we bought yesterday, and this splendid cassoulet, we can eat in today most grandly. So let's get to the task at hand."

Victorine shifted uncomfortably. "This isn't my area of expertise, and to tell the truth, I don't even know how to begin."

The silence of Drake and JP conferred their agreement, and Caverlock paused for a moment before bending down to touch the sawdust covering the concrete floor.

"It is not my expertise either, but let's draw upon the expertise we do have and timeless sources such as the Utilitarian Hume and Bernays, the philosopher of persuasion. Drake, you're in marketing," Caverlock said, drawing a circle in the dust. "I'm confident you can pen a persuasive summary."

Tracing another circle and connecting it to the first circle, he said, "JP, you know what sparks Mandarin-speaking audiences that might also gain the attention of the media in China." Glancing at his client, he added, "Victorine, we never discussed your work."

"I'm in the non-profit world," she said. "Grant-writing, proposals, that sort of thing."

"Then you must have a contact list full of people keen to right exploitive wrongs," Caverlock observed. "And much of what you do is marketing as well."

Drawing a third circle, he said, "I have the poorest prospects, but there's a few old contacts who might be useful. And we have an auxiliary force in Carlito, who has networks quite different from ours."

Enclosing all three circles in a larger circle, Caverlock stood up. "Drake, your office seems the place to be." Unaccustomed to Caverlock's deference, Drake made a show of letting Victorine lead the way, followed by JP and Caverlock carrying the boxes of food.

At Drake's insistence, Victorine took the office chair while the other three sat on the overturned buckets.

"The first step is to identify each audience, and design a pitch for each one," Drake said. "Gerard has already done that for his groups but we should work on our own."

"Splendid," Caverlock responded. "My suggestion is that we try to emulate the messages that had an outsized impact on people we know. The world is awash in marketing, and so what makes a message cut through the clutter?"

"Empathy and outrage have been worked to death," Victorine commented. "Emotional appeals don't work."

"Then we should stick to facts," JP suggested. "Fact, there is no grain shortage, fact, speculators are trying to push prices up for their own gain."

"Facts have limited impact now, too, as they're quickly degraded by counterclaims," Caverlock observed.

Taking the yellow legal pad and pen from the desk, Drake jotted a note. "What seems to work is presenting people with a simple action they can take that boosts their ideal self, the self they seek to be."

"Presenting a choice, brilliant," Caverlock enthused. "For traders, their ideal self is a brilliant speculator who cuts against the crowd. For those seeking to signal virtue, a moral stance is their ideal self."

Arising, he busied himself with laying the fruit from the farmer's market on the desk for communal consumption. Selecting an apricot, The Consulting Philosopher said, "How about this: *Who wins? A few speculators or everyone who eats rice and bread?*"

After a meaningful pause, Drake added to his notes. "We need to propose an action they can take."

"Send this to everyone in your networks," JP offered.

"That might work with my audience, but what about the commodity traders?" Victorine asked. "If they had a conscience, they wouldn't be speculators."

Drake shivered as if struck with a shower of ice, and Caverlock mused, "Opportunistic greed is part of human nature. Nothing wrong with appealing to that."

"Fairness is also part of human nature," JP countered. "We should talk about the unfairness."

"Let's each compose pitches for our audiences and then compare notes," Caverlock suggested. "The perfect is the enemy of the good, as time is the key determinant. We need to launch our best shots soon." Biting into the apricot, he began pacing the tiled floor with an air of intense concentration.

Victorine and JP opened their keyboards, and once Caverlock had reduced the apricot to a clean seed he pulled a small notebook from his back pocket and began scribbling.

The four worked in silence for a time, and the chirps of birds in the courtyard peach tree provided a tranquil background to the tapping of keys.

After a brainstorming session, the group agreed that each person would select the messages they reckoned most likely to sway their audiences. The work on four keyboards was over soon enough, and Caverlock reported, "Gerard has nothing new to report, and we've added our four grains of sand to his efforts. I sent our pitches to Carlito and asked him to alert his network. Now we await results, if any."

There was no celebratory cheer in the room; the price of grain appeared poised to continue its ascent, and web searches turned up no sign of Gerard's counter-campaign.

Caverlock transported the savory-scented cassoulet to the kitchen upstairs to be reheated while JP set the desk with the borrowed plates as an informal dining table.

The luncheon of cassoulet, bread, fruit and rosé wine had a slightly funereal air; after desultory comments on the wine and fare, each diner fell into the well of their own thoughts. Even the four *Mille-Feuillet* patisserie did not brighten their spirits. Jet lag, anxiety, a somber fear of failure and a swarming host of other worries weighed on each, and Caverlock issued a yawn worthy of a gorged tiger. "I need a nap," he announced. "We'll regroup in the evening."

While JP caught up on personal messages, Victorine and Drake slipped out. An hour later, as the afternoon sun warmed the old stone house, Caverlock entered the office in a rumpled short-sleeve white cotton shirt, having shed the turtleneck. Holding their hats in hand, he said, "JP, I shall go mad confined to this charming prison. Let's take a walk. From satellite imagery, it seems this road extends beyond the village into a delightful valley of small farms."

Once the pair had left the last houses of the villages behind, Caverlock breathed deeply of the hay-scented air and swung his arms in circles. "A bit warm today, but ideal for a jaunt. Tell me, JP, did your childhood include any visits to a family village deep in the countryside?"

Her reluctance to speak of her own life loosened by the setting, JP described her mother's family's ancestral village, nestled in mountains at the end of an unpaved road, effectively cut off from the bustling urban world of China's megalopolises. "No young person stays in those villages," JP stated. "It's too boring, everyone is a farmer and poor."

"It's a peculiar world, isn't it?" Caverlock replied. "The people who grow the food we need and enjoy are poor while those who can print money out of thin air by speculation own private jets and posh villas."

Adjusting her hat to block the afternoon sun, JP chided him, "But you're a speculator, too, printing money out of thin air."

Removing his weathered fedora to wipe his brow, he replied, "Ah, but a principled speculator. It's like playing chess for money. Nobody loses except those who choose to sit at the table. Nothing is created out of thin air. Wagers are placed and won or lost. It's brutal but fair."

The road made a sharp turn and JP stopped to gaze over the verdant valley, checkerboarded with a scattering of recently mowed fields of hay adjoining stone farmhouses bordered by neat rows of vegetables and corn.

Glancing at his companion, Caverlock said, "In your chic hat, sunglasses and embroidered peasant blouse, you look right at home here."

"How about you, Boss--did you ever live in the countryside?"

"Yes, my aunt's house was in an impoverished rural county of abandoned homesteads and elderly farmers. It sparked my interest in growing things, which was a profound revelation. Did I show you the Japanese pumpkin vine that's taking over the hillside below my office? It's one of my private joys."

Resuming their walk, they were surprised to meet Drake and Victorine returning to the village. The front of Drake's peasant shirt was darkened with sweat, and beneath her broad-brimmed hat, Victorine's face and shoulders were flushed.

"Greetings, strangers," Caverlock joked, and Victorine explained, "Drake showed me the farm where he's been staying and working. A couple about our age are making goat cheese and growing vegetables for the farmer's market."

"Marvelous," Caverlock said. "I would dearly love to taste their *fromage*." A battered white truck streaked with rust rounded the bend and wheezed down the road into the valley, trailing a faint stench of diesel.

"We'll see you back at the house," Drake said, and the couple started for the village. Caverlock watched them round the corner and then bent down to examine a patch of bright-gold wild poppies on the side of the pavement.

"They didn't look too happy," JP remarked. Caverlock plucked a single flower and stood up to hand it to JP. "No, they didn't," he responded. "They are each in a difficult position, and they must make wrenching decisions on their future together, assuming they have one."

JP accepted the flower and after a moment's hesitation, placed it in the top buttonhole of her embroidered white smock. Glancing up the road, Caverlock said, "Let's walk to those chestnut trees at the end of this splendid little valley. I'd rather walk here than pace in the half-finished house."

"At least it's cool in the house," JP protested, and Caverlock replied, "We're both peasant stock, JP. Deep in our genes, we're accustomed to a bit of suffering. It's our stoic nature."

Removing her hat, JP wiped the sweat from her forehead with the back of her hand and murmured, "If that's supposed to make me feel better, it didn't work." After a sigh, she dutifully accompanied The Consulting Philosopher as he resumed their walk.

The house was quiet when they slipped from the courtyard into the office some time later. Caverlock took two bottles of water from the box and handed one to JP, who half-drained her bottle and flopped down on the cool tile floor.

Checking his laptop, Caverlock brightened. "A colleague I've never met in Paris just published a denunciation of the speculation in grain in a journal he edits. It's a small audience, but it's a start."

Her eyes closed, JP asked, "You never met him?"

"No, but we've had a multi-year discussion of *decroissance*, DeGrowth in English, and the failure of the Marxist critique to account for the DeGrowth movement."

"Boss, could you hand me my tablet, please?"

Caverlock complied and after scanning her correspondence and news feeds, JP reported, "Nothing in China yet."

"Check with Gerard and Carlito," Caverlock said. "Maybe they've generated some coverage."

Despite his overheated state, Caverlock could not resist pacing while they awaited reports from Gerard and Carlito.

A half-hour later JP received their reports. "Nothing yet," JP said, and glanced up at The Consulting Philosopher. "It's Sunday," he said by way of an excuse, but his attempt at appearing confident flopped.

Closing her eyes again, JP murmured, "I'm tired," and Caverlock sat down on an overturned bucket. "Me, too. With our hectic travel schedule across so many time zones, how could we not be tired? And yet we must arise at the open of pre-market trading in New York to execute our initial trades. We must retain our wits for another 24 hours."

The quiet of the hot still air of late afternoon was broken by the first movement of Dvorak's *New World Symphony* streaming from the adjoining house.

"It's our good fortune that our unseen neighbor has a refined taste in music," Caverlock mused. "Another piece in E minor, if I'm not mistaken, this one by Dvorak. Take note of the sumptuous color of the first movement, with horns, fanfares, dramatic percussion and melodies that move from lilting to the deepest minor-chord depths and back, as if crossing open sunny meadows and then entering a towering forest."

The two listened to the first movement and JP commented, "My Mom made me take piano lessons, but it wasn't fun."

"Like all difficult things, the fun comes after a grueling learning curve."

JP absorbed this and asked, "Boss, do I get overtime on this consulting job?"

Caverlock smiled sheepishly. "Dear JP, I've neglected your compensation in the press of things, and I apologize. I am rarely conscious of being an employer. By all means, calculate whatever strikes you as fair, which in a utilitarian ethics would be what you would pay your employee were you the employer."

Surrendering to her fatigue, JP lay down on the cool tiles. "How much of my savings should I put in this bet that grain prices will fall?"

Caverlock pondered the question and replied, "We'll hedge whatever sum you risk, but one must always assume the entire sum will be lost. This is the only way to get clarity on one's appetite for risk."

"Aren't you afraid of losing such a big amount of money?"

"Of course it would sting very badly for a time," Caverlock conceded. "But I've committed to the trade for other reasons. As you so insightfully noted, I would be crushed were I denied this opportunity."

"But how can you be sure you won't lose it all?"

"The hedge," he explained. "I'm betting against myself as well. No hedge is perfect, but it will limit my losses. And I trust Ben's assessment and my own intuition."

Her eyes still closed, JP said, "I don't see how you can make money based on your feelings. Everyone else who guesses like that loses."

"It's a constructive question," Caverlock replied. "In some ways trading is like music. The more you know, and the more experience you have as a player, the more you hear. The average person hears very little because their ear is untrained. Trading is the same way. Those with little experience see a jumble and are thrown by their fears onto the opinions of authorities, who cannot be trusted for one profound reason: if a financial guru is any good, they can make as much money as they want by trading, and so they don't need to sell their services."

"You mean like Ben," JP said.

"Precisely," Caverlock replied. "Ben doesn't sell his expertise. Why give away one's hard-earned secrets? Use them to your own advantage and keep quiet."

"And what's your secret?"

Caverlock chuckled. "I've already told you, dear JP, but you dismissed it as rubbish. As the Taoist sage Zhuang Zhou explained, the Tao flows when the hand guides itself without thought. Concentration is present, but empty of effort as the beginner understands it."

"But how do you trade that?"

"Good trades are rare," Caverlock explained. "The good trader never forces a trade. The good trader scans for extremes of sentiment and asymmetries of risk. It's like a wood worker looking through stacks of lumber. The average person sees boards that look alike. The master is alive to grain, knots, and patterns that can be matched. The board the amateur rejects as flawed might be the prized piece the master immediately grabs."

JP mulled this discourse, and Caverlock continued. "This trade is different, as we know it's a manipulation and not the result of thousands of traders' emotions and decisions. The deck is stacked, and the only way we can win is to scatter the cards to the winds. I fear we've run out of time, and my annoyance with the feckless Drake rises when I think of what might have transpired had he confided in Victorine two weeks ago."

As if beckoned by the mention of his name, Drake entered the courtyard through the gateway, two paper bags in hand, followed a moment later by Victorine. The couple entered the office and displayed their purchases: savory meat pastries and a selection of raw vegetables with a bottle of dressing, and a chilled white wine.

"A splendid dinner at home is the perfection of contentment," Caverlock declared, and Victorine and JP ascended to the half-finished kitchen to slice the carrots, broccoli, zucchini and cucumbers and clean the tomatoes and lettuce leaves. Caverlock reviewed Ben's trading plan with Drake, and concluded, "As soon as the New York pre-market opens, place a bet the grains decline with your margin account. Then later, sell half your investors' stake in one fell swoop. That should arouse the curiosity of commodity players when they awaken."

Drake nodded, but his expression was troubled.

In a quiet voice, Caverlock asked, "Do you have second thoughts?"

"No," Drake answered. "I'm just thinking about what to do if we fail."

"The same thoughts weigh on me," Caverlock said. "I tell myself this is a test of my detachment, but I cannot put my mind at ease. There is too much at stake."

"I would rather you didn't risk your own money," Drake said, and Caverlock paused before responding. "We must each do what we reckon is required."

Drake slouched in the office chair and began toying with the pen. "Any news from Gerard?"

"None."

Drake opened his laptop and busied himself with correspondence, and Caverlock called Ben to confirm the trading plan remained unchanged.

JP and Victorine arrived with plates of raw vegetables and the warm savory pastries, and Drake opened the white wine, now beaded with moisture, while Caverlock readied the small glasses that Yvette and Michel had included in the box of kitchenware.

"I propose a toast," Caverlock said once Drake had half-filled each glass. "To we four, exasperatingly persistent individuals who are constitutionally incapable of capitulation, to borrow a phrase a Churchill."

The four sipped the chilled wine, and Caverlock nodded approvingly. "Since Ben is not here to raise the ante of my Churchill quote, I will say on his behalf that *it is neither necessary to hope to undertake, nor to succeed to persevere.*"

It was a fitting phrase, for the dinner party was enlivened by the forced joviality of the condemned; each of the group felt the shadows of failure lengthen with each passing hour. To ease the stifling air of defeat, each sought to humor the others with jokes, often at the expense of Caverlock, who bore the brunt with the amusement of one practiced in self-deprecation.

After the meal, the desk was cleared of dishes and Drake opened the local Languedoc red wine. As Caverlock poured, Drake produced a deck of playing cards with the exaggerated flourish of a magician.

"Let's play Hearts," Victorine said, and when JP professed ignorance of the game, Victorine patiently explained the rules and the strategy of winning, including the counter-intuitive *Shooting the Moon*, in which the player who manages to end up with all the hearts and the Queen of Spades—the cards everyone typically avoids as they add unwanted points-- saddles the other players with 26 points while earning zero points for their feat.

"As in life, in Hearts the way of the Tao is reversal," Caverlock said, and JP protested, "Boss, don't confuse me with Chinese philosophy."

The open door let in a zephyr of cool evening air, and the red wine induced a tipsy competition. Caverlock won the first round, but Victorine took the next two, while a jubilant JP took the fourth. Drake was either unlucky or skilled at losing on purpose without appearing to do so.

The party broke up amidst infectious yawns, and JP claimed first rights to the bathroom's handheld shower. She emerged in her spaghetti-strap peach nightgown, her long hair twisted in a damp knot atop her head, and Victorine took her turn.

Caverlock let the other three go first, and when he crept up the stairs to the maid's room, he found JP was sitting in their bed, clutching her knees and gazing up at the moon through the half-open skylight.

"I thought you'd be asleep," Caverlock remarked, and JP said, "Look how beautiful the moon is tonight."

Caverlock joined her and peered up at the crescent moon illuminating the edges of slowly drifting clouds that imagination conjured into dogs and dragons.

"I fear you are infected with the same anxiety I suffer from," Caverlock murmured. "There is nothing to be done, so we must detach our minds."

"I'm not worried about tomorrow," she replied in a soft voice. "We've done our best."

"Then something else is weighing on you," Caverlock ventured.

JP made no reply, and Caverlock said, "Though I don't make much of a show of it, I am a good listener."

Letting go of her knees, JP lay on her side and pulled her pillow to her.

"Forgive me for saying this," Caverlock said, "but I do love hearing you speak Mandarin to your Mom and Aunty. Your voice is sweeter than your English voice. I feel like I'm hearing your unshielded self when you're chatting with your Mom and Aunty."

"Boss, are you trying to make me cry again?"

"What a dreadful accusation," Caverlock said, and then pointed at the illuminated clouds. "Look, a ferocious bunny is about to eat a poor helpless shark."

JP giggled, and Caverlock glanced at her with a smile. "That cloud-bunny frightened me so badly, I may have another nightmare in French."

Seizing Caverlock's pillow, JP playfully walloped him, and then clasped both pillows to her chest. "Now you lost your pillow."

"Alas," Caverlock replied good-naturedly, and JP covered her face with one of the pillows. When she lowered it a moment later, Caverlock was still gazing at the night sky.

"When I messaged my classmates about our campaign," JP said in a soft voice, "I was thinking about how successful they are. One is a junior professor, another is finishing medical school and my other friend is a government official. They already own investment flats, and two are already married; the other one is engaged. Compared to them, I'm a failure."

"Comparing ourselves to others is a path to madness," Caverlock murmured. "You managed to go to university and immigrate to *Meiguo* on your own. Those are accomplishments few manage. And now you have time for self-cultivation that your classmates can only dream about. And who is to say that they married wisely? Perhaps they felt pressured into taking the first qualified fellow through the gate to please their parents, just as Drake took on this swindle to please his father."

JP was silent and Caverlock said, "I know there's no prestige in working for a consulting philosopher, but prestige doesn't guarantee happiness. If you want an impressive title, then choose what you want and we'll print up cards. Or if working for me feels lowly, start your own company and I'll pay you under contract. When we visit China, I'll be your employee. I'll make notes on a tablet, open the door for you and bring you tea. Dressed in something stylish from Paris, you will cut a very impressive figure, and your friends will envy your unconventional freedom and success."

Shifting onto her side again, JP's youthful face was faintly illuminated by the moonlight. "You already open doors for me and bring me tea," she said in her sweetest voice.

"You feel something is lacking," Caverlock said, "but there is nothing you need beyond what you already are."

JP turned away, and a moment later she launched a pillow at the Consulting Philosopher.

Retrieving the pillow, Caverlock lowered his voice to a rough whisper. "As punishment for your beastly pillow attacks, I demand you share a bottle of champagne with me the minute we return to Paris."

Chapter Seventeen

Squinting at the morning sun flooding the courtyard, JP entered the office wearing her white cotton dress with a frilly hem, now wrinkled from days stuffed in her luggage.

"Why didn't you wake me?" she demanded of Caverlock, who glanced up from his laptop with a forlorn expression. He was wearing a pinstriped Oxford shirt and his black jeans, a marked contrast to Drake, who was the picture of informality in his khaki shorts and a faded surf-brand T-shirt.

"You couldn't have bought in pre-market trading with your limited account," he replied. "Besides, nothing has changed except grain prices have moved higher all morning. The London market opened an hour ago, and the continental bourses have just opened."

Looking over Caverlock's shoulder, JP asked, "Nothing from Gerard?"

"No. He's perplexed and frustrated. I suspect his campaign is being suppressed. Or perhaps nobody cares about grain prices rising."

"How about Carlito?"

"Seven hours ago, it was 5 pm in San Francisco, and he said he was working on something."

JP rubbed her eyes and yawned. "What happened when Drake sold half his bet?"

Caverlock heaved a deep sigh. "The price dipped briefly but quickly recovered. I placed a bet for a reversal and hedged that position with a bet that price will keep climbing. So far, our hedges are up and our primary bet is down."

Victorine emerged from the passageway holding a flat cardboard box which she nimbly held level while crossing the courtyard. Setting the box on the desk, she removed her hat and sunglasses, and Caverlock glanced at the coffees and croissants and then at her sleeveless red batik-print sundress. The scent of her perfume accompanied her entrance and Caverlock smiled in wonderment. "That shade of red suits you," Caverlock commented as JP requisitioned a café au lait and Victorine handed a cup to Drake.

Turning to give Caverlock a coffee, Victorine's green-brown eyes flashed with humor, and Caverlock played along, saying, "It's too bad your third suitor Jules isn't here to compliment you in French."

Both glanced expectantly at Drake, who appeared too lost in the thickets of his own thoughts to have heard the repartee intended for him.

JP also missed the humor, as she was focused on her tablet screen.

"Boss, look at this," she said, and the excitement in her voice caused Caverlock to stand up and look over her shoulder. "A financial site got hacked with a big warning about speculators' manipulating grain prices."

"Carlito's crew has drawn blood," Caverlock said. "It's a good start but far from enough."

The sound of an electric drill in the front room announced the return of the construction workers to the premises, and Caverlock closed the heavy door to the hallway.

"Boss, I want to make a bet in my own account," JP announced, and Caverlock gave her an appraising look. "You'll have to follow Ben's plan and buy a hedge."

JP nodded, and Caverlock glanced at his watch. "Trading in the U.S. market opens at 9:30 am in New York, which is still six hours away. You'll have to wait until then."

A loud knock on the door announced a visitor, and a wizened old man wearing faded overalls and a jaunty corduroy cap entered apologetically. Caverlock greeted him with a polite *bonjour*, and the man spoke in a voice loud enough to be heard over the drilling. Caverlock exchanged a few phrases in French with the gent and ushered him from the room.

Turning to the group with alarm, he announced, "He says we must leave immediately. He doesn't know why, but we're being shut down. It wouldn't surprise me if gendarmes were on their way to arrest us for squatting or some other bogus charge."

Drake snapped from the office chair as if spring-loaded and began disconnecting the digital equipment.

Caverlock asked, "Drake, do you reckon the farm is still safe?"

"As far as I can tell," he replied, and the urgency in Caverlock's voice increased. "Have you taken a mobile phone there?"

"No. I used my co-worker's phone a couple times for local calls, and I keep an airport rental phone disassembled for emergencies."

"Very wise," Caverlock said. "Is there another route to the farm other than the road?"

"Yes, a pathway that starts behind the old silk factory."

Caverlock turned to his client. "Victorine, grab your bag and accompany Drake to the farm on foot. We have five minutes to disappear, maybe less."

Victorine stuffed her tablet in her travel bag as Drake slammed his laptop shut and grabbed the disconnected equipment. Reaching beneath the desk, he pulled loose two small black boxes taped to the underside of the desktop. Tossing one to Caverlock, he explained, "Sniffers for hidden listening and tracking devices."

Catching the small box with one hand, Caverlock said, "Excellent—only the paranoid survive. JP and I will get to the farm with the Deux Chevaux via a circuitous route. As a precaution, we should remove the batteries from our mobile phones."

Caverlock stopped Drake and Victorine at the courtyard door. "How can we tell which farm is the one?"

"Their logo is a dragonfly," Drake replied. "You'll see the sign by the entrance. The driveway is gravel, and you can't see the house from the road."

"You know what this means," Caverlock said in a low voice. "They're afraid we might succeed."

The couple nodded acknowledgement and hurried across the courtyard and out the gateway. Caverlock commanded JP, "Get our bags, I'll wait here," and JP darted out the hallway door. Caverlock returned to the desk to retrieve the coffees and croissants, murmuring, "First things first."

*   *   *

Caverlock slowed the Deux Chevaux as they passed a small sign announcing a hamlet ahead, and JP said, "Boss, we'll never find the farm without a map or phone. We don't even know where we are."

Caverlock drove slowly through the scattered cluster of old houses and then gently pushed the accelerator of the clattering vehicle. "Patience, JP, patience. We must be absolutely confident that we aren't being followed. And I do know where I am. The Mediterranean is behind us and the Cevennes is dead ahead."

JP gave him a sour look and he chuckled. "I studied the map a bit that night in Paris, as we couldn't be sure we'd always have mobile coverage in these rural valleys." Spotting a narrow dirt track through a copse of chestnut trees, Caverlock pulled over and adroitly backed the car down the dirt road out of sight. "If they hired pros to follow us, they'll have a minimum of three cars," Caverlock explained. "One in front of us, one behind us in case we try a U-turn, and a tail, which only has to insure we don't evade the cars ahead and behind us."

No other vehicle came along the country lane, and JP said, "We're clear."

"I'm not so sure," Caverlock muttered. "They may have tricks I've not yet seen. Their move this morning speaks of a desperation to shut Drake down before our attack gains ground. I am not yet ready to declare us in the clear."

Starting the antique vehicle, Caverlock eased it onto the road and turned downhill at the next intersection.

"As I said right at the start, we have a knowledge problem," he said. "We cannot know how much the swindlers know about us, or the magnitude of forces they've assembled to foil us. I suspect Drake surprised them with his disappearance, and they increased their efforts in response. They probably underestimated Victorine and our efforts as well."

With a chortle of amusement, Caverlock said, "Imagine their confidence that I was nothing but an impractical eccentric after scanning the web and finding my monographs on labor-backed cryptocurrencies and the *Hikikomori* phenomenon. And what would they find on you, dear JP? Almost nothing in English, and precious little in Mandarin. As for Victorine, they probably made fatally inaccurate assumptions based on her film-worthy looks. Her will is flexible steel."

The Deux Chevaux leaned heavily in a turn and JP gripped the door. "Boss, be careful."

"Your worries are understandable but baseless, as I'm finally getting the hang of this old war horse," Caverlock assured her. "Your worry should be the sophistication of the operation they've thrown against us. Note the care Drake took to evade surveillance. He certainly didn't underestimate them. He took a page from Carlito's playbook by avoiding mobile phones, he paid cash for airline tickets and kept electronic sniffers to ensure his rooms weren't bugged and his possessions were free of tracking devices. He has done a remarkably thorough job for an amateur, and that's why I wondered at the start if he was following orders from a professional."

"So you underestimated him, too," JP said, and Caverlock gave her a sheepish look. "Yes, I confess I did at first, but my assessment changed when we discovered the clues in his flat. Now I'm trying to avoid underestimating our opponents. I felt we were being watched when we visited Gerard, and no wonder. Wouldn't that be one of your first actions if you were the swindlers trying to trace Drake?"

"So what do you think they're doing now?"

"We must assume they're throwing everything they can to stop us. I reckoned they had us followed to the TGV and Nimes, but perhaps Drake fed them enough misinformation that they decided that either we were on a wild goose chase, or we'd given up the search for Drake and were enjoying a trip to the south. What would you think if you'd followed us to Nimes and observe us meeting a family with two children? We didn't look like people hot on the trail of an elusive fugitive."

Caverlock turned onto a main road and shifted into high gear. "Drake's dumping half the position this morning must have alarmed them, and perhaps they belatedly concluded he was operating from here after all. Hence their hurry to shut down his makeshift office."

Frowning, JP asked, "But how did they find it?"

Caverlock lifted one hand from the steering wheel to gesture uncertainty. "Perhaps they traced the router, or maybe they followed us once they located the Deux Chevaux. Victorine cuts quite a swath, so maybe someone spotted her walking with Drake. Our precautions weren't extreme."

"So what's your plan now?" JP asked. "Wander around like we're lost?"

"We must be careful not to lead anyone tailing us to the farm," he explained. "I'm looking for a particular traffic arrangement that I can exploit."

JP looked at him over her sunglasses. "Maybe we're not being followed at all, and you're wasting time for nothing,"

"Perhaps," Caverlock said in an agreeable tone. "But consider the decision tree in terms of risk management. If we are being followed, and we blithely run straight to the farm, our chances of success dwindle very quickly to zero. If we are being followed but manage to lose the tail, then the odds of success remain unchanged. If we aren't being followed and I waste precious time being paranoid, we've reduced the odds of success somewhat, but we've gained the equally precious confidence that we aren't leading our opponents straight to Drake."

Caverlock guided the redoubtable old car through a medieval village choked with tourists and then along a winding route to a small town with a one-way loop that led to a roundabout of three roads and the entrance to a supermarket and hardware store. "This might do," Caverlock murmured, and turning into the expansive parking lot of the supermarket, he went back through the town and pulled to the curb with the engine still running.

"Are you trying to spot our tail?" JP asked, and Caverlock replied, "No, I'm waiting for an opportunity."

Time passed slowly and JP shifted impatiently on the hard seat. "If you're right, they're keeping their distance. Waiting here doesn't accomplish anything."

"True, but this will," Caverlock said, and revving the underpowered engine, he slammed the car into gear and raced down the wrong way of the one-way loop. An oncoming car swerved and honked its horn, and JP involuntarily braced for impact.

"Boss, you'll get us killed," she shouted, but Caverlock pressed on, jerking the wheel to avoid another oncoming car and a bicyclist, who loosed a stream of invective aimed at the speeding Deux Chevaux.

A third car stopped amidst an insistent blare of the horn, and a few seconds later Caverlock was in the roundabout and turning unsteadily onto a narrow road barely wide enough for two small vehicles.

Clinging on to the door, JP fumed, "Boss, did you do that just to scare me?"

Caverlock shot her a petulant glance. "I'm not that misguided," he replied. "No, that was a classic maneuver to evade a three-car tail. Our primary tail couldn't follow us down the one-way street, as that would reveal their identity, and with three outlets in the roundabout, the other two tails can't cover three roads. This road leads to several intersections, which multiplies our options of routes and leaves them with too many choices of routes and destinations to track."

JP loosened her grip on the door and stole an admiring look at The Consulting Philosopher. "Sometimes you're better than I thought," she said, and he chuckled. "Never underestimate the utility of the study of deception."

After several more turns at intersections of narrow local roads, Caverlock coasted to a stop by a gnarled vineyard clinging to a rocky hillside and turned off the engine. "I admit defeat, I am lost," he announced, and JP emerged from the cocoon of her own thoughts.

"Shall I turn on my phone? I doubt they can trace us out here."

"As a last resort, yes," Caverlock said gravely. "Time is passing, to our detriment."

In the silence, the steady hum of farm equipment from somewhere beyond the road was punctuated by the chirps of birds flitting about the grape vines strung along trellises.

While Caverlock pondered his dwindling options, two middle-aged matrons in khaki trousers and short-sleeved blouses leisurely cycled past the Deux Chevaux. Caverlock immediately hailed them, and as they slowed to a stop, Caverlock threw open the car door and trotted up to ask for directions. The bicyclist wearing a paisley scarf deferred to her blond friend in a maroon beret, who offered an extended rapid-fire answer in French. After listening politely, Caverlock withdrew his pocket notebook and asked her to sketch a map.

As JP watched the tableau from the passenger's seat, Caverlock reviewed the map and then thanked the pair profusely. As they resumed their ride, Caverlock returned to the car with a bemused expression.

"As you know, males are genetically programmed to avoid confessing ignorance of their surroundings, but the ladies couldn't have been more helpful," he explained. "Actually, too helpful, as the flood of French swamped my feeble comprehension. Finally I hit on asking for a map, and now we can proceed with renewed confidence."

*   *   *

"There it is, Boss," JP said, pointing to a painted sign of a dragonfly set back from the road that was partially obscured by a profusion of tall spindly shrubbery.

"I would have missed it," Caverlock exclaimed, turning the old car to enter the gravel driveway, which was little more than a narrow opening in the shrubbery that obscured the farmhouse from the road.

"It's certainly private," Caverlock observed as the car bounced over the potholed driveway.

Wrinkling her nose, JP said, "Smells like a farm," as the odor of manure, hay and damp earth wafted into the compartment.

"Help me look for a place to park our trusty steed," Caverlock said. "I want it out of sight of prying eyes, including those from above, which is to say drones."

"There," JP said, pointing to a dilapidated, rusting sheet metal shed with a decided lean. Caverlock pulled up to the shelter, and got out to move some wire-mesh boxes and rough-sawn lumber. Satisfied the area was clear of debris, he maneuvered the Deux Chevaux under cover, turned off the ignition and motioned JP to bring their laptop and tablet.

The old two-story stone farmhouse could have been a set for a 19th century drama, as the only signs of modernity were the telephone and power lines, and two impressive glazed pots as tall as a kindergartener on either side of the entry, one forest green and the other deep red. Each held matching bound clusters of decorative reed stalks and a bamboo walking stick. Two tall casement windows were open on either side of the vases, but no sound emerged from the interior.

No one came out to greet them, and after waiting a moment Caverlock and JP went to the planked front door and hesitantly knocked. "Come in," a voice they recognized as Drake's responded from behind a window.

Pushing open the door, they entered a large low-ceilinged room anchored by a heavy wood table that looked old enough to bear the scars of swordplay from the time of the Cathars. Drake greeted them with a conventional handshake, but Victorine rose from the table to greet them with a hug of relief. "We thought you'd been captured."

"No, the wily goats evaded the wolves," Caverlock remarked. Glancing round the room, he took in the light-green plaster walls and an ornately framed original painting of the farmhouse that took pride of place on the rear wall. "Where are your hosts?"

"They're delivering to the nearby villages," Drake replied.

Inhaling deeply, Caverlock said, "I detect the smell of fermenting grapes. Are they also making wine?"

"They've given some space in the shed to a friend aspiring to become a winemaker."

"Impressive," Caverlock murmured. "Now all they need is to host a baker, and they'll have the trifecta of rustic happiness: cheese, wine and bread."

Gesturing to a simple white-painted sideboard, Drake said, "There's some of their cheese, and local bread and olives, and a carafe of water."

"Wonderful," Caverlock enthused. "It's well past noon and we have yet to eat. Come, JP, let's dine."

Drake had connected their laptop and tablet to the router with cables, and JP studied the digital setup. "We disabled wireless on the router and our computers," he explained. "And we're using our hosts' router, so there's no new IP address for anyone to spot."

"Very wise," Caverlock affirmed. "I commend the care you've maintained from the start."

Nonplussed by this compliment, Drake offered a brief update. "Grain futures are still going up. A few references to manipulation of grain prices have been published, but they're not being picked up."

"That confirms my greatest fear," Caverlock said in a somber voice. "We've run out of time to derail the narrative. Our opponents may well be countering any selling with additional buying. That's the oldest and most reliable trick in the book."

Pulling out one of the wooden chairs arrayed around the old table, Caverlock sat down heavily. "I've lost my appetite," he said miserably.

Glancing at him with subdued alarm, JP went to the sideboard and prepared two small plates of bread, cheese and the local olives. Setting a plate and glass of water in front of Caverlock, JP scolded him. "Stop feeling sorry for yourself, Boss. You have to keep your strength up."

"You are a strict taskmaster," Caverlock complained as he placed a piece of cheese on the slice of heavily crusted bread.

"There's still time before the U.S. markets open," Victorine said, and Caverlock waved aside the whiff of hope in her tone. "That is the hour of our doom," he said dourly. "Whatever trends are in place at the open tend to accelerate. Our only chance is to reverse the trend before the American markets open."

The afternoon heat had finally seeped into the stone walls, and the radiating warmth raised a sheen on Victorine's face and bare shoulders. JP's frilly white dress clung damply to her, and Caverlock unfastened the top button of his wilted pinstriped shirt. Only Drake in his khaki shorts and T-shirt seemed unaffected.

Caverlock's effort to chew a piece of bread and cheese lacked his usual gusto, and he gently returned the crust to the plate. "The black dog has me by the throat," he stated. "We have come all this way and overcome multiple obstacles to fail in the last hour. I taste only the ashes of defeat, as if we are trapped in our own pathetic replay of Cannae."

Though no one understood the reference to Rome's devastating defeat by Carthage, his depression was reflected in their expressions and body language.

"I find nothing of solace in all my philosophy and all my faith," Caverlock continued, "save Buckminster Fuller's insight that our lives are not our own. Our accumulated failures and experiences must be applied to serve others. And so despite the certainty of defeat and the mockery of our victorious opponents, we must try to serve those who will suffer if this cruel swindle succeeds."

Wiping the sweat from her forehead with a paper napkin, JP gave The Consulting Philosopher an appraising look and said, "Boss, I can tell you have a plan."

"You are unfailingly observant," Caverlock murmured. "It's based on the premise that the overconfidence and disdain for their opponent of the apparent victor is their Achilles Heel of vulnerability. Our opponents reckoned they slapped us down easily enough, and a steady drip of buying has pushed grain futures higher."

Heaving a great sigh, Caverlock arose and began to slowly pace from the open casement windows back to the table. "To use the Battle of Midway as an analogy," he continued, "we have launched our strike force at the Imperial Fleet but at this late hour our torpedo bombers have been massacred and our dive bombers have yet to locate their target. All seems lost."

Now accustomed to Caverlock's disquisitions, the three members of the audience listened attentively. "Yet our dive bombers are still in the air, and though running dangerously low on fuel, we have a brief window to locate our enemy's four aircraft carriers." Gazing at his audience, Caverlock said, "You recall, of course, that when the small force of dive bombers finally located the four great carriers, the cream of the Imperial Navy, they needed mere minutes to transform all four into burning wrecks destined for Davy Jones' Locker."

Resuming his slow pacing, he said, "What are our opponents' greatest vulnerabilities? Political pressure that demands investigation, and unremitting selling that overwhelms their steady drip of buying."

Addressing his assistant, he said, "JP, disable the Wi-Fi in the laptop, connect to the router and call Gerard. We must arouse a firebrand politician seeking a larger stage. That seems to be our best leverage at this late hour."

Returning to the table, Caverlock stopped by Drake and asked, "Is there anyone who you invited to join the trade who can be turned against it? We need a seller willing to dump an absolutely crushing sell order to persuade Ben to pile on."

Drake's pensive expression darkened, and he made no reply.

Hovering as JP worked to contact Gerard, Caverlock murmured, "If you're bold enough to want to trade our last-ditch effort, now is the time to do place an order that will execute at the open of American markets."

JP's expression telegraphed her uncertainty and he reassured her, "There will always be other trades. Don't force a trade you don't feel right about."

JP nodded and opened her account. "Don't forget to hedge," Caverlock muttered, and she nodded again. A few moments later she closed her account window and said, "OK, I'm calling Gerard."

Gerard answered audio only, and began in an apologetic tone, "*Je suis desole*—"

Caverlock cut him off abruptly, saying, "Save the apology for after we fail. Gerard, listen carefully. Your theory depends on key influencers. We desperately need a firebrand politician who sees an opportunity here to make his or her name in public, defending the exploited and attacking the manipulators. Is there anyone in your networks who can recruit a firebrand? Make whatever extravagant promises of glory are necessary to inflame their passion, but we need a public demand for an inquiry and indictments within the hour."

The computer screen suddenly displayed Gerard's haggard face partially obscured by his outsized black cat, and JP laughed. "I'm already working with a prospect," Gerard said, and Caverlock replied in his booming voice, "We need your magic, Gerard, so let fly whatever incantations are required."

Caverlock next turned to Victorine. "There must be some firebrand in your network of non-profits who can stage a press conference on the fly to denounce a ruthless exploitation of impoverished consumers to enrich a handful of filthy-rich speculators. Call in favors, run the guilt flag high, offer to work for their cause for free, do whatever you reckon will work. We need a media-savvy speech within the hour."

Victorine's large eyes widened, and after a brief hesitation, she said, "OK, I'll work on it with JP."

"Bend them to your stupendous will," Caverlock advised, and turned his gaze to Drake.

Drake was deep in his own troubled thoughts, and Caverlock considered him closely. "You have someone in mind you might turn, but he's loyal to your father. And that's the rub, isn't it?"

Drake could not mask his surprise at this statement, and Caverlock said in a near whisper, "But you knew it would come to this sooner or later, didn't you?"

His expression mixed smoldering resentment and fear in equal parts, and Caverlock clapped his oversized hand on the younger man's shoulder. "Putting it off will only increase the harm to everyone," he said in an avuncular voice. "This entire experience has prepared you for this moment."

Drake nodded uncertainly, and Caverlock patted his shoulder. "You don't like being bested. So let's win this one. Everyone is giving it their all, but it's all for naught unless you deliver the sell order."

Closing his eyes, Drake readied himself and then dragged his chair and laptop to the corner of the room, stretching the router cable to its limit. Facing the corner, his back to everyone else, he made the call and began in the warm voice of an intimate friend.

To give Drake some semblance of privacy, Caverlock sat down beside Victorine and JP, but all three did nothing but listen to Drake's conversation as it transitioned from friendly banter to a confrontational tone.

"Look, I'm doing you a favor here," he said in a voice neither Caverlock nor JP had ever heard. "The trade's turning, this is the point of maximum profit. If you don't sell, you'll be sitting on a loss by the close."

After a moment listening, Drake barked, "I know you promised my father, but I'm about to unload our entire position, and so are my guys in Asia. I can't tell you why, but by the time you know it'll be too late."

Drake ended the call and swore under his breath. Without turning around, he said, "Caverlock, I'm dumping the rest of the position. Call your friend Ben and get him to sell now. This is it."

Peering closely at the laptop screen, JP's voice burst with excitement. "The Chinese news agency just blasted the manipulation in a big headline. There's no grain shortage, shame on the American government, blah blah blah."

Caverlock slammed his fist on the table and Victorine jumped. "Finally, something is going our way. JP, one of your contacts got to the right person, congratulations. Victorine, perhaps this clarion call from the Chinese will inspire some idealistic firebrand in your network. JP, please get Ben on the line. I hope it's not some hideous hour in Bangkok."

Consulting the laptop screen JP said, "It's about 7 pm in Bangkok," JP said.

"Excellent," Caverlock said, and a moment later Ben's good-humored face appeared on the screen. "Ben, the Rubicon awaits. Can you cross it with a financial army, or not?"

"Give me a status report," Ben said calmly, and Caverlock summarized Drake's upcoming sell, the Chinese news coverage and Gerard's political firebrand.

"Tell Drake to wait until the firebrand demands an investigation. Then we'll move together once the U.S. markets open."

"Affirmative," Caverlock said. Ending the call, he leaped to his feet and paced furiously like a caged beast. "By Jupiter, this will be a close thing," he muttered.

"Listen to this," JP announced excitedly. "A financial news network just reported that the grain shortage blamed for the rise in grain prices is false, there is no shortage."

Drake launched another call and his voice was alive with renewed confidence. "Hey, I wanted to let you in on a great trade, but you have to take it literally right now. Grain futures are about to U-turn, anyone going short now is going to make a killing. Check the news—there's no grain shortage, the Chinese are covering it, and my sources tell me an investigation is about to be launched any minute. You're the only shop I'm sharing this with, so can I count on you for some big numbers?"

JP's laptop chirped and JP said, "It's Gerard."

Caverlock hurried to look over JP's shoulder. "She's being prepped for the camera right now in Washington. She's only working from notes, but I think she's very good with improvising."

JP clicked on the link Gerard posted and a youthful woman with dark blunt-cut hair in a gray business suit approached the microphone with an air of incensed authority.

"Outrage does not do justice to the exploitation I'm about to describe," she began. "An exploitation that makes a mockery of our financial system, our economy, our criminal justice system and the values our nation was founded on. At some point, this exploitation of the innocent to enrich the few becomes so odious that we must throw a wrench into the gears and shut the machine down."

"The camera loves her," Caverlock murmured. "That's worth an entire army. JP, send the link to Carlito and get Ben on the line."

With the politician's passionate speech playing in the background, JP sent the link to Carlito and placed the call to Ben. "As promised, the speech is being delivered," Caverlock said.

"OK, it's a go," Ben said. "I've lined up some other pools who will jump at the first drop."

Drake had returned to the table to watch the fiery speech, and he motioned for Caverlock to join him. "I'll sell at the open, and I'm going short with my whole stake and the margin account."

"All in," Caverlock said quietly. "Excellent."

Gazing at Victorine, Caverlock asked, "Do you want to take a personal position in this?"

With a sheepish look, Victorine said, "I already did. JP helped me."

Caverlock chuckled, "My, my. Well, we're all in."

"She just called for an investigation," JP announced.

"The market just opened," Drake said in a tone of uncontainable excitement. Glancing up at Victorine and JP, he said, "All our open orders must have executed by now."

"This is the moment," Caverlock said in a low voice. "Sell your investors' position."

"Done," Drake said.

The room was quiet for a long, agonizing moment and then Drake issued a war whoop, startling the other three. "Grain futures just fell off a cliff," he reported. "The bad guys are trying to reverse it, some buying is pushing it up, no, somebody big just sold, another leg down. Woah, the bottom just fell out, Ben's group must have jumped in. It's a complete evaporation."

"Their fourth carrier just took a fatal hit," Caverlock said with satisfaction. "Overconfidence has a price."

"Still dropping," Drake said. "It's panic-selling now."

"A remarkable reversal of fortune," Caverlock said. "Now let's not make the same mistake as our opponents. This initial panic is an excellent opportunity to exit the trade. We can anticipate an end to the panic selling, and so we should sell everything in the first hour."

"But what if it drops further?" JP asked. "We'll make even more profit if we wait."

"The yin and yang of the market is fear and greed," Caverlock observed. "Neither is conducive to profitable trading. I'm afraid I must insist we liquidate our positions at the first pause in the panic selling. The successful trader takes the middle 60% of a trade and leaves the top and bottom to those with higher risk appetites. There is no guarantee we'll have higher profits in six hours; we might have considerably less."

While they watched grain prices continue cascading down, Caverlock issued a flurry of suggestions and tasks.

"Drake, I suggest returning your investors' capital and profits, which must be substantial since you sold before the decline, this very afternoon, without any explanation. Victorine, unfortunately you didn't have time to find a firebrand in your community, but given how many foundations and non-profits are funded by the ill-gotten gains of wealthy hyenas, it's something you may want to pursue as a much-needed airing of dirty laundry."

Glancing at the white sideboard, Caverlock asked, "Is there any wine we could open to celebrate?"

Arising, Drake said, "Sure. I'll get a bottle. They trade their cheese for local wines all the time."

"Splendid," Caverlock said, and then turned to JP. "JP, please make note of these tasks while they're fresh in my mind."

Tracing a path to the casement windows and back to the table, Caverlock spoke in his usual booming voice as he paced. "One, arrange to send a gift to Michel's aunt, check with him to identify what she would appreciate most. Two, check with Yvette's father on what sort of gift would be most useful to her and Michel and their delightful children. Perhaps a new car, something on that order. Cash is always welcome, too, of course. Three, send Gerard his well-earned fee and an offer to dine with him in Paris, his choice of the restaurant. Four, thank Ben, and find an appallingly tasteless tchotchke to send him. Five, thank Carlito for his absolutely critical contributions to the project, and harangue him to get his passport. And add a zero to whatever fee he presents us."

Drake returned with a dusty bottle of wine, an opener and four cut-glass wine goblets. Glancing at his laptop screen, he said, "Grain futures just took another dive."

Handing JP her tablet, Caverlock said, "Sell, sell, sell," and taking a chair across from her, he swung his laptop around and followed his own advice.

No one spoke as each concentrated on the task at hand, and when Caverlock looked up, he found the eyes of his compatriots on him. "It's done," he said. "*C'est tout.*"

JP's eyes sparkled and she allowed herself a small grin. "Boss, look how much money I made."

"Congratulations on your first successful trade," Caverlock replied. "Congratulations all around, all very well earned." Stretching his arms, he said, "I'm feeling a bit bedraggled, but happily so."

Drake opened the bottle and poured an inch of red wine into each glass. "To us," Caverlock proposed, and the four clinked glasses in a toast.

"Very pleasant," Caverlock said after sipping the wine. "In this heat, this will go straight to my head." Looking across at Victorine and Drake, Caverlock smiled slyly and said, "Dear client, I regret to inform you that substantial travel expenses were required to resolve your case. These expenses and the modest wages of my assistant will be deducted from your deposit. As a wedding gift, I waive my own consulting fee."

Victorine's fair features broke into a grin and she glanced at Drake, who looked down at the table in self-conscious bemusement.

Observing the couple's reticence, Caverlock asked, "What are your plans now?"

Taking Victorine's hand, Drake met Caverlock's gaze. "We've decided to stay here and help with the farm."

"A marvelous decision," Caverlock declared. "JP, don't you agree?"

Drake and Victorine turned to JP, and she blushed under their gaze. "Boss, you were right."

"Really?" Caverlock said in mock surprise. "About what?"

Her blush deepening, JP murmured, "You know. About love."

"Ah, yes," Caverlock said in an uncharacteristically quiet tone.

Victorine's smile softened and she said, "You were right about a lot of things."

Caverlock shrugged, and Victorine asked, "So what are you two doing next?"

Glancing round at JP, Caverlock said, "We haven't had a chance to discuss it, but I want to retrace our hurried steps and enjoy everything we rushed past, starting with Nimes. Italy beckons, a short train ride from Nimes, and I have a dear friend in Montreux, Switzerland, whom I've intended to visit for years, and I reckon JP won't mind doing a bit of research in his lakeside villa. Then there's the celebratory dinner with Gerard in Paris, something I'm looking forward to with great anticipation."

Flashing a rare grin, Drake asked The Consulting Philosopher, "And what about the money?"

Taken aback by the question, Caverlock paused and then shrugged again. "Ah, you mean our gains. I suppose we'll tally the winnings when we get home and render unto Caesar that which is Caesar's. Perhaps JP will want to refurbish her Mom's flat, or something along those lines. As for luxuries, savoring the memories of this adventure will be more than enough for me."

finis

43775583R00097

Made in the USA
Middletown, DE
29 April 2019